THE
FIFTH
DAUGHTER
OF
THORN
RANCH

A MODERN RANCH WITH AN ANCIENT SECRET

JULIA BREWER DAILY

ADMISSION PRESS, INC.
OKLAHOMA CITY, OKLAHOMA

First Edition, November, 2022

Names: Daily, Julia Brewer, author
Title: The Fifth Daughter of Thorn Ranch/Julia Brewer Daily
Description: First Edition. Oklahoma City: Admission Press, 2022
Identifiers: ISBN 978-1-955836-13-5 (hard cover) /ISBN 978-1-955836-11-1 (paperback) ISBN 978-1-955836-12-8 (e-book) /ISBN 979-8-218-03215-9 (audiobook)
Subjects: LCSH: Contemporary Western —Fiction./ Parent and Child—Fiction./
—United States.

BISAC: Fiction-Women FIC044000/ Fiction-General FIC000000/Fiction-Saga FI008000/
Fiction-Romance Western/

To Texas, our adopted state in "Life's Sweetest Third."
May the words of this story be a testament to how grand
and majestic your citizens believe you to be.

"Texas is a state of mind. Texas is an obsession.
Above all, Texas is a nation in every sense of the word."
—JOHN STEINBECK

CHAPTER 1

EMMA,
THE THORN RANCH,
SOUTHWEST TEXAS,
PRESENT DAY

Emma swore under her breath and reached down to where her stirrup had been. The leather supporting her foot had torn, and her leg dangled against the horse. *Damn*, she thought. *I should've taken a newer saddle.* Emma had been so distracted by her argument with Jeff Bower that she was off her game. Now, she was a three-day ride from the barn and unable to exchange any equipment.

Three mornings before, she had lifted her great-grandmother's saddle from its post, yearning for a connection to her long-gone Abuelita. The leather, hand-tooled by a master artisan, was exquisite, but the worn seat verified someone used it for more than horse shows or parades. Emma imagined her tiny great-grandmother herding cattle from this same perch and shouting commands to the vaqueros. She now fidgeted in her relative's saddle. *Will I ever have her instincts?* Emma often questioned her mother about what they required of her.

"You'll be this operation's leader," her mother always told her. "But you'll often be needed as an extra pair of hands, and you'll need to know about crops and care for the animals." There were more than five hundred horses and 7,500 head of cattle, far too many for Emma to say grace over. She wished she could ask her Abuelita Lola if she had ever worried about the expectations placed on her.

Like Lola and generations of Rosales women before her, Emma was an only child and heir to the kingdom surrounding her. *Kingdom* was a lofty word, but the pressures seemed as great as those faced by the King of England. Emma was twenty-two, but often, she felt as if she were twelve. Her hands on the reins dampened at the thought of her responsibilities. Emma felt strong yet insecure, accomplished yet lonely.

She never considered she would do anything other than managing the ranch until recently. Then, Emma began thinking about an animal practice in a small town.

Maybe knowing The Thorn was a million acres and larger than the cities of Los Angeles and New York City combined gave her pause. The Thorn was a living, breathing entity that demanded constant attention.

The ranch had a single fence surrounding 1,600 square miles of the property, spanning eight counties. Since returning from college in the spring, Emma rode the fence line daily. It always needed repair and gave her an excuse for being alone, so she carried a saddlebag of tools. Private rides gave her time to think about her future and offered uninterrupted solitude, rare in the hustle and bustle of ranch activities with vaqueros or her parents.

On this ride, she avoided Jeff Bower as well. She did not want to see him or think about his intentions toward her. Unfortunately, their last shouting match still echoed in her ears. It stung to think he was more interested in owning the ranch than having a relationship with her.

With a firm but gentle hand, Emma pulled the reins and stopped her horse under a tree. It was as if the land took a deep breath and when it exhaled, the scorching air screamed across the expanse. Hives broke out on her neck, exacerbated by a searing pant of blistering wind. Her thick black hair swirled around her face as it escaped its clasp, and she dropped her bridle to sweep it back into a ponytail.

Emma scribbled notes in a small spiral-bound book about borders requiring additional barbed wire or fence posts. They'd dispatch a truck for those. It was helpful to keep fences mended, but Emma was more interested in areas on the ranch she'd never seen than in repairing boundaries. There were miles of The Thorn where her mother claimed no one had ever ridden.

Ravenous Grand Canyon-like cavities traversed many sections where the magnificent Pecos and Rio Grande rivers crossed their property. The Rio Grande, which formed the boundary of their land with Mexico, was Texas's longest river. It was impossible to cross in places because of the swift current—unless you wanted to take your life in your hands.

In the shade of a leafy mesquite tree, heavy with frothy blooms, Emma examined the land more closely. Some of her college friends visited the ranch during school breaks. They hated the rocky terrain, especially those from states with the perpetual green of pine trees and the shocking purples and pinks of exotic azaleas or camellias.

When Emma visited those same friends in the south or northwest, their landscapes heavy with humidity and swollen with constant rains, she longed for the dryness of her corner of the world. Many thought the desert isolating and unattractive with its low scrubs for trees and cactus plants for foliage. But Emma saw beauty in the desolation.

She guided her horse around gigantic cacti that looked like eerie monuments reaching for the sky. She loved when the prickly pear blossoms were yellow against the spines of its body, and then rich red fruit burst forward.

Emma learned painful lessons from picking the fruit; hair-like needles embedding into her fingers. It took days for the minute spikes to wear out of her flesh. After that, she selected the fruit while wearing thick leather gloves and a hand-held torch to scorch the prickles. Then, her grandmother could handle them to make preserves.

Emma liked standing at the stove stirring a bright fuchsia syrup from the fruit. Abuelita Valeria, her mother Josie's parent, placed it into jars to save for the winter, and they spread the luscious jelly on toast in the mornings.

Suddenly, Emma noticed the darkness of the sky. She was far from the ranch house, spending the last three nights on a blanket under the stars. She'd always camped, alone when possible, and with her parents away in Europe for the summer, she was free to come and go as she pleased. Her saddlebag hung behind her, stuffed with beef jerky, Flora's cookies, and two water bottles. Emma knew where streams and rivers were if she needed refills.

Jagged streaks of lightning filled the sky and thunder rumbled. Fascinated, Emma watched the atmosphere light up like the explosions on the ranch when they celebrated with fireworks.

Skittish, Honey-Boy snorted, and his head darted from side to side. She sped him up, gripping her knees and pushing her weight into the one remaining stirrup for support. Cliffs of red sandstone rose around her trail, and she looked around for a place to shelter. Then, without warning, Honey-Boy lurched into a stumble that took him to the ground.

Emma pitched forward over the horse's head onto the hard granite soil. She heard a loud snap behind her as she hit the ground. Emma pulled herself to a sitting position on the hardened, cracked clay and rubbed her cheek. *What was that?*

The horse rolled onto his back and wallowed from side to side. Emma looked at his frightened eyes and heard his heavy breaths. She stared at an enormous gopher colony that camouflaged a knee-deep rocky crevice.

Please, no, not you, Honey-Boy, she thought. Emma made a lunge toward the writhing horse, speaking to him. "It's okay, Honey. You'll be okay."

She knew he would not be. A leg break like this wouldn't heal even if they were home. His break showed a compound fracture with a bone penetrating the skin. She had seen many of these on the ranch.

But, the flash of memory that rocked her back on her heels came from her childhood. When she was six years old, she had heard her parents whispering in the kitchen.

"You don't have any choice, John. His legs won't support him, and the vet won't be back for a week."

"It's Emma's favorite horse. She's claimed him for years."

"Just keep her away from the stall."

Emma snuck to the front door and ran to the barn. Her favorite horse, Shiner, lay in the hay. He tried to stand when he saw her, but she waved her hand at him to say, "Stop, stay down," and ducked into the next stall just as she heard her father open the heavy barn door. Emma listened to her father shuffling through the sawdust, and the enclosure hinges creaked. Then, a metal *click*.

"Wait, Papa, wait," she cried.

"Emma? What are you doing?"

"Don't hurt my horse. Shiner will get better."

"He's suffering, my girl. We have to help him."

Emma hid her face in her father's jacket. He held her behind him and placed a gun to the horse's temple. The shot sounded like a cannon in her little ears. Her shrieks continued back to the house. John walked Emma to her room and tried to explain how births and deaths on a ranch are daily occurrences.

"I'll never get used to killing," Emma's defiant voice declared.

That night, her mother Josie sat beside her on the bed.

"I'm sorry about your horse, Emma. But you must control your emotions and make good decisions for the animals. Everything on this ranch is about business. Crying won't change anything."

Emma stared into her mother's sculpted face with heavily fringed black eyes and tight lips. Then, she watched Josie's stiff back as she left. Would she ever be cool and detached like her mother?

Now, she took a deep breath and untied the saddlebag. Inside, she reached for her .357 Magnum pistol. Her stomach twisted like a metal coil.

Tears brimming in Emma's eyes caused her vision to blur, and her hands shook. "You were a superb horse. Go in peace."

The crack of the weapon stopped the horse's movements. Emma pressed her face into his mane, smelled the straw-like hair, and cried. Even after years of placing animals out of their pain, Emma never lost compassion for the remarkable creatures in her care.

Now she was all alone. Emma sat beside Honey-Boy, stroking his mane and whispering, "Remember when we rode all night just by the light of the harvest moon? You never faltered. You trusted me, and I trusted you. This accident wasn't your fault. I should have been watching the ground instead of the sky. Thank you, Honey, for being a good friend." A final tear dripped onto the horse's muscular back.

Emma dug in her knapsack, turned it upside down, and shook out the contents. She blew out a huff of air. *Could this day get any worse?* She had left a satellite phone at the barn. Now, completely cut off from civilization, maybe she was glad she was solitary. If they weren't in Europe, her parents would lecture her on the safety measures she had learned from a young age.

"Never ride out on the ranch without water and a phone or radio. Always give a ranch manager the approximate area where you plan to travel." Her mother's mantra bounced from ear to ear inside her head.

Well, I have water, Emma thought. *One of the three.*

The heavens seemed to have heard her statement and distorted at the contemplation of liquid with cone-shaped black clouds and swirling raindrops. Emma's clothes were drenched and clung to her skin in a few seconds while the wind slung the torrent into her face like stinging needles. She pulled her great-grandmother's saddle from the motionless animal and hoisted it onto her back. Emma looked once more at the four-legged friend beside her. She walked away. Emma was not frightened but knew she should be.

IF THEY SENT A search party for her, even if they found where Honey-Boy had died, his body would be long gone. A Texas clean-up crew—massive turkey vultures—stripped flesh off bones in little more than twenty-four hours. The birds wiped away all evidence of life and the bones they left would be dragged away by coyotes.

Her walk led her through deep fractures of rock, and she lingered to look at holes in the sides of the cliffs created from years of erosion by rivers and streams. Thunder exploded in her ears now, amplified by the stone walls around her.

It was difficult to believe she walked in territory few had ever explored on the ranch. But, the landscape, thick with mountainous peaks and valleys as deep as skyscrapers, prevented her family from using this ranch border with Mexico. It was wild and forbidding. Cattle couldn't graze here, and the crevices' depth made getting too close dangerous.

Emma's wet, stringy hair dripped into her eyes, and her soaked clothing, whipped by the wind, stuck to her body. She wanted to get out of the sheeting deluge, so she tossed her saddle into the next narrow opening of a cave she saw and followed it in.

Emma had come nose to nose with animals in dens before. So, she squinted as she looked around. She could hear if a rattlesnake was there with its angry hissing and rattles chattering. But, if there were a mountain lion or coyote, they would not warn her until it was too late. All was quiet.

She examined her immediate area still half-lighted by the outside illumination and yelled into the hollows, hoping to frighten any animals that might have shied into a corner. Emma used her saddle as a pillow and stretched out her legs. The howling wind roared against the mouth of the cavern, and flashes of lightning from the storm gave bursts to the dimness. She fell asleep within a few minutes, exhausted from her hike, and emotionally spent from losing her horse.

Emma awoke to the sound of rushing water. Gasping, she stared with wide eyes and saw a river within a foot of the cave's opening. Grabbing her flashlight from the knapsack attached to the saddle, she used the heels of her boots to shove herself backward. The rapid scraping of her feet stirred up a cloud of dust and gravel particles. Emma's heart slammed against her ribcage as she recognized the rising tide could swallow the grotto. She had walked through a dry riverbed without realizing it. During previous rides, she watched from afar as floods devoured acres in a few minutes. Trapped, Emma scrambled into action.

She crawled on her belly using her elbows and twisting her torso. Luckily, the cave widened and continued for quite a distance. The small opening contradicted the size of the underground cavity.

Would it fill up, or could she reach higher ground? Her pulse beat wildly in her neck and made her nauseous. She didn't want to drown tonight.

While slithering through the barely wide-enough tunnel, Emma's bleeding palms and fingernails embedded with coarse pebbles, pulled her forward. When the coolness of a more expansive cavern hit her, Emma scooted onto her knees and then stood.

Shining her flashlight, she saw that the fissure continued farther than she could see in the darkness. Following the narrow beam, she walked upward, taking care not to slip on the treacherous path.

The sheer size—the grandeur of the cavern studded with stalactites and stalagmites—took her breath away. She continued climbing, ducking her head under lower places in the ceiling. She and her parents had visited tourist attraction caves when she was younger, and this one was as large as any they had encountered.

Veering around an impressive formation that almost blocked her route, she discovered a lake. The dark surface rippled slightly as if a breeze blew from somewhere. Emma shivered, goosebumps covering her arms. A rocky, pebbled beach lined the water's edge. There, lying at the curve of the lake, was a dugout canoe. A hand-strung net lay over the boat as if to dry. It was bizarre.

Around the next bend was a set of stairs carved into the side of the wall. Looking upward, she saw light shining through a crack.

Clinging to the edge of the barrier, Emma trembled as she placed one foot in front of the other on the narrow stone sections. Reaching the top of the steps, Emma glanced through a fissure in the rock. She saw her position on a plateau and stuck her head up through the hole and into the daylight like a prairie dog.

In disbelief, Emma watched people milling around a sunlit pasture below her. The area sparkled from the sudden rainfall that lingered on tall grasses and glistened like jewels in bright shades of green and gold. Towering cliffs completely walled the pasture.

There were pens of horses and crops planted in square plots. Women and children laughed while bathing in a stream, and men stood talking around a firepit where they heaped stacks of wood. This gathering was not a picnic or casual outing. Emma could tell these people lived and worked here—on her family ranch!

Disoriented, Emma narrowed her eyes against the brilliant light and shaded them with her hand. She thought she must be suffering from vertigo or exposure to the elements. But, on the other hand, she might have a fever. *Am I hallucinating?*

The individuals by whom she was intrigued did not wear jeans or shorts. They did not look like the contemporary Native Americans who lived around The Thorn. Instead, they had a lighter skin color and wore animal skins and tall leather boots.

Was this a mirage? Who were these people?

CHAPTER 2

JOSIE

Josie and John landed in London and rented a pale blue Mercedes convertible. They planned to visit England for a few weeks before continuing to Italy and Switzerland. Josie shrieked as John swirled in the roundabouts on the wrong side of the road, her scarf whipping against her face and strands of hair landing in her mouth. They wound their way into the villages north of Oxford, where thatched roofs clung to the tops of stone cottages.

Josie wanted to stop and read each historical marker. Her family had been on the same land for generations, but these regions dated back into the 1500s and beyond. Narrow, winding streets led to castles and manor houses that had been converted into inns when the cost of maintenance on the elegant properties threatened to close the estates. They turned into the driveway of the one they had booked for the week. Sherbourne. Even the name was fancy. The long road leading to their first glimpse of the enormous structure, complete with a chapel and glass observatory, was breathtaking. Yellow daffodils lined the mile-long drive, and the green of the fields was lush with tall grasses blowing in the wind. What a contrast to the long brown summers of Texas.

The owners had divided the manor house into a dozen flats or apartments. A hostess escorted Josie and John to theirs and told them dinner was promptly at six. Josie knew from the brochures they must "dress" for dinner. That meant a coat and tie for John and a lovely outfit for her.

Josie usually wore slacks daily, primarily blue jeans, so it felt like they'd stepped into another world when they looked at each other in their finery. As a couple, they were spectacular contrasts with her straight brown hair, deeply set black eyes, and his pale skin and blonde crewcut. John grinned, lifted her hand and kissed it.

"Ready, ma'am?"

"I am, sir!"

Then, John led her down the broad stairs to the dining room. They were not late, but other couples gathered and toasted each other with burgundy wine in crystal stemmed goblets. It was like a typical cocktail party, except Josie and John didn't know any guests.

At first, being among strangers in an unfamiliar house in a foreign country was odd. But it seemed they were all old friends by the time the staff served dinner. One couple was from Scotland, one from Australia, and one from Canada. She and John were the only couple from the United States.

When the guests heard they were from Texas, they seemed intrigued.

"You live on a ranch? Do you ride horses? I can just see wagon trains in my mind."

"That was a long time ago." Josie laughed. "We drive cars now, although we spend much time on horseback."

"Are there still tribes of Indians?"

"Of course, but Native Americans are not like the depictions you've seen in movies." Josie felt a pang about how obtuse people could be concerning others.

She sat back and let the excited chatter of the guests surround her. Josie looked around the table at the elegant women with their creamy complexions, never exposed to the harsh Texas sun. She glanced down at her uncovered shoulders and arms, noticing sun spots against the tan. Josie remembered holding her mother Valeria's hand and running a finger over the enlarged veins stretching like lines on a map, spotted with brown age freckles. Her own hands would be a replication of her mother's.

Soon, Josie enjoyed the boisterous conversations among these international travelers. Her shoulders relaxed, and she realized how stiff her neck and shoulders were from the constant pandemic demands.

Covid had interrupted staffing at the ranch and required weekly visits from doctors to treat their ranch hands. Escaping to Europe after the quarantines relented was a welcome change of scenery, far away from the stress.

During the second week of their stay, she and John bought trail maps. England was unlike anywhere they'd ever hiked because the country considers all its land a national treasure, and anyone can open a gate and walk through someone else's property. Unheard of, especially in Texas. No one dared trespass on anyone's land, treasure or not.

John studied the intricate maps. Every few hours, they entered another village—quaint, with rivers running through them and local pubs offering a kidney pie or fish and chips. The chips were French fries, not potato chips like at home, and seated at the Iron Gate Pub, John smacked his lips, smearing sea salt around his mouth.

Josie's brow relaxed. She and John needed time together away from the ranch responsibilities. Josie leaned toward him to kiss his mouth, his breath sweet as syrup.

It would be a lovely vacation.

CHAPTER 3

EMMA

A hand snatched Emma and pulled her back into the cave. "Put me down!" she barked.

A tall man gestured toward the darkness to invite her to stroll with him. Instead of taking his guidance, she darted in the opposite direction. He caught her and signaled again. Emma shook her head and pushed against his chest. He threw her over his shoulder like a sack of animal feed and carried her. Emma stopped kicking. Her shallow, rapid breathing made her light-headed, and she lay still against a broad back, trying to determine her next move. Emma touched long hair when she clung to his neck with one hand. He carried her quite a distance, and she leaned more closely against his back when he lowered his head where the cave's height decreased. Finally, he dumped Emma onto the ground at the foot of a flickering campfire.

Her heart pounded so rapidly that it seemed to skip beats, and sweat was sticky on her skin. Smoke burned her eyes and caused her to cough, but she could see the surrounding area from the fire's light and a wide opening in the cave's ceiling.

Standing by the flames were four men in various stages of undress. All were bare-chested with animal skins fashioned into breechcloths. The men's hair hung to their shoulders, decorated with feathers and braids, holding it out of their eyes. They wore boots fashioned from hammered rawhide. All stared at her, their brows in bewildered scrunches. Emma could not tell if they were Native Americans, indigenous Mexicans, or both. She saw no signs of modern conveniences or clothing. Were they cave dwellers? Here on The Thorn?

They talked and pointed at her. Some laughed. Emma did not understand the language, but it sounded like Spanish words were in the mix.

The tallest man in the group grasped the arm of one nearest him, a heavy-set man with a chest covered in necklaces of bone, spoke harshly, and shoved him toward a tunnel. He disappeared as if sent on an errand. After several minutes, the man returned.

Beside him walked a deeply wrinkled older man, his bearing almost regal. He steadied his steps with a highly polished wooden staff; it glinted in the firelight as he neared. Without taking his eyes off Emma, he sat on a log vacated by the others for him. He had a long, pointed nose, and his eyes—a cold, piercing brown—stilled her breathing.

He spoke in melodic tones to Emma, tucking his gray hair behind his ears.

"What is your name, child?"

"You speak English?" Emma's eyes widened.

"It has been a long time, but I still remember." He seemed kind and spoke with a gentle, but hesitant, tone.

Emma's mind spun with so many questions that she did not know where to begin.

"Who are you, and what are you doing on my ranch?" Emma's words rushed out in one breath.

He smiled and moved toward Emma to sit cross-legged beside her.

"*Your* ranch?"

"Yes, my family's land."

"My people have lived here for many years. Perhaps your family lives on *my* land?" His eyes crinkled.

"My name is Emma Rosales. Five generations of my family have owned this land. We also owned the land across the river before they declared it the property of Mexico."

"I know the ancients traveled here long before your time and settled in these caves. They were the original stewards of this place. We have lived below the land for many, many generations."

"How do you speak English?" Emma's vision was blurry from the smoke. She blinked to clear her strained eyes as the echo of her question hung in the air.

"My great-grandfather married a woman who spoke several tongues. She taught him to speak your language, and he required it of his family. He thought it might prepare his relatives in case more English speakers arrived."

"Do all of you speak it?" Emma gestured to the men gathered there, watching her.

"No. Some."

"What's your name?"

"I am Chatpa, which means Rising Owl. I am the eldest leader of The People."

She peered at the other men. They watched her intently, with some whispering and others snickering.

He noticed her feverishly glancing at the ones in front of them.

"I understand your concern. You will notice curiosity from my people. They consider it of great importance that you have joined us."

Emma wrung her hands and shook her head. "I have not *joined* you." A soured taste like yogurt filled her throat.

"I am certain you will not be allowed to leave."

AFTER ALL THE MEN left the cave except Chatpa, Emma sat with her back propped against the wall, cold air seeping through the cracks. She crossed her arms against bent knees and lowered her head in prayer. Not many people had told her what she could or couldn't do, even when she was young.

Emma remembered the summer of her tenth year when she decided she wanted to be a bull-rider.

"I'm tough, Mama. I can do it."

Emma's maternal grandmother, Valeria, turned her head as she chuckled.

"Oh, you're tough, little one. But bulls are tougher," Emma's mother, Josie, replied.

"I'll try," Emma retorted, sticking out her bottom lip and narrowing her eyes. She saw her Abuelita trying not to laugh.

That afternoon, Emma marched to the pen where a longhorn bull stood snorting and pawing.

"Angel, get a saddle, por favor!" she shouted to the ranch hand standing near the pen.

"What are you doing, Miss Emma?" Angel's eyes showed wide and white, and he rushed toward her.

"I'm gonna ride this bull. Now, do as I say."

Angel strode toward the barn, and, instead of returning with her saddle, her father walked toward her.

"Where's the saddle?" she asked.

"Oh, Emma. You are truly a Rosales woman." Her papa wrapped his arms around her. "That'll serve you well, my girl, but will also bring you pain."

He held her hand and walked her back to the house.

The following January, Emma stood in line at the County Show Barn. She gripped the halter on the same bull she had attempted to ride months before. He towered above her and snorted in her ear.

"You behave, Dumpling, or no alfalfa for you tonight!" Her stern little voice and clutch of the leash proved efficient, and the large animal lumbered after her around the ring. She had graduated to heavily tooled and highly polished black cowboy boots instead of her childish pink ones.

Still, Emma knew she would clean them when she returned to the ranch because everywhere she stepped was a pile of manure.

Emma learned from an early age to be brave and expect more from herself than even her parents did of her. This memory had popped into her mind because someone else had offered her a challenge everyone assumed was beyond her.

Now, Emma looked up in disbelief at the older man. *Not allow me to leave?* If she wasn't scared before, she was now.

Chatpa pushed himself to his feet slowly and extended his hand. "Come."

Emma reached for his hand and jumped to stand with a ramrod-straight back. She would not show him fear even if her hands were shaking and a bead of sweat wound down her spine.

Chatpa led her away from the fire, and Emma squinted to see in the darkness. But, as they walked, she could see a few torches attached to the walls.

From what she could tell, there were rooms of various sizes along the path. Some walls appeared to have windows cut in the stone. Some rooms had holes in the caves' ceilings like *skylights*. She wondered if there was a pecking order for who got the most natural light. Emma longed for an iPhone to take photographs. *But, of course, no one will believe this.*

When Chatpa stopped before a large doorway, she hesitated. He paused until she entered, and then he joined her.

Emma's eyes darted around the space. It reminded her of the forts she had created as a child. Stacked in the corner were hides, instead of blankets, where it looked like someone slept. A firepit was in the center of the room. A window, covered by a curtain of woven branches, faced the pathway outside, and there was an opening to the sky where Emma could see fluffy white clouds passing over. *How does the room stay dry in a rainstorm?* A second room opened to the left of the central area, and Chatpa motioned for her to enter.

"This will be your place to sleep," he told her.

"I have to go home. I can't stay here." Emma heard pleading in her voice, her nerves on fire.

"My people would consider it dangerous to our protection if I allowed you to leave," he said, shaking his head. "The ancestors passed down stories of the few times they had contact with intruders who stole our horses, burned our crops, and killed some of our men. Our ancestors then warned us against strangers in our homes. Now that you are here, we cannot allow you to tell others of our existence, or we could experience warfare."

Emma's throat was so dry that she could barely swallow. "How is it you exist here without discovery?"

"The ancients came from tunnels and saw that cliffs covered our caves from the sky, and there are no openings, except on the side that faces our pastures. There is only one path in and out of these hidden lands. No one else knows the way, except The People."

Emma sank to the floor. Chatpa patted her shoulder.

"I am sorry, Emma, but you must stay." He left her there on the ground.

Emma covered her face with her hands and felt like someone had kicked her in the stomach.

IT WAS FREEZING IN the cave room. Every time Emma awoke throughout the night, she reached for a tablet. She chastised herself for extending her hand to an electronic device like all friends her age. The absence was like having a physical limb removed, and the sensation continued. *What an addiction.*

Emma had laid down on the hard rock floor to sleep after Chatpa left. Shivering, she awoke to find an animal hide placed over her during the night. Emma rolled herself into it and slept again.

When light beamed into the room from the opening overhead, Emma smelled smoke and heard wood popping on a burning fire. Wrapping the covering around her shoulders, she walked to the pit surrounded by stones and knelt there, feeling the rush of warmth.

"You are awake," Chatpa said, as he entered the room.

Emma gritted her teeth. "I won't tell anyone about your presence on this property. I need to go home to my family. Will you let me leave?"

"Not today."

Did that offer hope she could leave someday? Or did he merely intend to placate her to keep her quiet? She didn't know how many days she could stay here like this.

CHAPTER 4

EMMA

Emma stood at the door and looked down the corridor in both directions. She did not hear anyone coming, so she hurried out the door and into the darkness. She ran her hands along the walls and looked for any sliver of light.

Three days and nights had passed, and Emma had not left Chatpa's quarters. He checked on her several times and brought her warm broth to sip, a raw turnip root, or a piece of dried meat. Emma knew she could not find her way through the cave mazes, but she decided she would find an opening and escape to the outside.

When Chatpa left on the morning of the fourth day, Emma looked to the sky showing into her confinement, but the walls were too steep, and there was nothing to stand on.

Now, alone in the dark of the pathway, Emma furrowed her brow. Suddenly, she spotted a wide opening on the wall above her head. She reached up to locate a ledge and pulled herself onto her elbows. Then, with her feet scrabbling against the rocks, she shoved herself toward the light beam. *Free!* She landed in a heap outside the hole.

Her breath froze in her chest. She precariously perched on an unsteady formation that had seemed like a shelf before she tumbled onto it. It swayed in the wind with her as an anchor.

Emma gripped the sheer side of a cliff. Looking down caused her to gasp. She could not see the ground, only a deep, murky, and terrifying crevasse. Her stomach curdled, and she leaned back. A small pine tree sprouted on the mountain's rocky side, and Emma placed her foot against it to release her squat and stretch her legs.

She was in a dangerous situation, and the next powerful gust of wind could topple her off balance and into the precipitous ravine. A trail of sweat beaded on her upper lip and dripped from her hairline.

"Emma? Emma!" She heard Chatpa's voice calling from far below her.

"Here—I'm here!" Her voice quaked, and her eyes darted from side to side.

A man's scowling face appeared in the opening and he grasped her arm. Dragged toward him, she re-entered the hole, and he dangled her over the floor beneath them. She gripped his forearm until he released her. Emma slumped in front of Chatpa, who stood with his arms crossed, staring at her.

"You could have fallen to your death."

"Will you let me leave now, Chatpa?" The days-old request had been in many forms.

"My family at home needs me."

"Search parties will comb every square inch of this land to find me, and they will not be kind to you."

"Why are you keeping me here? I have to go!"

But Chatpa's response was always the same. "Not today, Emma." A now familiar refrain.

AFTER HER FIRST ESCAPE attempt fiasco, Emma stayed in the cave. Chatpa stationed a man to stand outside his dwelling; so, she had no choice but to remain imprisoned. She lost track of the number of days and nights she remained in his quarters.

Emma slept most of the time. Sleep was a form of escape and killed large chunks of time when she did not encounter nightmares that threw her back into consciousness with jolts. Chatpa slept in another area, and Emma did not notice when he came and went.

At her wit's end, Emma fidgeted and paced the small space. Even when occupied with daytime chores on the ranch, she had spent her nights watching Netflix or YouTube channels. Now, her time loomed before her without any distractions. It bothered her that she missed immediate entertainment by turning on a computer or television. *I would give anything for a cute kitten video.*

When Emma arose, she swept ashes from the floor with a broom fashioned from dried grasses and cringed when she noticed spider webs and bat droppings in the corners. She added branches from a stacked pile of wood to the firepit. Chatpa gave her two pieces of flint, and she had a small fire blazing when he arrived home at night.

"Tell me about this group you call The People."

"The People came out of tunnels many generations ago and found this hidden place to live. We continue to share the legacy of property and work they provided us."

"No one knows you are here?"

"Many years ago, strangers passing through this land came here, and we welcomed them at first. Then, they stole our horses and gave us little in return. We stay to ourselves, so our families are not in peril from outsiders. We wish to stay uncontacted.

That is why we cannot allow you to leave, Emma. You would bring danger to us."

Emma jumped to her feet and clasped her hands behind her back. "I'm the leader of my people, Chatpa. They will not rest until they find me. So, the only danger that would come to you is if you don't allow me to return home."

ONE DAY, AFTER A week of confinement, Chatpa watched her cleaning the cave and asked, "Do you want to feel the sunshine on your face?"

Nodding her head vigorously, she said, "Yes, please."

He motioned to her, and she walked behind him down a long corridor. They made so many turns and switchbacks Emma knew she would never remember the way out. Suddenly looming before them was the brightness she missed.

Stepping outside, Emma lifted her face. *Will I ever complain about the hot Texas sunshine again?* Even though it was partly cloudy, the sky's brilliance burned her retinas. She squinted and blocked the glare with one cupped hand.

They were at the edge of a meadow she had seen days before from the hole in the cave's ceiling. Emma walked toward horses tethered to stakes in the ground and ran her hand over their foreheads.

"These are good-looking animals, Chatpa. Where'd you get them?"

"They come to us in large numbers."

"Wild horses?" Emma blinked against the harsh intensity. Her eyes needed to become accustomed to the light again.

Emma had lost track of how many days she had lived in the caves, maybe a week or ten days. She wondered if Flora had alerted her parents to her absence. Probably not yet. Ever since she was young, she had camped on the ranch, and everyone trusted her to return.

But, wait, she was supposed to go with Norma to the Sharonville Dance Hall on Saturday night. Would Norma call the house when she did not show up?

Emma noticed several women staring at her. They sat near a stream.

"May I bathe in the water?" Emma looked at Chatpa.

"In the river's curve, you will be away from all eyes."

She walked toward the river, looked over her shoulder, and saw Chatpa motion to one of the girls.

Emma followed the stream and, except for the lone woman who shadowed her from a distance, she did not see anyone else. Skinning off the torn and filthy clothes she had worn for an eternity, Emma waded into the deep, rushing water. She ducked under the stream and scrubbed her hair. Immediately refreshed, she wished for a bar of soap and a towel.

When Emma bobbed to the surface, she saw the woman standing on the shore holding a garment toward her. Turning her back to Emma, she laid it on the ground and walked away.

Emma crossed her arms over her chest and walked out of the river. Instead of her dirty clothes, a tanned hide dress replaced them. Emma pulled it over her wet body. It was loose like a muumuu her mother once wore to a Hawaiian luau on the ranch. Next, she pulled a pair of leather strappings shaped like boots onto her feet. *At least I'm cleaner than I was.* Emma saw Chatpa waiting for her when she re-entered the pasture.

"Can we stay outside?"

"For a while." He smiled at her.

They sat on the ground in silence. Emma held her hair back with one hand and closed her eyes. The sun baked her head with its luxurious warmth and scorched her neck. The same woman who had brought her dress to the river sat behind Emma and braided her hair.

"You look like sisters," Chatpa remarked.

As soon as he spoke, a group of young men rode into the paddock at a fast rate of speed. They laughed as they bounded off the ponies and walked toward where she and Chatpa sat.

One man strode confidently toward her and grabbed a braid of Emma's hair, pulling her to her feet.

"Owww. Let go of me." She slapped at him, but he held her at arm's length.

Chatpa stood and rushed to her side.

"Do not ever touch this woman again, Chesma."

Chesma laughed and dropped Emma's hair.

Speaking to Chatpa in another language, Chesma motioned at Emma.

"It is time to go back," Chatpa said.

"What did he say?"

"He wants you to know he will be your husband."

Emma's face flushed, and she felt her pulse quicken. "You'd better tell him I'll die first."

CHAPTER 5

EMMA

Entering the cool, dark caves after being in the brightness, Emma felt her pupils shrink, losing her sight for a moment. She placed her hand on Chatpa's back and followed him down the long, winding path to their quarters. When they sat cross-legged on the floor, she turned to Chatpa.

"What did you mean by that man wanting me as a wife?"

Chatpa looked at her face and sighed. "You were sent to us by the ancestors to join our numbers."

Emma stabbed her finger toward Chatpa's face. "I'm not here to stay and be someone's wife. *My* people chose me to be *their* chief." Even as she spat the words, Emma's lips trembled at the thought of ruling her kingdom, The Thorn Ranch.

"You are to be chief, Emma?" Chatpa's eyebrows raised. "That is remarkable for a woman."

"Yes." Emma drew a sharp intake of breath.

Did he believe her? He seemed to look at her with new respect.

"I am still the leader of The People, but my grandson has more influence with the young people. We will discuss the matter with him," Chatpa said.

Emma huddled in the corner, shivering. *I won't ever gripe about my ranch responsibilities again if I can just get out of here.* How many women in her family had ever been in a precarious predicament like this?

Emma's great-grandmother Lola had lived in a casita on the ranch when Emma was young. On Sundays, she joined the family in the main house for dinner. Emma liked to sit next to her and hear stories about her childhood.

Lola often pointed to a framed photo hanging in the hall that showcased five generations of Rosales women—Camilla, a stern great-great-grandmother; Lola, the great-grandmother; Valeria, a grandmother; and Emma, a baby in her mother Josie's arms. Emma liked to think about the women surrounding her with love. Those women were tough, and most females in the Rosales family lived to be one hundred years old.

Lola had told Emma stories of her mother Camilla riding a herd of horses across the Rio Grande River. Camilla descended from Spanish nobility, and the king of Spain granted the noble families large sections of land. Camilla and her husband settled The Thorn property on both sides of the border, claiming hundreds of thousands of acres, but losing some after Santa Anna was defeated at San Jacinto in 1836. As a result, the boundary between Texas and Mexico became the Rio Grande.

There were tales about harsh living conditions in makeshift cabins with dirt floors. *No wonder Camilla looked stern*, Emma thought. Camilla did not put up with nonsense, especially from her family members. She'd ruled with an iron fist. Unfortunately, she died not long after the photo, so Emma never knew her, but stories about Camilla were legendary.

Camilla's daughter, Lola, learned the ranch life from her mother and passed those skills to Valeria, who taught Josie, who lent her expertise to Emma. After listening to the tales, Emma sometimes wished she could have ridden on the cattle drives to New Orleans in the early years, as her Abuelita described.

Emma had stood in the hall and looked at the portraits of those fierce women with pride and sometimes trepidation. After celebrating her twenty-second birthday, Emma studied the paintings and felt rather than saw her mother pause behind her.

"Mama, how do you know when you're ready to run the ranch?"

"I will know for you, my love. When I'm ready to live in Valeria's casita, and you are ready to take over this house, you'll assume all the ranch duties."

Emma shook her head from side to side.

"Not sure that will ever happen."

"Oh, I thought the same thing, Emma. But, one day, believe it or not, you'll want to be in charge."

At the time, Emma had not believed her mother. Instead, she felt a deep thumbprint on the top of her head pressing down on her ability to make a choice different than her relatives had made.

Now sitting in the dim cave with the memory of strong women in her family, Emma knew she would not readily submit to these captors. *I'll continue my efforts to escape.*

She tried to nap. Emma awoke when she heard Chatpa's voice speaking to someone.

She wrapped the hide tightly around herself and stepped into the adjoining room. Standing before her was a tall man.

When he turned to face her, she saw his resemblance to Chatpa. His skin was tan, and his arms and chest were muscular. Dark hair hung to his shoulders. If he'd been a student on her college campus, her eyes might have followed him. He was handsome and close to her age.

"Emma, this is Kai, which means Sparrow."

"Thank you for meeting with me. I want to ask you to allow me to leave to go back to my family."

"Please sit." Kai motioned to a woven grass mat next to the fire. "When you found your way here, our people took it as a sign the ancestors chose you for us."

Emma spit out her words. "I didn't choose to be here. I *choose* to return to my family."

"Perhaps you will change your mind."

She knew she wouldn't. But she was starting to see they'd never change theirs either.

CHAPTER 6

EMMA

Emma sat high in a tree and could not see the ground. Water crept up the trunk toward her, and she climbed higher, clinging to the limbs above her. Her feet slipped as she grasped upward. Her heart hammered in her throat.

Emma awoke with a start and sat up straight, her chest still heaving. Looking around in the dark, she realized she was in Chatpa's quarters, not in a tree. *I'm stranded, nonetheless.*

She sniffed the now familiar smell of his pipe. Puffs of smoke drifted into her room, and she knew he was tending the fire. She pushed back the blanket that covered her and joined him.

Kneeling beside him, she warmed her outstretched hands.

"Chatpa, yesterday a horse was injured by how a man tied him to a tree. I don't wish to become a wife to anyone here, and I don't expect to be here much longer, but I would like to help. I trained in animal health care and agriculture. I could advise you on your crops and help keep your animals well."

Animals had been Emma's weakness since her childhood. She could not bear for one to be neglected or mistreated, even if by accident.

Emma smiled at a flash of memory. Flora had set mouse traps in the pantry, but before she could catch any, Emma removed the traps and put cheese in shoeboxes. Her mother found the containers under Emma's bed full of baby mice.

"I am glad you are one of us, Emma," Chatpa said.

She squinted her eyes at him. "I won't stay but want to make the most of my time here."

Emma was bored and desperate with her captivity, so she couldn't help but offer. And, she thought she might find a greater chance to escape if she had more freedom.

"I will let Kai know of your special talents. He and I are the only ones able to heal the sick. You will be a welcome addition to The People."

That afternoon, Kai came to escort Emma out of the cave and into the enclosures for the livestock. The People had fashioned roughly hewn timbers into fences for the animals. Kai said they moved the area around the meadow for the animals to graze.

"That's a smart way to feed livestock, Kai. Do you use the same methods with your crops and rotate them to different areas, so you don't deplete the soil?"

He looked puzzled at some of her phrases and asked her about definitions when she used a word he did not understand, but it surprised her how knowledgeable he was about most subjects they discussed. Of course, he had no textbook learning, but he had better skills than she had with the land and animals, maybe from generations of trial and error.

As they walked, Emma noticed men standing near them and watching her. Her stomach felt uneasy, and her palms sweated.

Emma had never felt less than a formidable opponent with men on her ranch. Was that because they respected her position as a future owner, and she had grown up knowing most of them? Emma knew if ranch hands acted out or flirted with her, her father would shut it down.

She even felt more capable in a college town bar, discouraging or encouraging young men and being confident. Surrounded by her friends, Emma could laugh and say, "Not interested," or "Why don't you join us?" but not here. She wished for the hundredth time she hadn't left her gun in the bag on the saddle—now hidden in the bowels of the cave system.

Kai did not seem to notice her nervousness. He was busy making a poultice of mud and herbs he had picked from the pasture. The soil reeked of iron in the clay, and she wrinkled her nose. After all her animal science experiences, Emma had thought foul odors would not bother her. She recognized rosemary but was unfamiliar with the other broad leaves he chose.

The man's horse was lame. Kai wrapped the mixture around the leg and secured it with large leaves and vines, tying it firmly. The horse's owner appeared to thank him and offered what looked like venison jerky. Emma remembered her mother's stories about the years when a chicken, eggs, or a side of beef served as barter payments for services rendered on many ranches.

Emma wandered into the pasture and looked at the corn growing there. She motioned to the stalks, and Kai nodded his head. She gathered a few ears and shucked them on the spot.

Emma heard giggling and turned to see two young boys standing in the river with nets. One of them yanked a fish into the threads. They scrambled onto the bank and stood dripping.

The boys looked around eight years old, with straight black hair, browned skin, and deep brown eyes. Shyly, they offered her the fish. She pointed at herself, raising her eyebrows as if to say,

"For me?" They nodded and ran down the trail toward the bend in the river.

Holding her ears of corn and the fish, she rejoined Kai as he finished examining a baby a woman held. He dabbed a bit of salve on the baby's stomach.

"You have a feast planned?" He pointed to Emma's bounty.

"Yes. You're welcome to join us."

That night, Emma roasted corn, then speared the fish and smoked it over the fire in Chatpa's quarters. Kai brought plums, and Emma passed around small pottery dishes of the food.

For the first time since they discovered her in the cave, Emma enjoyed a quiet meal with her captors. The smoky tenderness of the fish melted in her mouth, and the corn crunched in her teeth.

"What if we make this my *last* supper here with you?"

CHAPTER 7

EMMA, AGE TWENTY-ONE

Emma walked quickly toward the Texas A&M Veterinary Medicine Center, an imposing building. She remembered thinking as a first-year student, she would never find her way around this one building, much less the entire campus. Her only worries now were finding a parking space and not being late.

Her class team had a presentation on animal heart murmurs today. She handled the PowerPoint illustrations for her group. Jeff Bower, their team captain, had led the experiment and would speak about their findings. She was happy to be on his team. He was intelligent and capable—being handsome did not hurt him.

Fingers crossed, today would be the day he asked her to join him for lunch. She had been hoping for an invitation for weeks, but he always remained after class talking with a group of students, and she usually just grabbed a coffee on her way back to the dorm.

Panting, she jogged up three flights of stairs and arrived at the classroom early. Jeff was the only person there.

"Hi," she gasped, out of breath.

"Hi, Emma. Glad you made it, so we can make sure everything works."

She reached into her bag and found the memory drive with the presentation stored on it. Tossing her purse on a desk, Emma joined him at the projector and desktop computer. She deftly booted up the PC and pressed the stick into the USB port. The presentation bloomed to life on the large screen in front of the classroom.

"Perfect," he drawled. "Terrific work."

Emma smiled. A heart was beating on the screen, and the sound echoed throughout the room. *Ba-bump, ba-bump, ba-bump.* Emma hoped it was from the presentation and not her own. She could not keep her eyes off Jeff's smiling face full of freckles with a mop of curly reddish-brown hair falling over his blue eyes.

Later, when applause filled the classroom, Emma nodded toward her teammates. Her stern professor, Dr. Waller, said, "An excellent presentation. You other teams, take note." That was the highest praise he ever gave. They were successful.

"Let's celebrate," Jeff announced to the team. "Everyone meets at the Dixie Chicken in an hour?"

Emma tried to look nonchalant but dashed out of the stuffy classroom and down the stairs. She had time for a quick shower and to look more presentable.

Drying her long, thick hair took too much time, so she yanked it into a high ponytail and smeared a little foundation on her bronzed cheeks. *I cannot not decide what to wear.*

A heap of discarded clothing on her bed grew taller. The floral skirt looked too fancy, and her cut-off shorts were not nice enough. Finally, she pulled denim trousers out of a drawer and opted for a soft blue sweater. Emma decided against cowboy boots. She leaned over to fasten on a pair of sandals instead, then grabbed her car keys, skipped the steps, and entered the parking lot.

When she arrived at the Chicken, Emma scanned the room.

Well, again, I'm the first to arrive. Then she saw Jeff perusing a menu at a four-top table in a back corner. Glancing up, he waved her over.

"You're always punctual." He tilted his head to look at her.

Emma could feel her face grow warm, and she laughed. "Years of having to show ranch hands I wasn't a lazy teenager. I had to get up before dawn to impress them."

"You grew up on a ranch?" Jeff leaned toward her for her reply, but the other two team members, Danny and Cathy, interrupted them. The conversation halted as everyone ordered beers and fries. Emma requested a Diet Coke because she had never developed a taste for the bitterness of the students' preferred drink.

"Here's to an A in the hardest class in college!" Jeff raised a frothy glass and clicked it against his table mates' drinks. "You each played an important part in our team score," he continued.

They all seemed comfortable, and the night was pleasant, with tasty snacks and comparisons of which instructors they preferred or detested. Emma sucked her teeth to remove the slick melted cheese from the nachos lingering there.

She angled her chair in Jeff's direction to see his face. Emma handed him extra napkins when his hands became coated with sticky sauce from the chicken wings, and he licked his greasy fingers. *Am I being too obvious?*

After their celebration, Emma walked out with Jeff and clicked her key case to open the driver's side of her Jeep.

"Nice ride."

"Thanks. It was a graduation present from my parents." She looked over at the shiny Wrangler. Black and with all the bells and whistles, it zipped around the campus and town but could climb a rocky hill just as quickly.

"Well, see you around." He closed her door after she climbed in and wandered down the sidewalk.

Emma gripped the steering wheel and maneuvered into the street. She chewed on her lower lip. Emma liked Jeff but could not tell if he liked her or was just being polite. Were there signs she was missing?

Emma could trail a wounded deer for miles or identify wild animals by their prints on the scorched ground. She flirted easily with guys for whom she held no attraction.

Why don't I have the same instincts with guys I really like?

CHAPTER 8

EMMA

After Emma's first excursion into the fields with Kai, he came to Chatpa's quarters each morning and drank whatever brew she was heating. She longed for one of Flora's tortillas and a stiff cup of coffee at breakfast.

Then, Emma and Kai discussed how many of The People had ailments or which animals needed tending.

Emma followed Kai to other cave dwellings to tend to a child's cough or a man's leg infection. Kai's skills of mixing herbs to calm a fever and his steady hands impressed her as he used a sharpened bone and sinew to stitch a wound.

"How long have you been treating your tribe?" Emma asked as they made their way through darkened hallways.

"My grandfather taught me after my father died," he said. "Chatpa knows every plant in the pasture, and we pick and dry them to use. I will show you the medicine room."

Turning toward light flickering into the darkness, they stopped to climb rock steps fashioned into the side of the cave. Emma blinked as they exited the dim light into the brightness.

They were standing on the top of a rocky plateau. No one would believe there were hundreds of caves underneath their feet. She walked through rows of slatted wood with herbs of every hue drying in the glare.

Emma recognized a few of the dehydrating plants. She had helped her mother choose peppermint from her garden for iced tea and, as a child, had picked bouquets of dandelions to present to her grandmother, Valeria. But most Emma could not identify and yearned for her phone to take a photo, google the plant, or ask Alexa. So instead, she pointed to the leaves as she walked, while Kai answered with names she did not recognize and told her how he used them as remedies. His lesson reminded her of Pedro teaching her about seeds.

"The root of the wild carrot is delicious when stewed but helpful for women who are having trouble conceiving a baby." Next, he pointed to a lacy flower with a tuber attached. The flower looked like the Queen Anne's Lace she rode through in the fields at the ranch. "You must know the difference between this one and one that looks very similar but is poisonous."

"Kind of like mushrooms?" She picked up a dark fungus drying on a board.

"Yes," he said. "Some will cause terrible nightmares, even when you are awake."

Emma smiled at his version of a hallucination.

He told her that the dandelions she recognized were for ridding the body of toxins and the peppermint for digestion issues. Kai was as knowledgeable as a compounding pharmacist. And he put his experience to use every day. It seemed there was always someone to treat or with whom to share food.

"Grandfather is one of our Eagle doctors. Our tribe considers the Golden Eagle revered because it flies highest in the skies and is closer to God. So, we call our most trusted healers Eagles.

"What else does an Eagle doctor do?" Emma leaned toward him.

"He interprets dreams. Our braves often fast without food and water and go to our sacred spaces to receive visions. Then, Chatpa tells them what they mean."

"Can *you* interpret dreams?"

"Sometimes, I can see what a dream means in my mind." Kai's dark eyes rested on a distant hill as he spoke.

Emma sighed and blew out her breath in a huff. *When will this encounter end? What would I see if I were a dream interpreter about my returning home?*

By now, the ranch hands would believe she was missing and send out search parties.

Would her parents have returned from Europe to investigate for themselves?

CHAPTER 9

EMMA, AGE TWENTY-TWO

Emma stood at one side of the quad and watched as younger siblings visited their college-age brothers and sisters. Many grabbed each other and hugged tightly. They laughed and made jokes, and Emma felt her singleness acutely. Her stomach had ached with loneliness since childhood; she missed young relatives to keep her company. *Did I want a sibling so the ranch's pressure on me alone would not be so great?*

Emma always wondered why her mother did not want to fill their house with children. Having the neighbor kids visit their ranch several times each year made her desire for more family members stronger.

Once, she remembered asking her mother, "Mama, why do you and Papa just have one child? All the ranchers have many children."

"Humph. We hire our helpers; we don't birth them."

"I want to have a brother or sister." Emma pouted and stuck her lower lip out.

"When you have a perfect child, there's no need to duplicate, querida." Josie laughed at Emma's puzzled expression. "The Thorn has had a one-woman heir for each generation. No need to change the formula that works."

Emma remembered overhearing her parents discussing the same topic she and her mother had argued.

"It would be nice to give Emma playmates," her father had pleaded, his blue eyes looking forlorn.

"She has friends on adjoining ranches, ranch hands, and all the animals she could want. So why would we need to have more children?"

"What if, God forbid, something happened to her?" Her father lowered his voice to a whisper that Emma could barely hear.

"Nothing's going to happen to Emma!" Her mother's voice sounded angry as if he had summoned the gods to will such a tragedy. Josie barely weighed a hundred pounds, but her presence was like dark electricity sparking through the room.

Emma stopped asking for siblings, and she guessed her father did, too. None arrived.

THE COLLEGE PLANNED END-OF-THE-YEAR activities and Emma picked up an events program. The organizers had arranged for a picnic on the West Campus, where Emma attended most classes. Then, the agricultural and veterinary colleges' get-togethers, graduation ceremonies, Corps of Cadets Aggie Band and Singing Cadets' performances, and the Corps' final review rounded out the schedule.

Emma loved to hear the all-male choral voices harmonizing across the Quad. In addition, there were always shouts of "Howdy" as the official school greeting when students passed each other. She thought about introducing the welcome saying back on the ranch. Her parents would get a kick out of it.

Emma and her friend Norma walked to a party just off campus, where lines of cars and loud music from the backyard signaled they were at the correct address.

An emailed invitation encouraged the guests to expect a "hot but sweet time" to celebrate the end of their senior year. Emma liked a theme party, and everyone was instructed to bring ingredients for s'mores.

Emma looped a grocery sack holding a bag of dessert ingredients over her arm, and Norma held skewers fashioned from two wire coat hangers. They made their way through the crowded house and into the backyard, where a dozen firepits were blazing. Norma and Emma chose one without many people gathered around and pulled up two folding chairs. When the marshmallows were toasted, they placed them on chocolate squares and graham crackers.

"Enough of those to share?"

Emma looked up from where she squatted before the fire.

"Oh, hi, Jeff. Sure. Join us." Emma felt her cheeks blush, not just from the heat of the fire. She scrambled to her feet and handed him her wire hanger, then stuck a blue-colored marshmallow on the end.

"I haven't seen you around campus," Jeff said.

"Just packing and attending some of the last activities." Emma noticed Norma watching her. She grinned back.

"Jeff, this is Norma. Norma, Jeff. We were in a class together." Emma watched Norma nod knowingly.

"Ha. I think the woman understates her involvement too much. She pulled our team project out of the fire." Jeff cackled.

"Everyone helped. It turned out well," Emma protested.

"I'd say. First A for me in quite a while." Jeff winked at her.

"Emma never makes less than an A," said Norma. "She's a wonderful tutor, too, and increased my scores over the past four years."

"I wish I'd known that earlier," Jeff said.

Their trio sat and studied the leaping tongues of fire as they danced over the hangers and caught the marshmallows ablaze. Jeff huffed and blew on the blue molten lump that had burst into flames. He grinned but stuffed the morsel that now looked like ash into his mouth.

"Just like I like it. Burned to a crisp."

The girls laughed and rotated their spears to avoid the same occurrence. Norma's hot sugar melted the creamy chocolate on her cracker, which oozed onto her crisp white blouse.

"Yikes! I just bought this shirt! Y'all excuse me. I'll run back to the dorm and see if I can soak this chocolate out."

Emma's eyes followed her friend as she dashed away and then returned to Jeff.

"I don't know much about you, Emma."

"Not much to know."

"What will you do this summer?"

"I have an internship with Dr. Abelson in town for a month. Then, I'll be going home. One dorm allows those of us with jobs to stay there for such a short time."

"That's nice. I'm going home to Abilene. My father has a construction job lined up for me. I wish I were doing something in our major, like you."

From his tone, Emma could tell he was envious of her shadowing the vet, who had the most extensive practice in town.

She felt a little embarrassed that her mother had just picked up the phone and secured her daughter an exceptional summer job.

They'd mapped out all her summers long before graduation. Emma had had a full rotation of every medical and agricultural experience she needed to make her degree work for her. She once felt she was preparing a resume for a job search; instead, her mother had planned her career. Emma would return home to the ranch for her lifetime of work. But, more than once, she'd questioned her mother about that permanent decision.

"Mother, what if I decide I want to go to vet school and own a veterinary clinic in Fort Worth?"

"Fort Worth?"

"Well, anywhere." She moved her wrist in a circle.

"Why, querida? Why would you want to be anywhere else? You have the largest practice in Texas right here."

"A small clinic might be nice." Emma's eyes darted from her mother's stern gaze to her own hands folded in her lap.

"This ranch will be your life's work, as it has been mine, your grandmother's, and all the women before us."

"Everyone should be able to plan their own lives."

"Those who don't have the land we do may have that choice, Emma. We do not and would not choose differently if we could."

I know you would not make a different decision, Mama, but what about my alternatives? Emma knew the odds were not in her favor. There were a million reasons she could not leave her ranch—a million *acres* why.

Emma snapped back to the present after a sugar rush dipped her head and drooped her eyes. Then, she felt Jeff wiping her lip with his thumb.

"What?" she mumbled.

"You had chocolate on your lip."

His face was inches from hers, and she could feel his breath on her skin. Before she could create a snappy reply, Jeff kissed her softly.

"Still chocolate on my mouth?" Emma grinned.

"Yep." He reached for her hand, and they sat quietly watching the flames and glowing embers.

"Emma, maybe I can visit you this summer while you are here in College Station."

"I'd like that."

"Will you put your number in my phone so I can call you?"

"Sure." Emma typed her mobile number into his iPhone.

"Looks like it will be a great summer, after all."

Things are certainly looking up, Emma thought.

CHAPTER 10

EMMA

Emma stepped from the darkness into a cool breeze blowing across the pasture. She glanced around and saw swirling rusty red and orange leaves blowing into the creek's water.

Her thoughts jumbled. Had she spent the rest of the summer here since returning from her internship at College Station? The weather announced fall in the air. What were her parents thinking about her disappearance after all this time?

Since her capture, she sometimes felt a tiny sense of reprieve, like she was on a summer vacation. Her responsibilities were less in the caves than being bound to the enormity of the ranch. Emma felt guilty, but she still felt conflicted about her ranch obligations.

The days were a blur of helping Kai with the animals and sick members of the tribe. She became adept at the homeopathic healing he used. When they diagnosed the illness, she now went to the storehouse and mixed the herbs needed for treatment without his supervision.

Today, for the first time since her arrival, she noticed men standing in huddles, pointing to horses, and examining their bows. It looked like an intentional gathering.

"Kai, what are the men discussing?"

"They are talking about the night they will ride out of the canyon and hunt for meat to dry for the winter ahead."

"I'd like to go with the hunters."

His expression showed amusement. "Why, Emma? You have not trained like the men."

"I've been on many hunting excursions. I know how to skin a deer or field-dress a wild hog."

Kai's face showed surprise. "You are a woman of many talents."

"May I hunt?"

"The women do not travel with the men. It is not done. The men will spend a night away from our home, and it would not be safe for you to be among some of them."

She could hear the meaning of the warning between his words. He feared that Chesma would take advantage of her.

"Come with us. You can protect me." Her eyes begged him.

Emma knew Kai realized she would not give up, despite knowing her for only a few months.

"Let's talk to Chatpa tonight." Kai sounded resigned.

Emma replaced the dried plants on the shelves in the storehouse.

"What are we waiting for?"

They stepped across the threshold of Chatpa's cave and saw him sitting in the corner smoking a pipe.

"You are back early, Emma." His voice was gravelly.

"We're here to make a request." Emma sounded braver than she felt.

Chatpa saw Kai standing behind her. "Hello, my son."

"Hello, Grandfather."

"What is the request?" His eyes flickered between the two of them.

"I'd like to ride with the hunting party, Chatpa. I'm an excellent hunter and can be of help to them."

Chatpa's eyebrows raised, and he looked over her head to Kai.

"Are you suggesting such a thing?"

"This is entirely her idea. If you consent, I will accompany her."

"I am not sure the other hunters will permit it."

"I will speak to them."

Chatpa bowed his head toward Kai. "If you wish."

Emma clapped her hands.

"Not so fast, Emma. The other men may not be as soft as Kai and me." Chatpa smiled, and Kai nodded.

"I trust Kai can make it happen."

He ducked his head to leave the cave.

"I think you have a protector, Emma." Chatpa puffed on his pipe and blew the sweet smoke into the dim space.

Emma looked fondly at Chatpa. She would miss him when she escaped.

CHAPTER 11

EMMA, AGE TWENTY-TWO

The day after the marshmallow roast, Emma rushed from the dorm to the parking lot to meet Norma. They planned to eat lunch together. Instead, Emma saw Jeff leaning against her Jeep, talking to her friend. Their backs were to her, and they did not see her approach.

"She said she grew up on a ranch," Jeff said.

"Not just any ranch. My folks own a ranch that would fit in Emma's compound. Haven't you ever heard about The Thorn?"

"*The* Thorn? Are you telling me Emma's family owns the largest ranch in Texas, maybe anywhere?"

"Yep."

Emma pressed her lips tightly together and squinted. Since childhood, her family warned her about letting people get acquainted with her before discovering The Thorn was her ranch. As a result, they were less likely to see her as an heiress and just as a friend. Unfortunately, Norma had spilled the beans before Emma could get to know Jeff better.

Sure enough, when he turned to look at her, he stared with what looked like stars in his eyes.

"Hey, Emma. Want to go to the last dance with me tomorrow night?" He moved closer to her.

"Thanks for the invitation, but I've got to pack my room to move to another dorm." She had hoped to get to know him better during the summer. Now, she was not sure she could trust his intentions.

The following day, she hugged Norma goodbye and drove her overpacked Jeep to another dorm, where students stayed while they held summer jobs in College Station. Emma's internship for a month assisting in a veterinary practice would be her last time living in her beloved university town, and she would make the best of it.

JEFF WAS TRUE TO his word and visited Emma on two of the weekends she interned in College Station. He was charming, held her hand, opened car doors for her, and paid for their meals.

On their last date, before she headed home, Jeff gathered her into his arms and kissed her until the windows in her Jeep fogged in the early morning cooler temperatures.

Finally, she thought. But still, Jeff asked many questions about her family ranch and seemed in awe of the immense property. He even clipped articles about The Thorn and brought them to their dates.

The summer was nearing an end, and Emma's expertise in handling dogs and cats and, less frequently, a rabbit or bird endeared her to the vet for whom she interned, and he offered her a permanent place at his practice. But at the moment, Emma knew her parents expected her at The Thorn.

Was she lingering in College Station to avoid the inevitable decision to accept her destiny on the ranch? Just to hedge her bets, she asked the vet if she could discuss the possibility of her working for him after the summer break.

She called Jeff to tell him she was headed home, but no answer. So after many trips up and down the dorm stairs and with her Jeep stuffed to the gills, she traveled toward the now-familiar highway south. She dialed the radio to a country station with oldies, sang along with Willie Nelson, and crooned to Patsy Cline. Emma's phone dinged and a text popped up from Norma, so she stopped for gas and lunch and wrote her back.

Norma: *Are you still on the road?*
Emma: *Yep. Just stopped for lunch.*
Norma: *Let me know when you get home, and we'll talk about the dance in a couple of weeks. I want to know what to wear.*
Emma: *Standard—blue jeans and boots.*
Norma: *I knew you'd say that.* ☺
Emma: *LOL. Talk soon.*

Stuffing the rest of her taco into her mouth, Emma pulled the nozzle out of her gas cap and climbed back into the Jeep. She arrived home before dark.

"Buenos días, Miss Emma!" She did not have time to open the front door before Flora threw it wide. She dove into Flora's powerful arms and laughed when the woman exclaimed she had grown two inches.

"You say the same thing every time you see me. I must be six-foot-five by now."

"It's true. You're not our little girl any longer. You are a grown woman."

"That's scary, isn't it?"

Emma's mother rushed down the hall to get the next hug.

"We're happy you're back, little one. We have a couple of weeks to catch you up to speed on the ranch before your father and I head to Europe."

Her parents escaped the Texas heat for a couple of months every summer. Sometimes they went to Europe, sometimes to the mountains of Colorado. Of course, they always invited Emma, but she preferred Texas to anywhere else.

"I don't complain about the heat because I don't like the cold," she told them. They smiled and said she had Latina blood in her veins, loving the sun's warmth as she did.

While Emma's mother carried one of her suitcases to her room, Flora hustled to the kitchen to complete a celebration feast in Emma's honor. Whenever she returned home from camp or college, her favorite foods were always on the menu—tamales with a squeeze of ketchup or salsa and tres leches cake. The thick, well-seasoned masa and shredded pork of the tamales were a perfect combination with the moist, three-milk dessert. Her mouth watered just thinking about it.

"Any boyfriends to tell us about?" Her mother winked at Emma.

"Are you trying to marry me off?" Emma groaned.

"Oh, heavens. Far from it. I know you'll find the right one in your own time."

Right one. Emma wondered if she'd recognize her life mate as a lightning bolt like her mother and grandmother had before her.

"Well, all I want to do is ride horses and explore the ranch."

Josie grinned at her. "You'll have plenty of time to do that. Are you sure you don't want to go to England with us?"

"No, thanks. Ancient cities and crumbling cathedrals hold no appeal to me. Why would anyone want to leave Texas?"

Her mother laughed and said, "Wash up and come on down. We have a homecoming supper to share."

All of Emma's college years had continued in the same vein. She rarely went to the ranch during the school year, except for holidays. Often, she took her friend Norma with her, but most of the time, she made the long drive alone, and her visit always began the same way—celebration supper, followed by an extended visit with her parents in the den.

Her father made the pretense of studying her grade sheets, but she knew he didn't worry about her marks. Emma had a double major in her senior year and graduated with the highest honors. However, her mother often tested her ability as they did chores around the ranch.

If Emma did not know the answer to one of Josie's questions, her mother would question the integrity of the college education for which they paid. They expected her to use the skills and knowledge she learned at the university to improve the ranch.

From different inoculations for the livestock to new methods of crop rotations, Emma always shared her ideas with her mother. Josie would make the specific decisions and then hand the implementation to Emma's father. Her parents made a good team. *I hope I will have a partner one day to share the responsibilities.*

The celebration supper was the same as previous years, but that summer would be one none of them would forget. That summer would be when Emma rode off on her horse and did not come home.

CHAPTER 12

EMMA

That following day in the caves found Emma hatching yet another escape plan—easily her fifth or sixth, by now. When the men pursued game, she wanted to ride along. It would be a hard sell because no other women went with the hunting party. But she knew if she could get a horse away from the mountainous barriers, she could travel toward home.

She had already convinced Chatpa and Kai. Now, she needed to persuade the other men of her worthiness. Emma was an expert marksman with a rifle and a fair shot with a bow and arrows. She would begin today with a show of confidence.

"Chatpa, let's set up targets and get the men ready for their season's first hunt. What do you think?"

Chatpa looked at her with a quirky smile crossing his face. "Are you interested in providing The People more meat to eat or providing amusement for yourself?"

"I've grown to love my life here and want to share new ideas with our people."

Emma shrugged and felt a tinge of guilt for deceiving the kind older man. But she needed a ruse to escape, and if that meant lying to him, she must do it. As lovely as he was, he was still her captor.

Kai greeted them as he passed their dwelling.

"Kai, Emma has a plan for increasing our food supply."

When Emma explained how a clay shoot works with various stations and challenges to test one's shooting ability, Kai nodded vigorously.

"Let's try it."

They began in the pasture by creating dummies made from hay, blankets, or skins. Some targets were small to replicate rabbits on the ground; others were in trees like doves or larger ones the size of deer or antelopes among the boulders. They spaced them around the meadow and laid a stone where each person would stand to shoot.

Passers-by questioned their game and offered to help. When Kai explained the competition to the men, they chuckled.

Word spread quickly; the following day, every man, woman, and child awaited the beginning of the contest. Emma counted sixty people in the pasture.

Men brought quivers of arrows and tightened the strings of their bows. Women nursed babies and chatted excitedly among themselves. Toddlers and older children ran and played in the stream.

Kai lined up the men and asked Emma to help with scoring. At each station, it sounded to Emma's ears as if the men were joking and taking bets on their abilities. By the middle of the day, two men were ahead of the rest. Kai was one of them.

"You and Jacco must break the tie with one last target." Emma pointed to a tiny piece of pottery in a tree across the stream.

Jacco's first arrow stuck into the tree trunk. Kai's sailed through the branches.

"May I try?" Emma questioned.

Jacco laughed and murmured to those around him.

Kai handed her his bow.

Emma spread her feet apart, grasped an arrow in her hand, and placed the notch on the taut string. She pulled the arrow back, and it soared into the air. Immediately, a cheer erupted. Emma's arrow found its mark. She split the dish in half.

After the show of her hunting expertise, Emma noticed The People gave her preferential treatment. Women ducked their heads and smiled shyly at her, and the men addressed her by name instead of ignoring her presence or making what she supposed were lewd remarks.

Emma continued her full-court press on Kai to warm him to the idea of her going on the next hunting excursion.

"Emma, you are excellent with the bow. I have been talking to the hunters about you riding with us."

Just when Emma thought her idea was a lost cause, Kai told her they would hunt that night. He said it would be a full moon and easy to see their prey. Emma quivered with excitement.

"Are you saying I can go?"

"Yes. But you must ride with me."

Emma's stomach dropped.

"I want you to prove yourself to the other hunters and not cause any problems. Please stay away from Chesma. He is not a good man."

Emma could tell Kai was still distrustful of her and her intentions. Her plan would not work riding double on his horse. But, looking on the bright side, if she proved herself this time, she might get her own horse the next.

At dusk, a dozen riders met at the corral, and Kai offered a hand to lift Emma to the horse's back behind him. They rode through the canyon, following the stream until it crashed into a waterfall. Emma did not understand why they were coming to this dead end.

The horses continued. Down a rocky path beside the rushing water, Emma held tightly around Kai's waist. She did not want to fall off the steep descent. The horse pitched and slid. Suddenly, the horses secured their footing and found a trail out of the canyon, to Emma's delight.

Could she find this precarious exit on her own? Not in the dark without the benefit of a full moon. The moon shone brightly; it looked like the dawn instead of night.

The corridor led to a flat pasture with a forest alongside. Deer were nose down ahead of them. She watched as each hunter slowly reached for a bow and pulled an arrow from a bag on the horse's neck.

Wump! Wump! Wump! The arrows found their targets. Three enormous mule deer lay on their sides.

Emma and the men jumped from their horses and got to work. She had field-dressed many animals, and she helped cut tender-loins and skin the hides carefully. Emma knew not one morsel of these animals would go to waste. This hunt showed how people had survived for generations.

Kai looked at her with admiration sketched on his face. "I am happy you are my friend, Emma. You are a good help-mate."

But, Emma's shoulders slumped, and the butterflies of antici-pation in her stomach dissipated, knowing her own goal would not happen that night.

CHAPTER 13

EMMA, AGE TWENTY-TWO

The week Emma returned home after college, she walked from the stables into the house to find her mother sifting through a stack of papers in her office.

"What're you working on?" Emma asked her mother.

"Choosing candidates to work in our ranch management program this year," her mother answered without looking up.

"Anyone interesting?"

"Several are. Quite a few from A&M. See if you know any of them."

She handed Emma a stack of applications and resumes.

"I know Pam Bergman. She studied with me in one of my small groups. Very knowledgeable."

Emma paused as she saw Jeff Bower's name on an application. She blew out her cheeks.

"What's the red mark on the top of Jeff Bower's application?"

"That means your father has already hired him. He'll arrive next week to work an internship for a year. He gave your name as a reference."

Emma seethed. Jeff should have contacted her first to ask if she'd mind. She did not want to think he planned to make himself indispensable and woo her simultaneously. How would she distinguish between his having valid feelings toward her while working at the ranch he coveted?

She would avoid him at all costs.

THE RANCH'S ANNUAL VAQUEROS competition for its Pride of Texas award began in the early morning, the last weekend in June. The overall cash prize was $1,000, but bragging rights and the bronze trophy of a bucking bronco were just as important. The few times Emma visited the ranch hands' quarters, trophies occupied places of honor in screened windowsills above the bunks where the winners slept.

The Thorn Ranch's staff numbered 250, and the competition was stiff. However, the categories for prizes had changed very little from when the event began in the early 1900s. The activities included calf roping, bull and bronco riding, eagle eye target shooting, and even a pie-eating contest. Ranch hands could sign up for as many events as they wanted. There were division winners and an overall champion.

When Emma was young, she took part in calf roping and pie-eating, but she climbed on the bull and bronco as she became a teenager. Sometimes, she lasted as long as most of the men. Her father didn't like it, but her mother said, "Just let her try." Of course, it embarrassed the men when she defeated them, but they admired her nerve.

The annual contest, after Emma graduated, began with a bugle sounding "Reveille." Men rushed from their barracks and moved toward the registration table to choose their activities.

Emma stood on the porch when she spied Jeff Bower among the men. Her breath caught in her chest. After he walked away, she went to the registration table and looked at the sign-up sheet. He had chosen skeet shooting and the riding marathon. Emma decided on the spot to make those her activities as well.

Skeet shooting began in a pasture near the stables. Tables there held shotguns, safety eyeglasses, and ear protection. Helpers filled mechanical launchers with clay disks.

Watching the shooters, Emma waited. They launched the first clay high into the sky, then a low one close to the ground. Next, two clays were thrown together, and the participants had to target the high first, then the low. She watched as the first contestant missed a target and had to re-shoot. Time dragged because each person had twenty-five shots, with the final one called the *shooter's option* for a choice of targets.

Now Emma saw Jeff picking up a two-barrel gun from the table. Of course, he chose an "over and under" gun. That weapon provided the surest method of getting two fast blasts.

Emma nudged her way to the front and stood next to Jeff.

"You don't mind if I join you, do you?" She smiled sweetly.

"Of course not." He looked a little sheepish.

Emma chose a pump gun. It required the most skill, with the shooter pulling the forearm back and pushing it forward. To be successful, one must have speed, consistency, and precision.

Jeff looked surprised at her choice of weapon.

"Would you rather use a semi-automatic?"

"Oh no. I like a challenge." She winked at the scorer, Mike, standing beside her. He rolled his eyes. Mike had seen Emma shoot many times.

Jeff raised his weapon and said, "Pull." The clay target soared high and right. He missed. The next one, high and left. The clay shattered into dust. Then, a disk flew just a few feet from the ground, and his shot was accurate.

Jeff stepped back and doffed his cap to Emma.

Emma called, "Pull" before Jeff had time to distance himself. Then, out of the corner of her eye, she saw him cup his ears with his hands.

One, two, three. Targets exploded in rapid succession.

"Wow, Emma. I didn't know you were an expert shot."

"Never underestimate me, Jeff." Emma held her arms high in a "Rocky" stance. Then, she whirled around and left the area.

The day's trials were in a speedy sequence. The last two events were the horse marathon, a race across the ranch similar to a cross-country run except on horses, and the pie-eating contest.

Emma chose Prince for her steed in the race. He was fast, but he had endurance, too. She stroked his sleek coat. He was tall and almost jet-black. While most men sported western saddles on their horses, Emma chose an English one. It was minus a horn to hold, and she could lean flat against the horse's neck.

Walking Prince to the starting line, she glimpsed Jeff with the horse Whisper. Whisper was a more petite red horse but quick and used for gathering herds.

Emma saluted Jeff's choice of horses and thought she would not beat him based on their mounts' differences.

When the horn signaled the beginning of the race, some horses reared up. Emma did not turn to watch the commotion. She and Prince were already leading the pack.

Stakes with colorful streamers pointed the route. The first leg was across flat land, but soon the path turned rocky and steep as they rode into the mountains. Prince's footing was sure, and

Emma urged him forward. Going down the other side was more stressful than rising. Emma sat far back in her saddle to help balance the horse's weight distribution.

When they hit level ground, they were off. Streaking along, Emma sensed riders gaining on her. Her eyes darted to the side, and she saw Jeff on Whisper next to her. Leaning completely flat on Prince's neck, Emma wrapped her arms around him and kicked his flank. She could see the flags waving at the finish line. Three horses flew across the chalk line. Prince by a nose!

Jeff jumped off his horse and led her around to Emma's side. He extended her a hand, but she ignored it and jumped off the saddle.

"I almost had you," he said.

"Try the pie-eating contest," Emma drawled as a smile crept across her face.

CHAPTER 14

EMMA

As Emma sat stirring a venison stew over the fire one night, Kai walked into Chatpa's cave.

"Tomorrow is a big day here. You will need your rest."

"What's happening tomorrow?"

"A competition."

"Another shooting competition?"

"No, Emma. A competition to impress a wife."

Emma felt the blood drain from her face, and her stomach tightened.

"I thought you said women can make a choice here. Why is this time different? Say I'm not the one they're competing for."

"You can choose from the men who wish to impress you. They consider you good luck and want to see you married." Even when saying these words, the expression on his face looked pained.

Emma's pulse quickened. "I'll choose my husband when I want. You can't make me marry someone."

"You will have the finest man we have. He will best all the others."

"Kai, you must let me go. You do not want to see me married when I am not ready."

Kai leaned down to her ear and whispered, "You are my friend. If this scenario does not turn out the way you desire, I will help you."

"To go back to my people?"

He nodded.

Emma felt a surge of hope for the first time since she arrived. She turned and left Kai standing next to the fire. She wrapped herself in a tanned hide and crawled into a corner of her room.

"Please let Kai keep his promise."

EMMA FELT SHE HAD not slept at all. Visions of a man forcing himself on her made her nauseous. She could picture the vilest man of The People—Chesma.

Chatpa woke her and gave her one of his hot herbal drinks. She bet the ingredients removed anxiety and calmed one's fears. She swallowed the hot liquid, not caring whether it burned her tongue and throat.

"Here is your wedding dress, Emma."

Draped over Chatpa's arm was a soft, cream-colored tunic. Someone had painstakingly woven bits of bone, shell, and colored stone around the neckline. The sleeves were fringed, and there were soft shoes to match. Did all the women wear this dress when they married?

Emma shook her head to rid herself of such frightening thoughts. She pulled the dress over her head and slipped her feet into the shoes. Although they were a bit snug, she pulled them on. *Maybe I will be their first runaway bride.*

Chatpa nodded his approval when she walked back into their living area.

"Come with me. The gauntlet will begin soon."

Emma and Chatpa walked down to the pasture. It looked like someone had arranged an obstacle course. A tall pole with a bright cloth blew in the wind like a flag. The deer dummy they had used for target practice stood in front of the stream. This competition reminded her of the one they held yearly on the ranch, where the hands competed against each other for trophies, prizes, and bragging rights.

Kai told Emma what the schedule of events would be that day.

"First, the men will race their horses. The one to grab the cloth will be the winner. Then, there will be a wrestling match in the circle and a target competition. The one to win the most contests will be the man you may choose as your husband."

Emma's stomach cramped, and her nerves vibrated. "You know this isn't right. I've told you I do not *choose* anyone here." Her bravado didn't ring true. She bit the inside of her cheek until she could taste blood.

"You will not be forced. You will make a choice. Emma, you are one of us now."

Suddenly, Chesma ran toward her. He wasn't much taller than her, but his arms were muscular and his chest broad. He snatched her into his arms and tossed her into the air.

His hair slapped her face, and his breath reeked like the wild onions in the field. She leaned back to place distance between them, her cheeks burning with anger. He laughed and pointed at himself and then at her. She could not understand his words, but his intentions were obvious.

Chesma dropped her unceremoniously and strutted back to his friends. They slapped him on his back and threw back their heads, laughing. He seemed like the ring leader of a few bandits.

Emma shivered involuntarily. "What did he say?"

Chatpa shook his head and murmured. "Chesma is not a good example of The People. Most men here consider women to be sacred."

"What did Chesma say?" she demanded.

"He said he will see you in the marriage bed tonight."

CHAPTER 15

EMMA, AGE TWENTY-TWO

Emma's father draped his arm around her shoulder. Then, someone handed her a trophy and a big blue ribbon.

"Guess we should have a woman riding that bronco on the trophy instead of a man." He winked at Emma.

Emma saw Jeff watching the festivities. She wanted to be magnanimous and walked over and gave him a one-armed side hug.

"I guess the best person won," he said. "Is there anything I can do better than you, Emma?"

"The pie-eating contest?" she sniped at him. *Try to be more gracious, Emma.* Her words tumbling out of her mouth had sounded flirty, though.

"The pie tasted better. I'm eating crow right now."

Emma flicked her ponytail over her shoulder and walked toward the house. She needed a shower. *Am I still angry at Jeff?*

She emerged an hour later, refreshed and wearing tight jeans and a white cowboy shirt. Her silver belt buckle was as large as a saucer and proclaimed her a rodeo champion, but it pressed against her rumbling stomach as she smelled barbeque roasting.

Neighboring ranchers gathered to toast the winners of the events and determine if they could entice some of them to leave The Thorn and join their operations. A few ranch hands longed for greener pastures, but those usually returned after a short stint. Known throughout Texas and far beyond, The Thorn was the best ranch for excellent salaries and good working conditions. Today's challenge was just one example of the perks of the job.

The band tuning up reached Emma's ears. Lights hanging in trees and on tables illuminated a dance floor with benches as far as her eyes could see. It would be a fun night of eating, dancing, and swapping tall tales of the day's activities. Then, they would announce the winners from the bandstand, and the applause would be deafening.

Someone grabbed her arm from behind, and she found herself face to face with Jeff. Emma felt butterflies scrambling in her gut. *Why do I still like him?*

"Let's show this crowd what a two-step looks like," he bragged.

Emma took a deep breath. Then, spinning around, they joined couples circling the floor. The music sounded loud and enthusiastic.

Emma knew her mother chose her favorite Texas musicians and gave them dates far in advance to ensure their schedules were available. Josie and John smiled at her from a table at the edge of the dancers. She grinned back at them as she swirled, sliding her boots along the slick floor sprinkled with sawdust.

When the waltz, "May I Have This Dance for the Rest of My Life," began, Emma led Jeff to a bar nearby.

"I'll have a lemonade, please," Emma said.

"And I'll have a Lone Star."

They leaned against the tent's posts and watched the couples' dance skills.

"Have you been avoiding me, Emma?"

"I haven't seen you to avoid you."

"That's what I mean. You know I'm working here. I thought you would seek me out."

"I have chores on the ranch. Not much time to entertain."

"I want us to continue to get to know each other."

"We'll see."

He reached for her hand, and they joined the dancers once again. She realized she had forgiven him for applying for an internship without her knowledge, and Emma wondered if he could feel her heart beating furiously against his chest.

CHAPTER 16

EMMA

Emma sat on the edge of the pasture watching the contests. Shirtless men sweated and strained to entice her to choose them for marriage. *How can this be happening? Am I living in an alternate universe?*

Twisting and turning each other in a defined circle, two men pinning each other to the dusty ground mesmerized Emma. They announced the winner by tapping him on the shoulder. One had survived to fight another. Where was Kai? Was he competing for her?

Dizzy with the realization that these men wanted her to claim them today, Emma walked to the stream, removed her tanned shoes, and plunged her feet into the cool water.

Without a sound, a young woman dropped to the ground beside her.

"You are fortunate to have many competing for you," she whispered.

"Not my choice," Emma replied. "Is your name Flana?"

"Yes."

"Your English is excellent. How many of The People speak English?"

"Probably half of us. We once numbered one hundred here. Now, maybe sixty?"

"Are you married?"

"To Cato."

"Is he kind to you?"

Flana cocked her head as if she did not understand the question.

"Does he treat you well?"

"He is a worthy man and an excellent hunter."

Emma lay back on the ground and closed her eyes, oblivious to the grunts and moans of the competitors behind her. When she sat back up, Flana motioned to her to sit still. Flana braided Emma's hair and added a few sprigs of fern to the sides. *She's decorating me for my wedding night*, Emma thought. Her breakfast sought its way back into her throat, tasting like gasoline.

Emma could no longer watch the proceedings. She crossed the meadow and climbed the rocky path to their cave. Reaching the dim of her room where she had spent months, she lay down on the floor and drifted off to sleep. Emma missed her family so much that her chest throbbed. She dreamed of childhood memories and events on the ranch.

When she was twelve, she lay awake in bed listening to the grown-ups in the living room. Above the loud chatter and lively music, she heard her mother. The musical tones of her mother's laughter were unique, much like the woman herself. Emma wrinkled her brow and imagined her mother's broad smile and sparkling eyes.

Emma believed men always felt a magnetic pull toward her mother. First, they commented over and over about Josie's eyes. Then, finally, her mother would grasp Emma around the waist and say, "My beautiful girl has the same eyes. For five generations, the women in this family have passed down the same traits: dark eyes, determination, and the ability to get the job done."

Whenever she made that statement, a man would tip his hat to her and agree. Not only were the Rosales women beautiful, but intelligent and capable as well. *Spitfires*, her daddy often said.

Emma thought her daddy and mother made a handsome pair and hoped it was a love match. But she had overheard her grandmother Valeria telling her mother, Josie, that men in the family were there for one reason, just like bulls on the ranch. Emma knew about bulls. Something confused her, though, because bulls produced many calves. Every woman in the Rosales family produced only one offspring—a daughter.

After hearing her grandmother's statement about men in the family, Emma observed her father and grandfather more closely. They were more alike than different. Both were quiet men who deferred to their wives and spent most of their time working cattle. And, Emma had listened to enough adult talk to know that the Rosales women ruled the roost and that the men were in supportive roles.

When Emma pitched a tantrum or demanded corn instead of beans, her grandmother, Valeria, laughed and said, "We have another strong-willed woman on The Thorn." From her Abuelita's approval, Emma learned early to speak up for what she wanted.

The morning after her parents' party, Emma placed tortillas in a black cast-iron frying pan. She liked to help in the kitchen when she was not riding her pony. Their housekeeper, Flora, handed the white circles to her one at a time and warned her not to touch the hot skillet.

When the tortilla blistered, Emma used her thumb and index finger to flip it over. Lightly browned and puffy, she removed the delicacies and placed them in a fabric bag to keep them warm for breakfast. Her mouth watered as she thought about slathering them with butter and rolling them to take a bite.

"Okay, missy. Let me cook your eggs. Your papa will be looking for you, and you haven't eaten breakfast yet." The housekeeper's dark eyes crinkled in contrast with the harshness of her voice. It was just how Flora ruled the kitchen, and Emma knew she was not angry at her.

Emma wiped the flour off her hands on her jeans and moved out of the way. She was hungry. Sitting at a small kitchen table in the corner, she opened the bag of warm tortillas.

"May I have a cup of coffee?"

"You know you're not supposed to."

"No one will know." Emma smiled at Flora.

"Here." Flora placed a saucer before her and poured a small amount of scalding coffee. "Let me add some cream."

Emma lifted the dish slowly, watching the steam curl around her nose. She loved the deep bitterness and cream together. She had just finished the concoction when her father strode briskly into the kitchen.

"Aren't you finished yet?" His deep voice echoed against the walls of the breakfast nook.

"I'm ready, Papa." Emma stuffed two tortillas into her jacket pocket and followed him to the back door. She turned to wink at Flora and watch her slowly grin as if they shared an important secret.

Emma and her father rode together into a far pasture. Then, he began to count *one, two, three.* She knew the signal for their favorite tune. Together, they belted "You Are My Sunshine" lyrics at the top of their lungs. Emma loved the way her papa made her feel like she was the sunshine in his life and he in hers.

Then, he began to fade away. *Wait, Papa, don't go. We haven't sung the entire song yet.* Emma could hear someone else calling her name. The dream of home vanished as quickly as fog on a hot Texas morning.

"Emma, come meet the winner of the competition."

Emma cocked her head back and moaned. She wanted to be in her childhood just a little longer.

Walking into Chatpa's room, she saw the back of a tall man. He turned to smile at her.

Kai. Emma didn't know whether to laugh or cry. Was she relieved or still furious? He had made her a promise to allow her to choose or return home. She would hold him to his oath.

"I do not choose you, Kai." Then, for a split second, Emma noticed a pleading expression on his face.

"You have time. We will get to know each other." He turned to her side and gave her a knowing glance. Emma realized he said this statement for Chatpa's benefit.

Emma saw Chatpa looking like a proud father. Was this where in the wedding ceremony they ask, "Who gives this woman to be wed?"

Chatpa gripped her forearms. "You are my daughter, child. Choose Kai as your husband. He will be good to you." Chatpa mumbled a few phases foreign to her, and he disappeared into his area.

"Would you like to see where I live?" Kai asked, with a nervous tremble in his voice.

He led Emma along the path to a cave high on the side of the mountain. Unlike Chatpa's, which was lower and farther into the side of the hill, Kai's possessed an open side with a grand view of the cliffs surrounding them and the beauty of the pasture, stream, and trees below.

"Well, you chose a spectacular condo," Emma said.

"Condo?"

"Never mind. Listen, Kai. In my world, I will meet someone I like. We will get to know each other. Then, if we are truly compatible, we will fall in love before getting married."

"What is compatible?"

"Like the same things, understand each other."

Now that she was safe from the other men, she would have more opportunities to convince Kai to send her home. He had made her a promise.

Kai smiled and guided her around the cave. The open-air side held a narrow ledge like a porch. She assumed that dried grasses were scattered there to sit and watch over their surroundings.

Emma gasped at the sky. The cliff's height was spectacular and their bird's-eye view showcased the most dazzling sunset she'd ever seen.

Saturated with the intensity of color and hue never duplicated by talented artists with oil paints, the patterns of the heavens made Monet's art look like a child's drawing. Pink bathed the cliffs with the palest shades, making the caves below look like stylish dwellings in Cabo San Lucas or a Riviera seaside. She must have stood there so long in awe; Kai touched her arm, and she re-entered the cave to continue the tour.

A living area was just off the porch, complete with a pit for cooking. A separate room for sleeping showed piles of hides on the floor. There was no bathroom, and Emma knew his daily constitution was like hers in the woods, with baths in the creek.

"Thanks for showing me your space. I'll go back to Chatpa's now."

Kai saw the eagle feather in her braid. He touched it lightly.

"It means good luck to you," he murmured. He bowed his head.

I'm going to make my luck soon. Very soon.

CHAPTER 17

EMMA, AGE TWENTY-TWO

Emma smiled when she remembered the Ranch Hands Competition the previous day. She had one photo on her phone of Jeff in the pie-eating contest with his face buried in the sweet crust and another with blackberry juice running down his chin.

Was she falling for him? He had given her no reason. But she blushed when she thought of him kissing her. After her morning coffee, Emma saw Jeff walking to a corral to check on the goats there. The creatures had performed in the roping competition the day before and were lying down, still exhausted, and ready to return to their pasture and tender grass.

"It's a beautiful ranch, this place you call home."

"It is, isn't it?" Emma looked around.

The hacienda extended long and low, with small oak trees lining a stone pathway to the front door. A large porch stretched the length of the home, and benches and chairs clustered in groups to allow for visits under the shelter of the red tile roof. A carpet of deep green fig vine spread across the white-washed stucco walls and crept toward tall twin chimneys. Yellow fragrant funnels of Carolina jasmine buzzed with bees and hummingbirds competing for its nectar as it wound its way up heavy oak posts lifting the porch's eaves.

Emma liked lying in a lacy hammock there or on the daybed swing her mother designed. Both were great for reading on afternoons too hot to be out in the Texas sunshine.

Jeff and the other ranch hands lived in quarters next to the stables, where they were near the animals that populated the immense acreage. When a vaquero married and started a family, Emma's parents built them a house on the property. The small stucco buildings with red-clay roofs lined a road that extended for miles behind the main house. There was a one-room school house for the numerous ranch children and even a chapel.

"How many acres is The Thorn, anyway?" Jeff casually dropped the question.

Emma learned from an early age not to answer questions about how many acres they owned. Her mother said the question was impolite and like someone asking how much money was in your bank account. In Texas, ranchers owned land by sections, not acres. Only strangers to this neck of the woods would venture such a question.

When Jeff asked her about the ranch's size, Emma felt a prickling on her skin. Was she being protective of her status?

When Emma was a student at A&M, she wondered if living in a small Texas town and getting to know all its citizens through their cats and dogs might be a good fit for her. Since she was a young child, Emma brought needy creatures from the ranch into their kitchen to try to mend whatever ailed them—a bird's broken wing or a fawn forsaken by its mother. Vet school seemed inevitable. And Emma remembered how being in College Station invigorated her. The town's many restaurants, bars, and movie theaters gave her options a remote ranch did not provide. She enjoyed having choices and making her own decisions. The ranch took all those away.

"I've got a surprise for you later," she murmured as she and Jeff parted instead of addressing his acreage question.

Emma picked up mitts in the kitchen and reached for a bubbling apple pie in the oven. She would take it to Jeff to remind him of his ineptitude at the contest. Emma was sure he never wanted to see another pie—at least for a long time. Bringing him this one would make them both laugh.

Emma left the house by the back door and skirted the staff quarters until she strolled between two buildings. She heard male voices laughing in the distance ahead of her. Emma did not want to show preferential treatment to Jeff in front of the other hands. She knew that would embarrass him and her.

Then she recognized Jeff's voice above the laughter.

"No, I mean it. Why do you think I'm hundreds of miles from home? I'm using this year to get close to Emma. She won't know what hit her. We'll be married, and I'll own this ranch before she wakes up from our honeymoon."

There were snorts and snickers from his audience, but Emma did not hear the subsequent statements. She halted as if she'd slammed into a brick wall. The hot pie in her hand matched the heat radiating from her face.

CHAPTER 18

EMMA

The morning after the first night of their "honeymoon," with Emma at Chatpa's and Kai in his own space, they met on the roof to survey the medicines at their disposal.

While creating liquids from herbs, Kai talked.

"When I was a child, my mother took me with her berry hunting. I scratched my hands and arms, reaching into the briars, but the ripened berries were delicious. I ate most of them and had stains all over my face from the juice. My mother noticed I had no berries left in my pouch. She laughed and sent me to swim in the stream while she gathered the fruit. I hope I learned kindness from her."

Emma whispered, "When I was a little girl, my mother told me I could be anything in the world I wanted. I don't think any of the options were living in a cave with a strange man."

They walked to Kai's space, and he sliced an apple for them to share. Then, Emma heard voices on the porch. She still wore her wedding attire and walked toward the sounds.

Flana, from the day before, stood next to a man who held a basket woven of colorfully dyed reeds.

"Hello, Flana," Emma said.

The man behind her said, "I am Flana's husband, Cato. We are bringing you The People's wedding basket to wish you a long life and many children."

Emma felt her cheeks bloom, and a knot in her stomach rose into her throat to strangle her.

She reached out her arms to receive the gift.

"Thank you" was all she could muster.

CHAPTER 19

EMMA, AGE TWENTY-TWO

Emma charged around the corner and confronted a startled Jeff. He propped one foot on a stump that Emma used as a child to climb onto the back of a horse. Jeff held court with four other ranch hands, who began backing up when they saw the look on Emma's face.

"Just biding your time, pretending to like me until you can get your hands on this ranch?" Her ears rang, and she had a narrow vision of him through her squinted eyes. She saw his hands fly up as if in surrender.

"I don't know what you thought you heard," he said, looking around and noticing that he was now alone and in Emma's cross-hair.

"Really? That's all you've got to say? Not even an apology?"

Jeff stared at her with wide eyes and raised eyebrows. "Aww, Emma, this is all a misunderstanding. And, just when we were getting to know each other."

She felt like spitting on the ground before him and barely restrained herself.

"The only misunderstanding is that I tried to convince myself you were a nice guy."

"I'm a nice guy."

"Not from what I just overheard."

He looked down at the toe of his boot and dragged it in the dust.

"Is it wrong to think of us being together and running this ranch?"

"Well, that's the first honest thing you've said." She tapped his chest with her index finger hard enough to leave a bruise. "Let me make this clear to you. No man will ever run The Thorn, married or not."

Ignoring her declaration and making one of his own, he stepped closer to her.

"Why would you say that? We'll make a great team."

"You're welcome to work as a ranch hand here on The Thorn. But the only ownership you'll ever have is a trophy for the pie-eating contest." Her voice quaked, but she moved in one fluid motion.

Emma smashed the pie into his face and ground it with a windshield wiper motion. He sputtered and spat crust and sticky apples onto the dirt at his feet.

Emma whirled around and entered the house before Jeff could wipe the remaining dessert off his face and dunk his head in the horses' water trough.

Later that afternoon, her parents informed her they would leave soon for their summer in Europe and hoped she would reconsider joining them.

Scorching temperatures in Texas soared over the hundred-degree mark, and a vacation in the mountains of Switzerland and a tour of England seemed like a cooler alternative. Emma considered escaping with them briefly, but Texas was her country, and she would not allow Jeff to send her packing.

Emma seethed and saw red over more than the weather. When her parents departed, she would get as far away from Jeff as possible and still be on the ranch. She planned a week's camp-out on the outermost regions of the vast property. It would be a relaxing adventure.

To keep busy and her mind off Jeff, she helped Flora cook in the kitchen daily. Emma watched as Flora pinched a small dough ball and placed it between her palms. Flora explained, "Some like to use a press, but there may be times you don't have one, so this is the way to learn."

Emma plucked a piece from the bowl. It was like squeezing-Play-Doh. She thought of kindergarten and the smell of the sticky concoction they pulled out of cans with colored tops that matched the contents. She had mixed the colors until they were a muddy brown or forgotten to replace the lids and returned to find a dried lump to greet her.

Now, the moldable mixture in her hand became warm.

"Quickly, Emma. Pat until thin. Rotate and make a delicate circle."

Flora showed an example, and Emma tried to follow her technique. By the end of the morning, her efforts paid off, and although her tortillas didn't look as perfect as Flora's, they were presentable enough to spoon taco meat into them for supper.

That night when Emma told her father she made the tortillas, he laughed. "Are you going to be a chef?"

Her mother snorted. "Of course not. But Emma can help feed the ranch hands on a cattle drive."

CHAPTER 20

EMMA

Every morning as Emma lay stiffly under her hide covering, she wondered what time Kai arose. It was still dark, so she used a piece of kindling to stoke the coals and brush away ashes from the night before. Rarely were any fires in the caves wholly extinguished. The People needed warmth and a way to cook their food.

She held an earthenware pot in her hand and added water and herbs for a morning toddy. *Emma moaned and wished for real coffee.*

She chewed on a piece of sassafras root to freshen her breath and teeth as Chatpa and Kai entered the room and accepted cups from her.

"Tonight will be a full moon. Do you want to go hunting?" Kai asked.

Emma's pulse ratcheted, and she answered, "Yes," a little too loudly.

"I have something for you." Chatpa rose from a crouch and walked into his private den. When he returned, he had hoisted something significant on his back.

"What?" Emma exclaimed. He laid her grandmother's saddle beside her crossed legs. "Who found it?"

"A man fished in the cave lake and saw it near an opening. He brought it to me."

Emma could barely breathe and choked out, "Thank you!" *This saddle is so important to me—an omen I will return home.*

"I repaired the broken strap with sinew from the last deer."

Emma wondered if a leather smith could have done as fine a job. Her stirrups were as good as new.

"I will use it tonight for the hunt."

"Kai, will you allow Emma to ride a horse?"

"Now that I have a saddle, he will!" Emma replied without allowing Kai to answer.

Emma carried the saddle into her space and sat alone with her new good luck charm.

Her fingers stroked the leather tooled saddlebag attached to the back. Emma opened the clasp and reached inside. To her shock, the contents were still intact. *He must have forgotten to check the bag,* she mused. *Surely, if he'd seen what was inside, he'd have confiscated it. Or, did he not know what it was?*

She now had a gun and ammunition.

LOOKING AROUND THE CAVE, Emma said a silent goodbye. If all went as planned, this would be the last time she saw this place.

Men gathered around the ponies at dusk, collecting their bows and arrows and speaking quietly. Emma and Kai made their way down the hill to the group. Kai patted a paint horse and nodded at Emma, but she shook her head and pointed at a large black stallion.

"Emma, that horse is a devil."

"I've seen Ponta ride him."

"Even Ponta says he is difficult to control. He just wants to fly without restraints."

"I like a fast horse."

Kai shrugged his shoulders, and she walked toward the stallion. He snorted and pawed the ground. Emma threw her saddle across his back, but he did not stand still. It was the first time a strange implement touched his back and stomach. She rubbed his nose and spoke to him.

Quickly, she stepped into a stirrup and swung her other leg over the saddle. The horse danced from side to side, trying to rid himself of the object. But Emma held on tightly and steered him toward the others.

As the group rode out of the canyon, her horse passed all the mounts, eager to be in the lead.

They did not immediately see any game when they left the tall cliffs behind and entered a flat valley. Hours passed. The men were getting frustrated and spoke of returning to camp.

Emma could not allow that to happen. She needed the men to focus their attention on the physical act of field-dressing deer and give her the time she needed. She pointed to dark figures standing near the woods. Two deer grazed there.

Horses halted, and men slid off their mounts and dropped silently. They crawled toward the unsuspecting animals. One of the deer fell to the ground. The other disappeared into the trees.

The men stretched out the downed deer and gutted it. Emma remained on her horse. All the men were a hundred yards in front of her. Suddenly, she reared up on her horse and waved her arms frantically. The horses standing nearby bolted away from where they nibbled.

Emma kicked the horse's flanks sharply, and he took off like a shot. She leaned over and gripped her knees tightly to stay on his massive back. The moon showed a path. She knew she had to find her way due east.

Emma was a three-day ride from home, but she knew if she controlled a head start, The People could not catch her.

The landscape was rocky and steep just out of the plateau, and Emma's horse stumbled more than once. Then, the wild horse crashed through a jagged stream, spraying water around her legs.

She raced the horse, just like when she'd won the marathon on the ranch. This horse was a superb creature and seemed to love the fast pace. They were one, racing against time and anyone chasing them. She felt confident her lead would be enough.

A memory of the death of Honey-Boy flashed in her mind. Emma silently begged the stallion to avoid holes. Her wet legs dried quickly in the wind, and she reined the horse to dodge boulders that stood like statues in the desert.

Emma saw her path ahead by the dazzling display of constellations and the mellow light of the orange moon. First, she glanced over her shoulder to ensure she was the only one in this race. Then, suddenly, without warning, Emma sensed someone behind her.

She kicked the horse and urged him forward.

A horse gained on them. Emma could not tell by furtive looks who sat on the horse after her, but the brown and white spots on the pony seemed to glow in the moonlight. Its rider yelled into the wind, but she could not understand his words.

"Go, boy, go." Her voice quaked. The hoof sounds behind her were getting louder. She tried a zigzag to see the rider's distance from her—less than a hundred yards. The granite outcroppings were making the chase noises echo off the canyon walls.

Emma knew her horse could not keep this pace for much longer.

If she could only discover a hidden path or place to hide. It was difficult looking for an exit when she struggled to stay on a horse, running at full speed. Her heart beat in her throat to the rhythm of the horse's pounding hooves.

How could one of the paint ponies be this swift? She chose the fastest horse in the group. But here was someone in close proximity. *Will they punish me for escaping?*

The hot breaths of a horse seemed to be in her ear. She could feel the paint bumping into her leg and saw a hand reaching for her reins. Emma reached behind her and flipped open her saddlebag. She grasped the pistol in her hand while lurching forward as the horse continued its harried pace.

Emma cocked the hammer and pointed the gun over her shoulder. Desperation seeped from her body as bitter sweat. She fired one shot near the approaching horse's head to scare him. It seemed to work, but her ears rang from the explosion, and she lost hearing. The horse following her veered away.

Adrenaline pumped through her veins like scalding water. Fate had not smiled on her yet. Could she shoot this man? She'd never killed anyone before.

Suddenly, the horse leaped back into her peripheral vision. Emma squeezed the trigger aiming high again. The second shot frightened both horses, and they skidded together, bumping their bodies. Emma's horse turned sharply, and she surged into the air. Her back hit the ground, and she rolled in the dust and gravel. The stallion continued to run.

Emma tried to get to her feet but crumbled back to the ground. *Did the shot hit someone?* A terrible sensation ran through her body. She shivered. Would he kill her now? She felt around in the dirt for her pistol. No luck.

The paint pony appeared at her side. Emma saw a man's bulk with the moon behind him but could not make out his features.

"Are you hurt?" The man on the horse looming above her was Kai.

Emma sat on the hard clay, her knees lifted and arms draped on them.

"Just let me go, Kai. Why didn't you just let me go?"

Kai reached a hand toward her and pulled her to her feet. She grasped his arm and pulled herself behind him on the horse—another failure.

Kai's horse seemed grateful for a slower pace as he turned and headed back toward the caves.

A cloud overhead moved away, and with the sudden brightness of the moon, she could see blood staining Kai's back. *My bullet hit its target.*

She moved one hand up the front of his chest and felt sticky, warm blood on his shoulder.

CHAPTER 21

EMMA, AGE TWENTY-TWO

Still trying to keep her mind off Jeff, Emma followed Pedro into the garden the day after tortilla-making. He motioned to her to pick the ripest tomatoes and dig potatoes.

The garden produced enough to feed the county. It wasn't a small garden for a hoe but required a tractor and tiller. Pedro cracked open a watermelon when they were both exhausted and offered Emma half. She buried her head in the fragrant sweetness. Pedro laughed at her abandonment and pointed to the black seeds dropping onto her shirt.

She mentally made a to-do list. Kitchen and garden, check. What else could she do today to drown her thoughts?

The sounds of vaqueros separating cows from the calves struck her ears, and she walked to the pens and jumped into the circle. The cows charged at her, and she swiped at them, sending cows into one pen and calves into another.

It caused her heart to melt a little when the little animals began mooing for their mothers. Although she knew it was necessary to wean the calves, it was still difficult to hear. Had she ever cried for her mother? Or was she always required to be tough?

Next up was sorting equipment in the barn. When Emma arrived, the stalls were already clean and piled with fresh hay, so she went into the tack room and folded and stacked colorful blankets the horses wore under their saddles. Emma used leather soap, polished equipment, and wiped down bits and reins. Finally, she placed the saddles on wooden sawhorses to keep them off the ground and maintain their shapes.

Emma heard Pedro calling her, and she walked toward his voice.

"Do you want to help me sort seeds?" he asked.

"Sure." She walked into the shed and saw shelves of glass containers with metal tops.

"How long have you been saving seeds?" Emma asked.

"My grandfather collected them and his grandfather before him." Pedro shrugged. "Now, stores sell those like you see here and call them heirlooms. Of course, everything is organic these days, but that's how we've planted for generations. Our seeds and crops are legacies from our ancestors."

Emma wanted to learn more. It was difficult to identify most. Some looked like the vegetable they would become, like corn or lima beans. Others were harder to name.

Pedro asked her to scoop a handful from each jar and call out the name until she knew them. Then, she went to the office and returned with a roll of masking tape and a black marking pen. As she tore off a section of tape, applied it to the jar, and wrote, he would call out a vegetable name. Their game helped Emma learn.

Walking out of the shed, Emma ran into a man standing at the corner of the building.

"I'm sorry, I…." She looked up to see Jeff's chagrined face.

"Emma, can we talk?"

"Not interested." She tried to move past him, and he grabbed her arm, pinching her flesh.

"You're hurting me," she barked.

"Just listen!" Jeff yelled.

Emma jerked her arm out of his grasp and shoved him.

"You don't tell me what to do." As Emma turned to walk away, she saw Pedro in the doorway, watching her and Jeff with a seething expression.

Jeff's last remark sent Pedro striding toward him.

"You'll be sorry, Emma; you'll be very sorry."

EMMA SURPRISED HER FATHER and rose before dawn to meet him in the stable the following morning.

"I want to ride with you today, Papa."

"What a pleasant surprise. I'd love that."

She led them out of the paddocks and into the fields. They stopped the horses and allowed them to forage while she and her father admired the sunrise. A thin line of pink smeared on the horizon. Colors washed into the dark sky until it filled with the most glorious blaze of orange light. Emma smiled. She wanted to savor her time with him. They were rarely alone, and she would remember every moment.

"Tell me a story, Papa."

"You haven't asked for a story since I tucked you into bed long ago."

"I want to know how you and Mama met and when you knew she was the one."

"You've heard this story a hundred times." He chuckled.

"Well, make it a hundred and one."

He looked into the distance. Emma thought he could see the memory play in his mind like a movie.

"I was just out of high school working for Mr. Daniel on the Prickly Pear Ranch. He held a rodeo there every summer. His ranch was famous for producing vicious bulls, and men came from all over the country to try their luck riding them."

"And you looked into the crowd and saw Mama?"

He grinned because Emma knew the story well. But he continued.

"I helped at the chute and got men settled on the backs of bulls before they rode into the arena. I'd never attempted such a feat. Most didn't last three seconds. The bulls hurt some terribly." He shook his head.

Emma's words tumbled out. "You looked into the crowd…"

"Yes, I looked into the stands, and there was the most beautiful girl I'd ever seen. Her hair fell to her waist, and her eyes were so deep, I thought I would drown in them."

Emma moaned at his romantic descriptions.

But he continued. "Josie sat between her parents. They were there to see the rodeo and eat barbeque, but Josie's father, your grandfather, wanted to buy a bull for his ranch." He laughed and threw his head back.

"The other hands kept pushing me off the top rail where I sat. I wasn't paying attention to the bulls or the riders, and the men laughed as they watched me stare at Josie. Then, suddenly, I had an idea to get her attention. I would ride the bull. I'd never even tried to get on a bronco. The men thought I was crazy. 'Maybe he has been too long in the sun,' they said."

Emma watched his face intently as she removed a tube from her saddlebag and smeared thick white zinc across her nose. "Papa, that wasn't smart."

"I asked one rider to let me borrow his chaps and gloves. He showed me how to hold on to the rope and raise one arm high. I climbed on the back of the most vicious animal in the lot. His name was Killer—appropriate, no? My skinny arms were shaking, and my legs jerked. The bull must have thought, 'This is going to be an easy one.' Maybe the gods were smiling at me. I don't know. The gate swung open, and the bull walked into the arena. Walked, not jumped, not ran, *walked*. I don't know if the men took the flank strap off the bull. It's usually cinched tight against the bull's torso before releasing it. It causes discomfort, and the bull bucks to rid itself of the belt."

She shook her head. "That's pretty cruel."

"I rode Killer into the arena as if we were walking in a downtown parade. When I realized the bull didn't buck or try to rid himself of me, I began waving at the crowd like a pageant queen on the back of a convertible. The crowd erupted into laughter and cheers. I pulled back to stop in front of Josie. I took off my hat and waved it at her. Her father and mother stared at her and then at me. Josie covered her mouth with her hands and bent over double, she laughed so hard. I jumped off and circled out of the arena while the other hands rounded up the bull. I saw Josie and her parents when they were leaving, and I introduced myself. I asked Josie's father if I could call on his daughter." John smiled at the memory.

"Her father pointed at Josie and said, 'You'd better ask her. She certainly won't take my advice.' He snickered and walked away."

Emma's lips twisted to one side. "Mama's father said that?" she said.

"I didn't know they were the owners of The Thorn. Or that your mother was heiress to such a place. I lost my heart at a rodeo and did not want to let her out of my sight. After that day, as your grandmother used to say, 'If I threw a pail of dishwater out the window, it would hit him in the face.' It just meant I always followed her around."

As the sun rose higher in the sky, her papa began to sing the song he had sung to her since she was a baby. Emma joined him on the chorus and belted out the words they both loved.

"You are my sunshine, my only sunshine. You make me happy when skies are gray. You'll never know, dear, how much I love you. Please don't take my sunshine away."

No one else had ever made Emma feel safe and secure. If she was his sunshine, he was undoubtedly hers. Her papa was her first love.

When their song ended, Emma studied her father. Did he know when he pursued her mother that he would be called "Mr. Rosales" instead of his last name? Sometimes, Emma forgot that her father's legal last name was Brewer. Hers was Rosales on her birth certificate. Once, when she inquired about how he felt about taking her mother's name, he said, "I forget Rosales isn't my name until I see my paycheck." Everyone knew men in this family took their wives' names.

All Texans knew it was Rosales land.

CHAPTER 22

EMMA

Emma strained her neck to look around Kai's chest. His eyes were closed, his hand rested on his shoulder, and blood seeped between his fingers. She reached for the reins, and Kai leaned against her.

She wanted to escape so badly, she had shot this man. Kai was heavy against her, and her hands shook. *Would he survive?* The motion of the horse and the rusty stench of blood made her seasick.

"Kai? Are you conscious?"

No response.

Emma lifted his bloody hand. She felt the wound on his back and sighed with relief—the bullet had exited his shoulder. *At least I won't have to do surgery to find the shell.*

Kai moaned.

"Hey, okay, good. You're going to be fine."

Kai looked confused.

"What happened?"

"You were chasing me. And I shot you."

"You shot me? You are an expert hunter, Emma. Few could hit their target with an arrow at full speed on a horse."

Emma ducked her head and did not tell him about the gun. He might have seen weapons from traders traveling through this place and from the thieves Chatpa told her visited here. But she did not think he had ever owned one.

"It was the perfect time for you to let me go home, Kai. You did not have to chase me. My life is elsewhere."

"You did not have any supplies with you. You said your home is far away. What if you died in the desert?"

Now, Emma felt even worse. He stopped her escape because he feared for her, and she might have killed him. Kai might not regain use of his arm. He might bleed out. Tearing the hem of her dress, she wrapped a long section around the bleeding area and tied it on top of his shoulder. Then she devised a sling from another strip and secured his arm against his stomach.

"We'll have to use one of your herbal remedies to prevent infection."

Emma resigned herself to the return.

She looped her arms around Kai so he wouldn't fall. Emma held the reins around his stomach, and they walked.

No one waited for them where they shot the deer. Emma knew it had taken time to gather the horses and return to the caves. She did not look forward to seeing the hunters the next day. They would be unhappy with her planned escape, mainly because she shot one of their leaders.

Reaching the gulley just as the morning sun peeked over the horizon, Kai propped his free arm on Emma's shoulder as they climbed the path to his dwelling.

Emma settled Kai onto the rushes and looked at his collection of herbs. She chose several and made a paste. Removing the hastily applied bandage, she packed the solution into the frontal wound and then did the same on the back.

The bandage was worthless, soaked through with his blood. Emma tore another strip from her dress. Her knees showed after the subtraction of material. Kai was drowsy but twisted from side to side with pain.

"What is the strongest herb for infection?" she asked when he quieted.

"Pour hot water over sage and help me drink it."

She did as she was told and held his head when she looked up and saw Chatpa standing in the doorway. Was it anger or confusion contorting the frown lines across his face?

"What have you done, Emma?"

CHAPTER 23

JOSIE

Josie and John had just returned from a hike during their third week of vacation when the phone rang in the manor house room.

It startled Josie.

"Maybe it's our host?" she asked.

"Hello, this is the operator. I have an international long-distance call from Flora Lopez. Will you accept the charges?"

"Yes, yes, of course." She held her hand over the receiver and spoke to John. "It's Flora!"

She chewed the inside of her mouth. What could be the matter?

"Flora, can you hear me?" The people in the next room could hear her.

"Josie, Emma's missing."

John stood up from the chair by the fireplace. "What did she say?"

"Calm down, Flora, and tell me why you think this." Her hand trembled on the receiver as she gripped it tightly.

"Well, she packed supplies, took a horse, and rode out on the place."

"Oh, my goodness. You frightened me. Emma won't get lost."

"That's what I thought when she left. But she hasn't come back yet."

Josie was now a little irritated. Why had Flora called all this way to say they lost Emma?

"Don't you worry, she'll be back. When did she leave?"

"It's been more than two weeks."

Josie sank onto the bed and pulled the phone line taut. "Two weeks? Are you sure? Could she have returned and gone to a friend's house?"

"No. I asked the stable manager. That horse she rode—Honey-Boy? He's not in the barn."

The pounding in Josie's chest rose to her temples with a white-hot headache forming. "Listen carefully. I want you to call the sheriff's office. Tell him they need to begin a search party. Get the ranch hands to help with whatever they need. Then, we'll be on the next plane we can catch."

She hung up the phone and sat staring at the receiver.

John stared at Josie, his brow furrowed. "Did I hear Flora say weeks?"

"That's what she said." Josie felt numb. Emma's disappearance couldn't be true. They would cut their vacation short and fly home to discover Emma lying on her bed. When they rushed into her room, she would say, "What are you guys doing home this soon?"

That is what Josie expected, but they could not take the risk. Josie's mind leaped to the worst-case scenarios. Emma had a hunting accident and shot herself. A coyote mauled her. She fell off the cliffs on the property. The caverns that ran through the ranch were as spectacular as the Grand Canyon. Not as large, but just as awe-inspiring. Now, she could see her daughter lying still at the bottom of one.

"Let's get packed. We need to catch the next flight out." Her voice quaked.

The weather around Heathrow Airport in London did not help their efforts to fly home quickly. Storms prevented planes from departing or arriving, and the system halted in gridlock. It looked like the earliest flight would be the following morning at 2:00 a.m. John wanted to get a hotel room until their departure, but Josie paced around the terminal, refusing to sit down.

She ordered the most oversized coffees she could buy and checked at every gate for someone who could change their return tickets to earlier flights. Manic, she raced around the airport like a madwoman. Then she slumped onto the uncomfortable seat next to her husband and laid her head on his shoulder. She could tell he tried not to move, and his arm was probably numb, but the armrest between them kept her from stretching out.

When most people had boarded another plane in the international terminal, Josie sat on the floor in front of massive glass windows and watched the aircraft and the blinking green and red lights climbing into the air. She sat there staring until her head nodded and her eyes closed. Then, finally, Josie stretched out and lay back on the dingy carpet. She was out.

John roused her at 1:00 a.m. to be ready for their flight. She dashed into the restroom and splashed water on her face. The line to board the plane snaked around the corridor and into the bowels of the aircraft.

Josie looked over her shoulder at her husband as they walked to the back of the plane. *Great.* They were seated in the very last row. When she tried to recline her seat after takeoff, she realized those seats did not push back. *No sleep tonight.* Or this morning, or in whatever time zone they were passing.

As she relaxed, flight attendants made their rounds and asked if anyone wanted a soft drink. Emma loved Dr. Pepper, so Josie ordered one and began remembering every time Emma left the ranch when she was in high school—mostly on dates.

Of course, there weren't many occasions because the ranch was too remote. But the adjoining ranchers got their children together for socialization, and the ranchers' sons asked Emma out.

The boys must have been interested in Emma, driving more than an hour each way to pick her up, going to a nearby town for a meal or movie, and then driving her back. From the time Emma walked out the front door until Josie heard the gravel crunch under a car's tires, she watched her husband. He was always on edge. Usually quiet and still, Josie knew his mind went into overdrive when it came to his only child, and he wondered if Emma and her date were in a ravine or had hit a deer.

Traveling after dark was treacherous in their neck of the woods. The wild game did not see many cars, and they stood in the middle of the road until blinded by headlights.

It would amaze her if Josie were not familiar with the over-abundance of animals. No wonder hunters flocked to south Texas. It was essential to thin the herds, so the animals did not starve from eating on the same acreage.

The thought of hunting caused Josie's mind to swirl with the possibility of Emma being shot. No, it wasn't hunting season. But on the other hand, a poacher on the property might not respect state laws. Josie waved at a flight attendant and asked for an eye mask.

She turned to ask John if he wanted one but noticed he was asleep. *Men could sleep standing up.* She knew he was just as fright-ened as she was, but exhaustion and fear took a toll on him, and his reflex was to sleep while hers was to become unnerved.

The flight attendants handed out magazines, and Josie peeled off her mask. If she couldn't sleep, she would read. Flipping through the pages, Josie could not keep her attention on the latest fashion trends or a celebrity's newest home. She placed the magazines back in the seat pouch under her tray table. Then, Josie clicked on the screen in the seat in front of her.

All the movies were sci-fi or murder mysteries. Finally, Josie placed earbuds in her ears and listened to piano music, hoping it would soothe her nerves. It was a long flight. Josie dozed briefly but did not sleep. Her nerves jangled, and her feet tingled like a thousand needles pricked her skin.

Josie was miserable when the wheels touched down in El Paso. The customs lines were at least three hundred people long. Finally, she sat down on the floor, waiting for the luggage. Josie asked if they could just forget the bags and head home. John said he did not think a few more minutes would change anything.

Josie could not prevent how weepy and inconsolable she became when a ranch hand finally lifted their luggage into the back of a truck. Nowhere was close in Texas. Three hours to a pleasant restaurant, two hours to a friend's house. Now, four hours to the ranch from the airport.

After quizzing their driver and finding he knew no more about Emma than they did, Josie stared at the back of John's head or out the window. John sat in the co-pilot seat next to the driver, and she was directly behind him. As if for the first time, Josie noticed he had a bald spot forming. Wonder if he checked out her flaws as she did his? *Am I blaming him for not being more emotional?* He seemed too calm, and she couldn't stop fidgeting.

When John talked to the ranch hand about the vet's visits, Josie could hold her tongue no longer.

"Are you kidding me? Our daughter is missing, and you are

worried about how many more vaccinations are needed?" She slung her head from side to side.

"I'm as worried as you, Josie. I'm just making conversation."

"Well, don't," she spat.

JOSIE FELT SHE'D BEEN gone for much longer than a few weeks when The Thorn's familiar gate allowed them entry. She burst through the front door, and Flora gathered her into her ample bosom.

"Sit down, Flora. Fill us in on everything you know about Emma." John perched on the arm of the sofa where Josie sat.

Flora's eyes looked wild, and she twisted her apron in her hands. "I haven't seen Emma in two weeks. She rode out onto the ranch and has not returned. I kept telling myself it was like all the times she had gone out before, but more days passed, and I worried. Pedro sent ranch hands out to see if they could track her, but they did not see any sign of her. I told her not to go far. She did not listen. She did not listen." Flora shuddered, and a tear snaked its way down her leathery cheek.

"This isn't your fault. Of course you would think it was like Emma's other camping trips. Tell me everything you remember about the last time you saw her. What was she wearing? What did she eat for breakfast? I have to get a firm image of her in my mind," Josie said.

"She ate a couple of tacos early that morning. It was Friday, and I thought we would see her on Sunday at the latest. I fixed spaghetti and a salad and put them in the refrigerator that night. I think they're still there waiting for her." Flora's voice broke.

She swallowed and continued. "She was wearing jeans and a blue shirt. I said, 'Dios te bendiga'—let me give you a blessing.

One hand said she told him she was taking her great-grand-mother's saddle so she could imagine her working the cattle years ago."

At the mention of her grandmother, Josie's insides quivered like gelatin. Lola died while herding those same cattle. During a massive drive, Lola's horse bolted and shook her free. She fell under the stampeding herd, and they trampled her. Josie could see it in her mind. She hoped it was not an omen that Emma used the same saddle as during Lola's tragedy.

Josie shook her head to dispel the image. "We'll talk to the sheriff about a search party and ride out first thing in the morning. Don't worry. We'll find her. Old Honey-Boy may have gone lame. She's probably leading him back."

JOSIE AND JOHN ESTABLISHED a command center to search for their daughter. Jetlag made their bodies weary, but their minds were on fire with ideas to find Emma despite their deep worry.

The rough-hewn planks of the table were barely visible with phones, stacks of aerial photos, and plates with remains of hast-ily eaten breakfast tacos. Josie barked orders to the men gathered there, made assignments, and pointed to a ranch map on an easel.

On the first day of the search, Josie assigned people to areas within a few hours of the main house. There was no evidence of Emma having been there. On the second day, they discovered a campfire site, ashes, and ants clinging to what looked like a piece of a protein bar.

"She's been here recently," her father said.

They continued their path, but the scenery changed rapidly from low grazing land to granite uprising and looming cliffs, making riding difficult. Finally, after two days of not seeing a trace of her, they returned home to the ranch and devised a new search plan.

"John, lead your team to these sections. I will go here." Josie pointed to two areas and circled them in red. The sections, each 620 acres and now color-coded, divided the areas on the poster.

After they swept a site by a line of horses or a hovering helicopter, the search committee dismissed it. The local sheriff's department assisted only a few weeks before placing their limited resources back in town and on other ranches.

"I'm truly sorry, Mrs. Rosales. We just don't have the deputies in our small office to cover a ranch this size." The sheriff hiked up his pants under his over-hanging stomach and looked sheepishly at Josie's flashing eyes.

Everyone knew the overwhelming task of combing a ranch the size of The Thorn. Only Emma's parents produced enough funds to continue. It had now been eight weeks since anyone spoke to Emma.

When the sheriff's department gave up the search, the national news stations received tips, and satellite trucks crowded the entrance to the ranch. Finally, Emma's father closed the gates and instructed the ranch hands not to talk to the media. After a few days of being unable to speak to the family, the reporters dwindled, and only a few local papers and the San Antonio and El Paso news outlets remained.

They stuck their microphones in her face every time she pulled out of the driveway.

"Mrs. Rosales, will you answer questions?"

"May we come in? We'll only take a few minutes of your time!"

Josie ignored their requests after a few non-productive encounters. Instead, she kept her nose in maps and concentrated on their search plan.

The missing heiress to Texas' largest ranch was big news, but not being allowed access to the ranch discouraged even the most tenacious journalists. Few wanted to remain in the extreme heat of the Southwest, where daily temperatures topped 110 degrees.

The reporters looked like bandits at the gate, with colorful handkerchiefs tied around their faces as sand and dust swirled around them. When dark arrived, so did the insects. Swarms of mosquitos descended on the pale flesh of the intruders, and while they slapped at the onslaught, tiny pests called chiggers climbed up their legs, leaving red, itchy welts.

The journalists arrived back in their studios, thinking no one could survive those conditions. Their reflections influenced their reports and pronounced Emma most likely dead.

Listening to their news reports fueled Josie's anger and determination.

"How dare they make such an assumption? Just because they are wimps and could not survive south Texas doesn't mean Emma is the same."

Without the sheriff and his small crew, Josie continued to work. Their dining room was her command center, and it hummed with intention. Every day was a replica of the day before.

"John, hand me that map."

"Mama, can you color this area red?"

"More coffee, Flora, por favor."

Josie chose a section for each day's search and marked it with a color. They dispersed ranch hands, some riding horses, others on four-wheelers fueled by diesel. Depending on the roughness of the terrain, horses could usually traverse the landscape easier. Helicopters flew where no one could navigate. This routine played out day after day, week after week.

The ranch hands looked physically exhausted. Josie's eyes were bloodshot from grit and flying insects by the end of each day. Her boots dragged heavily in the gravel as she faced Valeria, her tiny mother, and John waiting for her in the doorway.

"Is this a losing battle?"

"No, Josie. She will come back to us," John repeated day after day. "How long we can subject the entire ranch operation to this process is the question."

Josie had never considered the ranch anything other than her family. Now, she glared at the landscape like it was her enemy. Did the harsh climate and rough terrain devour her child? How could she resign herself to the fact she may never see Emma's face again?

NO ONE SAW THE agony that tore at Josie's insides like a wild, trapped animal. Only John commented on her sobs in the night, long after she thought he had slept.

"Are you crying? Come closer. Did you have a nightmare?" Pink light flooded the room from the lack of complete coverage around the window shades. John pulled her toward him and unwrapped damp sheets wrapped too tightly around her neck and shoulders.

Josie was not a quitter. She could not allow herself to believe her daughter was dead. But Emma would have made it home by now if not injured or her horse lame. It had been months since she rode out of the compound.

"You know our Emma's tough. She'll make it home." Her husband spoke as if to convince himself and to comfort his wife.

"I'm sick to death of your broad statements. If she were going to make it home, she'd have done it by now!" Josie hated how she'd begun to rebuke John for his consistent belief in finding their daughter, but she couldn't seem to quiet her sharp tongue. Josie raged; John sunk into himself. She hung her head when he slipped from the room.

Her mother's rosary hung from the mirror in her bedroom. Josie reached up and grasped the pink beads in her hand. It had been years since she attended confession.

She thought her place in God's world, and faith depended on her abilities and the land. *Dear God, the land was its own deity.* It was its own deity. Josie worshipped the ranch, giving her a sense of belonging, of knowing her worth and reason for living. Had she placed it above her own family? Its very existence demanded loyalty and commitment. It was the conqueror. They fooled themselves into thinking they controlled the land. But it influenced their every movement, their every thought.

It had finally cowed them. If it had swallowed their daughter, it won. There were no others to take over feeding the monster. The sacrifice—*were the gods happy with their offering?* With their daughter missing, Josie still worried about the damned land.

Always the land.

CHAPTER 24

EMMA

Emma stood and turned to meet Chatpa, who stood glowering at her. His face looked like the creases on it had multiplied ten-fold overnight.

"You knew I didn't want to be here. I want to go home." Emma's defiant words sprayed into the room.

"And, I told you that The People will not allow it. But Kai has been kind to you."

"I didn't think. I was on my way home and wanted to prevent anyone from stopping me." Her voice quieted.

"How is he?" Chatpa's angry voice now sounded anxious.

"I think he will be fine. The blood flow has stopped. The bull— arrow went straight through his shoulder. He will heal if we can keep the wound from getting infected."

"Come with me. I will make a concoction of herbs." Chatpa motioned to her with one hand.

She followed Chatpa along the now-familiar path to the medicinal area where they stored and dried herbs for many ailments. He opened lids on several pottery containers and mixed them in his hand. Chatpa rubbed them into a powder between his palms and chose a tiny vessel filled with a light brown liquid. He carefully placed the herbs into the liquid and shook it vigorously.

"Have him sip this throughout the day."

"I will."

He left her standing in the sunshine while he faded into the shadows.

EMMA NURSED KAI. SHE walked to the stream and brought fresh water to drink and cleanse his wound. She kept clean bandages, ready to change the soiled ones. Emma held his head so he could sip Chatpa's magic tonic, and she used her own mixture to apply directly to the damaged flesh.

After a week of rest, Kai's face looked healthier, and he could keep a meal in his stomach instead of only weak herbal tea and the bread they made in a skillet from crushed corn and animal lard.

Emma lay near him in the night's stillness and listened to his breathing. She could tell from quick breaths or moans if he was in pain and needed more medicine. They both slept when his pain subsided.

The routine assuaged her guilt. She was ashamed she'd hurt him. However, she was not at all sorry for the escape attempt.

When Kai became more coherent, they began talking while lying beside each other at night.

"Tell me more stories about your home, Emma." He turned onto his side to watch her face.

She did not know how much he would understand about her world. He grew up playing on the same land where she had. But his home hid him from view behind tall cliffs and jagged granite walls so high it would be impossible to traverse them.

"My ancestors created my home of wood," Emma began. "Many years ago, they cut trees, stacked them, and used mud, like in the stream, to stick them together. Over the years, whoever lives in the house expands it with stones or updates when someone invents new equipment."

"Equipment?" He slurred his words, rolling the unfamiliar one over his tongue.

"Instead of cooking over a fire as you do here, someone created another way to cook—without using wood." Emma struggled to describe the examples.

"What do they use?"

"Gas. A vapor from under the ground. Like the fog in the hills. It burns like sticks."

She could see him twisting his head and narrowing his eyes. Emma knew he thought of everything he did not know about the outside world. She felt like a time traveler trying to explain the oddities of the twenty-first century to those in the sixteenth. Almost impossible.

"What foods do you eat there?"

"We eat a lot of tacos." Her mouth watered, thinking about the spicy meat and cooling vegetables.

"Tacos?" His tongue tripped over the word.

"Like meat and other ingredients. People are always grilling, uh, cooking, over an open flame, similar to what we do here. Have you ever tasted a wild hog?" She made a face with a scrunched nose and used her index fingers to make tusks.

"Oh, yes. Commandoes. They are delicious but dangerous when attacked."

"Yes, they're quite aggressive."

"What about your family?" He watched her eyes darken.

"My mother is feisty, knows her own mind. She wants everyone to follow her lead."

"Like her daughter."

"Maybe. My dad is calm and kind. He is the peacemaker for sure." Her voice softened at the thought of her father.

"Where is your home, Emma?"

"It's due east of here, in the rising sun, at least a three-day ride, maybe more. There is a large gate with 'Thorn Ranch' above the arch. It has a rose in the brand—you know, a flower—because the Rosales women are always called the 'Roses of Thorn Ranch.'"

"Do you think your parents are seeking you?" His voice trembled in gentle tones.

"Of course. My parents won't stop looking for me." Emma was unsure how long she had been gone from the ranch, but she'd seen seasonal changes since arriving in this distant place.

"What will they do to us if they find you?"

She stared at him for a long moment, watching the shadows fall across his face.

Finally, she shrugged. "You won't have to find out if you let me go."

CHAPTER 25

JOSIE

J osie sat on a broad swing constructed of twigs on the front porch of the hacienda with her face in her hands. She imagined her daughter riding up, flinging her reins to the ground, and running to her.

Josie could almost smell her daughter's hair, scents from a tropical shampoo Emma loved with mango and coconut. It was like the sunscreen Emma lathered herself with as she sat by the pool.

When Josie had passed Emma's lounge chair, she could smell Hawaii in the dry Texas air. Josie always smiled when she rounded a corner and wondered if someone had concocted Piña Coladas but instead found her only child reeking from the aromatic mixture.

Now, those sights and smells of her daughter made her heart sink in her chest and her stomach pitch.

She recited the prayer she'd prayed for almost a year now.

"Please let the next person be Emma; please let Emma be the next person in the drive." She rubbed her palms raw where she stroked the rough branches that formed the swing's arms. But Josie overlooked the stinging of her hands when she covered her face to resume her chant.

A firm hand clutched her shoulder. Josie's eyes flew open to find her husband standing before her.

"Oh, it's you, John. I prayed it was Emma."

"I know. I pray every day riding on the searches. When I return home, I expect to see Honey-Boy standing in the stable and Emma with her finger in the queso on the stove."

His grin did not reach his eyes. Josie knew he was as exhausted and mentally spent as she was. Both were afraid they would never find Emma and more afraid they would. After all this time, no one gave them any hope of finding her alive.

The news broadcasters created their own scenarios for what had happened to Emma. She slipped off a cliff and fell into a ravine. A mountain lion dragged her to his den. Someone kidnapped her and held her for ransom. But that last theory did not ring true. A kidnapper would have contacted them by now.

Unless another conjecture was true, and someone inducted her into the sex trafficking trade that was now prevalent in Texas. Josie shuddered at the thought. *Don't think about it*, she told herself. *Don't even start.* Josie could handle most scenarios except that one. She could not bear the thought of her daughter being subjected to violent behavior and held against her will.

When Josie lost weight she didn't have to lose, John invited their physician to the ranch to examine her. He told Josie he had to intervene because he knew she would not see a doctor independently.

Josie submitted to Dr. Maben's examination, although she was peeved with John for requesting a doctor's presence.

Dr. Maben was a gentlewoman with whom Josie could share her feelings, and Josie listened when the doctor pointed out her dull hair and pale skin. Dr. Maben took vials of Josie's blood and promised to call with the results. But they all knew, without tests,

Josie was grieving herself to death over her daughter's disappearance. Finally, Dr. Maben told Josie a person could actually die of a "broken heart."

"Broken heart syndrome can happen when an extremely emotional or traumatic event triggers a surge of stress hormones. Those hormones can put you in short-term heart failure, which can be life-threatening." She stood, looking up at John.

John clutched a handful of his shirt against his chest. Then, looking incredulous, he whispered, "I can't lose both my girls. What can we do?"

"You're not going to lose me, John." Josie had been listening and watching his reactions when they assumed she was dozing.

Dr. Maben began putting her stethoscope back in her black leather bag. As Josie watched her, she remembered Dr. Maben's father, the town's doctor before her, visiting the ranch when Emma had fallen from a horse. The worn bag must have been his.

Tears welled up in his eyes as John reached out to the doctor's shoulders and turned her toward him.

"Josie must be here when our daughter returns home, right, Doc?"

Josie could tell Dr. Maben could barely look at him. She knew the doctor did not believe they would find their daughter after all this time. She was a woman of science but faith, too, so Josie knew she would continue to hope for the best.

"Josie, you may feel helpless in this situation, which aggravates the symptoms. What if you continue leading your search parties, even once a week? It may give you the impetus to get out of your head and feel you're creating worthy efforts."

John nodded slowly. "That may work. What do you think, honey?"

"I can try," Josie conceded.

CHAPTER 26

EMMA

Emma yanked a root vegetable from the stubborn dirt and squinted her eyes to examine it.

Turnip? Or maybe jicama? These variations did not match their pristine, shiny relatives in the grocery store or her home garden. The dirty orbs were twisted and distorted with green stalks that could be anything from carrots to beets. It didn't matter. They would prepare the tops for a salad and cook the rest like a stew. The People wasted nothing here. Every berry was precious, and they cleaned animal carcasses to the bone. Then, they fashioned bones for spears and arrows and hides for warmth and clothing. Emma had watched Kai hone small bones for fishhooks or a spoon.

One woman Emma liked, Essie, used tiny bones as weaving tools. Emma loved to stand behind her and watch her skillful hands patiently braid dried plant husks into mats for the floor or use the cane near the river for baskets. Essie knew which plants dyed the cane red or purple.

Emma lugged her bounty to the river to wash the vegetables. The men fishing there smiled at her. She was still an oddity to them. They whispered to each other as if she could understand them if they spoke louder. Emma had learned enough of The People's unique language to talk to patients who didn't understand English, but she could not carry on a complete conversation without faltering.

Essie appeared at her side, where she knelt. Emma could not become accustomed to how silently The People walked and how elegantly they moved. Essie reached for one side of the basket and helped carry it back to the caves. Emma motioned to Essie to choose some of the food. Essie smiled and lifted two large squash-looking pieces from the basket. Then she grasped Emma's hand and dragged her through the corridor to her own home.

Emma ducked her head and walked into Essie's abode. When she stood up and raised her eyes, she gasped. A gap in the rocks above their heads gave a skylight ray into the large room. It made the space cheerful and warm.

Essie's colorful baskets and woven mats made Emma think she was in a hunting lodge in Colorado—rustic and homey. Essie organized her food along one granite shelf, and a pile of hides was neatly stacked, like the quilts of Emma's mother in a cupboard on the ranch.

But Emma's eyes focused on the massive mural across the entire back wall. She had seen art of the tribes on other ranches, but nothing this spectacular and well-preserved. Essie giggled when she saw Emma staring at the art wall in front of her.

An artist or multiple artists had divided the scene into three sections. One looked like a hunting party with hundreds of riders on horseback holding bows. In front of the riders, large bulky animals shaped like buffalo ran in the opposite direction.

The following section showcased camp life with cave openings decorated with moons and stars. Stick children played there, around campfires and with what looked like dogs.

The final mural reminded Emma of a worship scene. People lifted their arms to the sky, a triangle skirt between outstretched legs and hair touching their shoulders. A glorious sun with a smiling facial expression dominated the entire scene.

Whoever painted this mural felt it was essential to capture their families, events, and religion from that time. Emma sensed a spiritual experience viewing this scene. Although the drawing had faded and the once bright hues were now soft and muted, she could not believe her eyes.

If discovered by the outside world, this find would bring archeologists in droves to the ranch. However, Emma's mother would not want to open their property for examinations, and now that Emma knew The People, she did not want their culture destroyed, either.

The cave was a remarkable dichotomy of life before her family, long before her relatives changed the ranch's name from El Espina to The Thorn. Her gasp and Essie's laughter brought her back to the present.

"Essie, who painted this?"

Essie shrugged. "Our people have been here for many generations. Leto's family has always stayed here, so maybe his ancestors?" She stammered with halting English, but Emma understood her.

"Are there others like this one?"

"A few. Not as large as this one."

Emma tried to quiz Essie on the making of such an art piece. Essie was an artist herself and explained to Emma the process of using animal fat and crushed minerals to make paint. She told her that a particular insect lives on the prickly pear cactus and is used to make red and orange dyes. Indigo plants gave paint the blue and purple hues.

Emma walked back to her cave, shaking her head. Essie did not realize she lived in an archeologist's dream.

EMMA AND THE OTHER women threw rotten rushes into a roaring blaze. A flood in the lower caves from heavy rains had soaked their floor mats and caused black mold to grow. They worked together to rid themselves of the swollen reeds.

The sound of helicopter blades beating the wind startled Emma. It seemed close. She sprang from her position, kneeling at the fire in the pasture. Squinting against the light, she covered her eyes with her fingers. She searched the few puffy clouds in a startling blue sky.

Emma knew where she would have the best view. She climbed two ladders and pulled herself onto the top boulder, where dozens of trays of herbs lay drying. Although it was a chilly day, the sun's harsh rays warmed her as she scanned the distance above and below her sightlines.

She stood like a statue, listening. *Where did it go?* Far in the distance, she could see a reflection like a mirror flashing a morse code. Was that it? Had it landed?

"Here! I'm here!" she screamed at the top of her lungs. "Are you looking for me?"

Would her cries echo far enough into the distance? Could they be her rescuers?

CHAPTER 27

JOSIE

The helicopter blades sliced the air directly over their heads. John smiled at her. She knew he thought his plan worked.

Josie crawled back into life and renewed hope that her daughter would return to them. Meanwhile, she devised a plan to search each week herself. The project yanked her out of bed in a darkened bedroom and into the hot Texas sunlight.

She handed the pilot the ranch section she wanted to fly over. Each week, she chose an original area of the ranch. She kept careful notes and colored pencils marked where they had already flown.

The pilot always gave her a salute each time the aircraft rose off the grassy pasture. He landed every Wednesday in front of the ranch house, and she and John met him in the early morning hours. Josie brought thermoses of coffee and bottles of water for their trip.

During the first hour of each flight, she always felt she was on an excursion. They had flown in helicopters in Alaska, looking for bears, and over volcanoes in Hawaii. Sometimes, they even used aircraft to round up a herd and point them in a different direction. But this was the first time they flew to search for a missing person.

When Josie was in the air, she newly appreciated the land she surveyed. The magnificence of the mountains was stunning, with the deep green hues of the lacy mesquites and dark-veined granite cliffs.

She caught her breath as they turned in a deep dive and followed the tremendous rush of the Rio Grande River barreling its way across their land. Her eyes misted as she fathomed the magnitude of this vast property and how impossible her task was. They were flying low, but even a giant elk or buffalo looked like an ant. How could they possibly find one tiny girl in this enormous place?

Josie sat back and bit her finger. Her ring finger on the right hand was the only one left with any semblance of a nail. Her cuticles bled from constantly being between her teeth. Her husband looked at her with what looked like sympathy.

John hurt, too, but he held it together more than she did.

"Emma's grown, Josie. She will be fine. She knows this ranch well. There are plenty of people here for her to rely on." This mantra, instead of comforting Josie, incensed her.

"Tell me why she has not returned, then."

"She will, Josie, I know it."

Josie made him eat every one of those words. She fed them to him spoon by spoon for weeks until he was sick. Of course, Josie knew Emma's disappearance was not his fault, and she could have insisted on Emma accompanying them to Europe, even though Emma never wanted to go. Josie was as much to blame as John. But she was not humble enough to admit it to him or anyone else.

When Josie tried to sleep at night, her guilt ate at her, nibbling away until she endured no appetite, no energy, and no more blame on others. Now, she often clung to John and wept openly about her part in their daughter's disappearance. Yet, all he did was stroke her hair and whisper into her ear, "It'll be all right. Emma will return to us. I know it."

She clung to him like a drowning woman without a life jacket. Josie wanted to stay afloat. She did not like the way her clothes hung on her. She knew she had lost the glint in her eyes and the sparkle of her laugh. Even their household staff avoided her. They knew her temper flared at minor details.

Flora over-salted the pork, and Josie dumped her plate into the sink, declaring it "inedible." Then, Josie chastised Pedro for the weeds growing in the garden or ranted at a stable hand for not having her horse ready when he was only a few minutes late.

Now Josie stared out the helicopter window again. This flight was like all the others. Josie and John flew for two hours, straining their eyes until they were gritty and bloodshot. Drinking all their coffee and water made staying in the air impossible for very long. Back to land in the pasture, they raced into the house to relieve themselves. Then, picking up a bag of tacos from the kitchen, they rose into the air for two more hours, flying in a different direction.

Suddenly, Josie lurched forward and cupped her hand over the small window. Was it fog? She squinted harder. Her hand clutched a bottle of water so tightly it sprayed against the seatback in front of her.

"There! Do you see that? Is that a campfire?" Her voice crackled like static in the headsets she, John, and the pilot wore.

Immediately, the helicopter turned on its side and descended rapidly, following her finger. They zoomed along the side of a large crevasse. A plume of smoke rose to meet them in mid-air.

Josie clutched John's arm until he pried her fingernails out of his flesh.

"Land the plane!" she shouted, causing John to jerk the headset off his ears.

The helicopter floated like a leaf on water and hovered in the smoke as it rose into the air. Josie sprang from the open door. She ran toward the fire.

Josie slid to a halt so rapidly that she felt she had run into an invisible wall.

Standing before her were a group of people with rafts and fishing poles. They were dipping water from the river to extinguish their fire. They looked as shocked to see her as she was to see them.

"What are you doing here?" she demanded.

"Ma'am?" A young man wearing a light blue quilted jacket and black pants stepped toward her.

"You're on private property," Josie screamed through clenched teeth.

"I'm a guide from Rio Grande Adventures. We have permission to camp along the banks of the river. Are you the property's owner? You can call my boss if you'd like."

John reached Josie and wrapped his arm around her shoulder.

"No need. We were hoping you were someone else."

Josie whirled around and trotted back to the aircraft. She looked back and saw her husband gesturing with his hands at the people standing before him.

When she climbed into her seat, something inside her broke open, and sobs shook her.

Leaning against the side panel, she cried away the excitement and hope seeing smoke gave her. Josie's nose dripped onto her shirt, and her hiccups pulled at her stomach, causing it to ache like she had completed sit-ups. Then, exhausted and spent, another day ended with realizing she had not found her daughter.

The flight back to their home was silent. Only the *whulp, whulp, whulp* of the chopper blades filled the space.

John offered his hand to help Josie out of the helicopter as soon as it touched down. She felt like she'd run a marathon. He propped her limp body against his side and led her into the house.

Walking down the long corridor to their bedroom, she barely noticed where she was. John gently removed her sweat-stained clothes and reached into a drawer to retrieve a cotton gown. He slipped it over her head and led her to the side of the enormous bed.

Throwing back the comforter and starched sheets, he tucked her into the layers as if he had inserted her into an envelope. Signed, sealed, and delivered to dreamland.

Would she see Emma in her sleep or the dangerous wolves that devoured her nights and woke her screaming?

She did not watch when she heard John tiptoe out of the room.

But, even with her eyes squeezed shut, she could still see the helicopter landing where smoke billowed, and people stood without her daughter.

CHAPTER 28

EMMA

Emma sank to her knees, and the granite rock cut into her skin. Was she hearing what she wanted to hear? As Kai described hallucinations, she produced a nightmare in the daytime.

Someone searched for her, and they could not find her.

Emma looked at the conditions surrounding her. Whoever chose this location hundreds of years before had the skill of a military strategist; no attacks would be successful in this location. The People carved caves out of the side of a cliff hundreds of feet in the air. Below her, the crevices were as deep as skyscrapers in New York were tall. The Rio Grande River made oxbow lakes from its meandering path and was a fierce opponent to anyone who dared cross its path.

She saw The People standing in the pasture beyond the caves and fishing in the stream. Granite crags surrounded the field, which would be invisible to the sky because the walls almost touched each other as if hands were nearing in a clasp.

Emma thought of the trees at home lining the road from the massive iron gate to the hacienda. The oaks, planted to decorate the mile-long drive, accomplished their task, and met each other with tremendous branches above the roadway. They gave shade and beauty to the driveway, just as the magnificent formations now sheltered the pasture below.

Beauty in this land could dazzle, but today, it stood between Emma and those who looked but could not locate her. Her screams were useless against the wind and distance.

"I won't give up. You don't give up on me, either." She waved in the direction where the mirror had glinted. "If you're here today, you'll be here another day. After that, I will go home."

She climbed down the ladders and dropped onto the path. Emma dragged her feet as she walked back to the cave.

Kai knelt by the fire when she entered the room.

"Want something to drink?" He held out a steaming cup to her. "Where have you been?"

She accepted the artisan-shaped mug and felt grateful for the warmth in her bare hands.

"Just watching the sky, Kai. Just watching the sky."

KAI RECOVERED FROM HIS wound but now played assistant to Emma as she nursed his patients. The People were hard-working, and Emma knew most of them would make good ranchers. She had established herself to them as an almost worthy substitute during Kai's absence.

"Push, Essie, one more push." Emma's hands invaded the wailing woman's body and twisted the child, who faced upward.

Sweat dripped off Emma's nose, and she turned to keep it from splashing on the face of the baby, who slipped into her grasp. Essie released her grip on her knees, slumped back, and moaned. Emma felt a rush of exhilaration and adrenaline. *I did it! I delivered a baby! Well, Essie had the baby, but I helped!*

Now, Emma gently bathed the newborn and handed the robust boy to his mother to nurse. Emma had spent the entire night sitting with the woman in labor.

Would the child have died if she had not been there? She grinned at Essie, who swaddled her brand-new baby into pieces of cloth. Kai stood in the doorway and waited until Emma ducked her head and walked into the main room.

"You did a good job, Emma."

"It was touch and go there for a little while. The baby twisted."

"I have birthed babies like that. How did you know how?"

"I learned in college. And, at the ranch, we helped many calves into the world that way."

"College?"

"Where I received training about animals and crops. Like you did from Chatpa."

"Oh. From a wiser person."

"Yes, many wiser people."

"We will prepare food for Essie and Leto. They will be busy with a new baby."

Emma smiled. The gift of food to someone with a new baby or after losing a friend was universal. Emma already thought of a hearty stew to nourish Essie.

It was not traditional for a man to cook, but Kai had lived by himself for several years since moving from Chatpa's home, so he prepared meals. He and Emma decided that night what they would cook for Essie from their storehouse of dried plants and salted meat.

They stored doves, carrots, and onions, and she cleaned and sliced the vegetables while he delicately removed bones from a dove's breast. Her mouth watered at the smell of the carrots and onions sauteing in animal fat over the fire. Why does food always taste better outside?

She and her father often camped on the ranch in pup tents and cooked what they shot or caught in the river over a campfire each night. Emma did not think she had tasted food as delicious since. Until now.

Kai added the meat to her vegetables, and she poured water into the sizzling mixture. Steam rose into her face, causing her to lean back and into his arms. He knelt behind her and held her close for just a moment. She allowed the tenderness between them and her pulse quickened.

Emma did not want to admit to herself she enjoyed his touch. He was strong and handsome, quiet, and understanding. If they were not in this situation—she shook her head.

I cannot allow myself to fall in love with this man. I won't be here much longer, Emma thought.

She pulled away, as Kai reluctantly released her, his hand lingering on her arm. Emma stirred the steaming concoction. After she thickened it by adding ground arrowroot, she ladled some into a bowl for Kai and one for her. They sat close, blowing on the spicy stew to cool it. Kai's eyes never left her face. She could tell he wanted to discuss their life together here, his growing feelings for her. But, instead, they ate hungrily, using fried masa to scoop the mixture into their mouths.

When they finished, Emma scrubbed the bowls with sand and refilled them. They walked the steaming dishes down the dark corridor to Essie's home.

She and Leto were sitting before the fire admiring their baby. They bowed their heads and touched foreheads as they marveled over the exquisite child.

Emma wished for a phone to take their photo. *Well, if I had a phone, I wouldn't be here!*

Then, watching the couple, Emma felt envious. She was jealous of the apparent love between these two people and for what, one day, Emma herself longed. A soft gasp escaped her lips, and they looked up.

"We brought you something to eat. Essie, you need to keep your strength and drink lots of water to feed your baby."

Essie nodded and smiled at her for a split second. Then, her eyes found her baby again. Kai stepped forward and offered his hands to Essie. She passed him the baby and received the bowl of food.

Emma handed her bowl to Leto. They both devoured the stew. Emma watched Kai gently cradle the baby in his arms. When Essie and Leto finished their meal, they stood to face Kai and Emma.

Kai spoke in his beautiful language with Emma understanding the words "blessing," "protection," and "long life." He held the baby up as if showing him to the ancestors high in the sky. Then, when he returned the baby to his mother, he asked, "What shall you name this child?"

"We will call him Adriel," Leto announced proudly. Kai whispered to Emma that the name meant "beaver" and symbolized skill.

"Adriel, we welcome you into The People today, where you will grow in courage and wisdom as your forefathers before you."

Emma felt her eyes brim. She'd been to babies' christenings before, but none any more lovely than this one in a dimly lighted cave on the side of a cliff.

CHAPTER 29

JOSIE

Josie perched on a worn tree stump she usually used to climb into her saddle and barked orders to the hundred men who stood before her.

"I placed a map of The Thorn in the barn with sections marked red where we have already searched. The blue areas are places where we have not been yet. You will divide into teams every morning and select acreage not already visited. Then, spread the horses out and search as you would for lost calves or a horse. You're searching for our Emma."

Gone were the days spent wallowing in grief and loss. Now Josie was perpetually angry.

The ranch hands avoided her until she returned from the helicopter hunts and held weekly meetings and gave daily instructions. She and John were putting their considerable assets behind the search.

"For the team who finds our daughter, we'll give one hundred thousand dollars. If one man finds her by searching on the weekends or his own time, he will receive the reward himself."

That got their attention. Not a day had passed since that

announcement when a single vaquero took a rest day. They were always looking at the maps and finding an alternative route to ride.

The ranch suffered from their lack of care, but Josie did not worry. What was the reason to prune the trees or mend the fences if the heiress to all this was missing?

Josie watched the vet ride into the ranch in his ragged 1972 Ford truck and knew he saw unruly patches of weeds growing on the caliche roads. He made a list of all the horses needing shoes. When he handed it to her manager, she saw him shaking his head, almost in disbelief at how much their animals needed. Then, she saw him watching some diligent hands filling the mechanical mules with gas and others throwing saddles on the horses, always riding away from the ranch before daybreak. Others just stood around looking lost. No one had ever seen The Thorn in this state of disrepair.

The electric gate needed a new battery to swing open from the touch of a button in their trucks, but they just propped it open.

"We'll get to that when we find Emma," was the standard excuse for anything going wrong.

Josie finished her pep talk, and the hands dispersed, one lingering to help her off the high step. Later, she overheard him tell his friends that she was as light as a feather when he placed his hands on her waist and lifted her.

No one remembered seeing her eat since Emma left. Until her daughter's disappearance, Josie ate heartily at barbeques, devouring a plate of ribs or a hefty steak. Now, she didn't have an appetite. She told Flora her longing for Emma settled like a stone in her stomach, its heaviness pinched her throat and prevented her from feeding it.

Josie walked back to the stable, her eyes still searching the map in her hands. That morning's group marked the areas they could cover, and she planned to skirt those plots and ride to the far side. That was her strategy each morning.

She knew John did not want her riding off alone. They'd seen what happened when Emma did that. So, she stayed within earshot of the searchers but far enough away to have her own space. She had developed a habit of chanting as she rode, saying prayers and wishes for Emma as if she could hear.

"I'm close to you, Emma. Come to your mama. Let me see you, and I will find you. We are looking for you. Come to your mama." She repeated the phrases over and over. Her eyes were sharp every morning, but by afternoon were sandy and dry, with dust and insects flying at her in the wind.

Josie left the barn each day with such high hopes to return home, dragging her expectations behind her. She stumbled onto the porch, held the side of the house, and used an iron jack beside the door to hoist off her boots. Then she staggered to the bedroom, filled the clawfoot tub with scalding hot water, and sank into it with a sharp scream. Plunging her head underwater, Josie remained there as long as she could hold her breath and emerged gasping and hair drenched. She slumped back and lay there until the water turned chilly.

The pattern of her everyday life was both tedious and necessary to keep her on the edge of sanity. Wrapping a thick white terrycloth robe around her, she padded to the kitchen in her bare feet. She watched John eat his tacos and swill a bottle of beer. She could barely stomach a tortilla, on which she spread butter and rolled it up like a cigar.

"How was your day, honey?" Josie's husband asked every night.

"Didn't see anything," she echoed every night.

"Maybe tomorrow," he said every night.

"Maybe tomorrow," she parroted.

HER SLEEP WAS DEEP when she finally slumbered. Her dreams were of vast deserts and wild animals. But, no matter whether her sleep was restful or not, Josie's eyes flew open at the same time every morning—4:05 a.m.

Time to search again.

John watched her as she poured a mug of coffee. She knew he worried about her. She looked as though she could blow away in the wind. Her infectious laugh was gone, and her skin was pale and lackluster.

Josie pulled her wide brim hat low on her forehead and headed toward the front door.

"Stay safe, my love."

"You, too." Her voice sounded tiny and without inflection.

Josie began her chants and rode the perimeter of where the ranch hands chose for today's search. What would happen when all the map was red with markings and thoroughly searched? What would she do then? Her chants stopped abruptly at the thought. Then, she remembered her nightmare from the night before.

Lost in a cave with just a candle for light, Josie tripped and ran into stalactites, striking her head against the icicle-like formations. She'd never been afraid of the dark, but now her heart contracted, as did her throat. Would she encounter a snake or a coyote? The cave continued for what seemed like miles.

There was a terrible stench. Josie pulled a handkerchief over her nose and mouth. The farther she walked, the more penetrating the rotten smell became. She could taste the odor in her mouth. Josie gagged. What could produce such a disgusting scent?

She felt around the side of a wall and stepped into something mushy. Her boots sank into the pile. Holding the candle down to the ground, she saw the rotten flesh and head of a horse. Not any horse. The body of Honey-Boy. The horse Emma rode when she left The Thorn.

Josie screamed, but John had already departed. Now that she remembered the horrific dream, Josie knew what she was supposed to do. First, she would have to look for caves on the property. Maybe this was a sign from her daughter.

Caves would be on the far side of the ranch in the granite cliffs overlooking the Rio Grande. No one in her family or employment ever went near the mountains. The entire area was dangerous to traverse.

Josie knew John would not want her investigating caves. Therefore, she must be careful with her requests or ask him to accompany her.

The mountain range was as vast as the acres Josie now rode—days of travel from the ranch house. The helicopter would have to deliver them each morning and pick them up every afternoon, or they would have to camp in the mountains. It was not an appealing thought but one she thought worth pursuing.

She would call the helicopter pilot as soon as she arrived back home.

CHAPTER 30

EMMA

Emma's days took on a sameness that became strangely comforting. She told herself she was not giving up her escape plans but making the best of her captivity.

Emma picked up a basket and took a path to the meadow and the communal gardens. She wore a thick jacket made of deer hide. Essie told her it was made by her grandmother and was too small for her to wear. Emma was pleased to receive it. It was wintry outside with a light peppering of sleet, but plenty of cold-weather vegetables were hardy and flourished. Certain varieties of kale and collards were almost waist-high. Emma picked the large leaves and saw bold heads of cabbage in the rows ahead. She would make a very green soup.

Another woman bent over the mounds ahead of her. Turning to meet Emma's eyes, Essie smiled. Strips of cloth strapped her infant son to her back, and a small blanket tucked tightly around him.

Emma leaned forward toward the tiny bundle.

"Hi, Adriel. You're looking well, little boy." He opened his eyes, gave her a steady gaze, then dismissed her. He scrunched his nose, yawned profoundly, and fell back asleep. His black hair stuck up, and static electricity from the woolen blanket shocked Emma's fingers as she patted his enclosure.

"This is a colorful blanket, Essie. Where'd you get it?"

"Leto's mother created it years ago."

"She was a weaver?"

"Yes, she shaved animals and made the hair into thread. Then she used a rack to weave the cloth. The designs were her own." Essie spoke with a mixture of The People's language and English. Emma had begun to understand more foreign language phrases that once were unfamiliar.

Emma marveled at the skills of The People. To be isolated and uncontacted by the outside world, they were naturally creative and industrious.

The two young women drifted along the strips of vegetables, chatting as if wandering along the rows in a grocery store. *People are the same in all corners of the globe,* Emma thought. *We make friends and enemies and watch our children be born and grow. We choose men to marry and become our partners. Is that my fate—to live here among The People the rest of my life? To have my parents long and cry for me, wonder what happened, and give up ever seeing me again?*

As Emma watched Essie wander around the garden with the baby on her back, she thought of another escape using a disguise. The men on their hunting expedition had informed Kai she was no longer welcome to travel with them, especially after she injured him, so she needed a new idea.

Buoyed by her new resolve, the following day Emma dressed and devised a package for her back like she carried a child. She braided her hair and allowed the blanket to dangle over her forehead to conceal a portion of her face. Would her cover-up work?

If it did, she could walk through the canyons before anyone noticed her missing.

Most days, the entire community noticed her actions. She knew they did not observe the other women in the camp as intently. Women came and went along the river, arousing no suspicions. Had Chatpa or Kai instructed the entire tribe to keep watch over her?

Kai had informed her that morning that he would be bringing more wild horses into their constructed pens. Most of the men would assist him. At least, that's what she hoped.

Emma glanced around the cave. She hated leaving her grandmother's saddle. Emma loved the silver and turquoise beads hanging from leather rosettes on the sides of the seat that jingled when she rode, but she could not carry it. Her camouflage would be for naught while lugging that piece of equipment. She wished for the gun she'd lost to protect herself from rattlesnakes or coyotes on the long walk home.

Home. It seemed like years since she saw the ranch. If her plan worked, she would make it to the massive gates of The Thorn, or the helicopter would return and she could alert it to her presence. Either way, she couldn't give up. She was at least a three-day ride from the ranch. But, on the other hand, it could be a week walking. Would she die trying? She'd been stockpiling food for this moment. And she had two large skin pouches full of water. Would that be enough to get her to a stream?

Emma shook her head to dispel the negative thoughts and the image of dying in the desert. She rearranged the pack on her back and left the cave. She took the long way down a rocky ridge and toward the far pasture, not the one immediately below.

Emma's footing was unsure as stones slipped beneath her

feet and the packet on her back threw her off-balance. Suddenly, she stumbled backward and used her hands to catch herself. The sharp gravel dug into her palms, and one wrist bent. *She hoped for no broken bones.* Then, turning to kneel and hoist herself back to a standing position, Emma pushed the bundle back into place and continued her descent. Looking to the right and left, she slid down the rest of the hill and landed in tall stiff grasses at the foot of the path. The weeds, nubby with seeds, clung to her dress, and she picked at the tacky passengers as she sat to catch her breath.

Emma scrambled to her feet and walked away from the pasture and toward the cliffs. Her heart beat wildly, and her breaths were rapid and shallow. In spite of the chill in the air, sweat rolled down her face and between her breasts.

Emma cautioned herself to amble and not draw attention to herself. She strolled at a pace she envisioned a mother might make with a baby strapped to her back. Emma stepped around the side of a granite wall and peeked back to see if anyone followed.

She was alone.

Emma peeled the fake baby carrier off her back. She pulled out a jug of water, venison jerky, and cowboy boots. Emma pushed her disguise between two boulders and jogged.

It was challenging to carry the supplies in her hands without a saddlebag. She should have thought of that. And she had a long way to go. Unless the helicopter she had heard a few days ago saw her. Right now, her only task was to get far enough from the camp that The People would not discover her absence until it was too late.

The sun was warm on her face, but Emma knew that the desert would be cold and full of animals seeking a meal when it set.

The granite outcropping kept her pace slow. Emma climbed up and down massive rocks and squeezed between the tall cliffs.

A horned toad scurried past her hand and grazed her arm. Unfortunately, the moss growing on the boulder camouflaged it, and she almost grabbed it by mistake. She grimaced. The prehistoric-looking creature considered her a predator and shot blood from its eye as a defensive behavior. He was pretty accurate because streaks marred the sleeves of her garment.

"Yuck. I won't harm you, ugly lizard."

Emma had studied horned toads at A&M and knew many species existed in the United States. She bet this one was a heavyweight record holder. Not as large as the reptiles encountered when she and her parents visited Puerto Rico, but big. She knew the State of Texas considered them an endangered species. Emma spied from the corner of her eye a pile of the lizards sunning themselves.

"If you could see all these, Governor, you would not consider them rare," Emma muttered.

Her foot slipped on the rock and slid into a bramble of thorny bushes.

"Ouch! I hate you, Agarita." She wondered at her ability to name the plants she hadn't seen in a while. Their summer clusters of fragrant yellow flowers belied their sharp needles. Only birds could get into the scrub, eat the bright red berries that followed the flowers, and get away unscathed. Now with all color gone, just thorns remained. Her arms bled, and Emma yanked a sharp needle from her palm.

"This isn't going well," she told herself. "Got to get to level ground."

She could not judge how much time had passed since leaving the compound. Were they aware of her absence yet? Had someone alerted Chatpa or Kai?

Emma quickened her descent, trying to prevent stumbling on

the loose gravel under her slick boots. This footwear was suitable for stirrups, not hiking in a mountainous area. She doubted the hide slippers she had worn that morning would have served her purpose better. The rocks might have pierced the material and lodged in her sensitive feet. In her present circumstance, she truly understood the meaning of the term "tenderfoot." She was one and had two.

The pass between two cliffs seemed wider. Emma did not turn sideways as much as she shimmied through. Her eyes widened as she saw a waterfall cascade directly in front of her. It was the same one they had passed on horseback, leaving the canyon on their nighttime hunt.

The tall wall of pink granite seemed to create a shower enclosure. A shelter formed from the erosion of water seeping through rock, and a deluge hung in the air. She inched her way around the narrow strip of rock surrounding the water and peered over the edge. The fall was at least one hundred feet and the rapidly moving cascade pooled in a pond.

"That must be the stream that runs through the pasture at the caves," Emma whispered. *Was she walking in circles?*

She leaned forward to see behind her, but the cliffs were too protective. Would the looming mouth of the falls swallow her?

Emma continued to inch her way around the plunging water, feeling a spray of mist on her face and arms. It cooled her hot cheeks and left her hair damp. The water muddied her path, and she left boot prints on the soft ground.

"I wish I could drag branches behind me to cover my tracks." But she was on borrowed time and climbed onto a rotting tree covering the path. Suspended between two boulders, it left little room to clear it.

Emma leaped from her perch, landed on solid ground, and saw for miles ahead. She had made it. She was away from the hills and now began the trek away from the setting sun.

After the sky left a thin line of orange sherbet on the horizon, it was as dark as a bottle of ink. A slim parenthesis of a moon was the only light. Clouds obscured the stars, and Emma wondered if she should walk with her hands in front of her.

Running into a tall cactus would be a very unpleasant greeting. Her horse, Honey-Boy, had broken his leg out here, stepping into a prairie dog colony. Her fate could be as severe. If she broke her ankle, her journey would be over. The desert and creatures of the night would consume her.

Emma gave up the impossible fight and decided to sleep. But unfortunately, there were few choices of shelter in the darkness, so she stopped abruptly and dropped.

Grasping her boot in her hand, she yanked it off. Her heels stung from broken blisters. Holding her foot in her hand, she felt more sores bubbling on her toes. Emma stacked the boots on each other and lay her head on them. She did not want fire ants or spiders to crawl into her ears.

Taking deep breaths, she laid her hands on her chest and tried to command her heart to slow its rapid beat.

Emma knew that by now, Chatpa, Kai, and the entire camp would know she was not there. They would send a search party to look for her by early morning. She could only hope they would begin in the opposite direction of her trek.

"No thoughts. Sleep, Emma, sleep." She stilled her erratic reflections about the ones who followed her and thought about the ones in front of her. Her dreams were of the massive gates of The Thorn and her family inside.

Emma may have slept a few hours, but she inched her way again before the sliver of a moon left the sky. She increased her pace to a slow jog when light burst upon the scene. Now her boots seemed much too small for her feet. Her ankles had doubled their standard size, and she was almost out of water. She thought she had enough to last but was swigging too much from anxiety. Nevertheless, she did not stop but chewed on jerky while keeping her legs moving.

"Please, God. Let me be going in the right direction." Emma judged by the ascent of the sun that she headed toward the ranch, but in this vast place, she could not be confident.

She was sure of the sudden movement of an enormous snake on her right side. It had coiled at the base of a barrel cactus and stretched out as she passed. Her boot struck its head, and his body reared up and struck.

Emma saw the piercing fangs enter her leg just above the knee. The rattler sprang back as quickly as he had forward and slithered toward a cluster of prickly pear cacti.

Emma sank to the ground and pulled back her dress. Two puncture wounds.

CHAPTER 31

JOHN

As it was now called, the campfire incident had the opposite effect on Josie. John thought it might give her a new sense of hope. They had seen fire and found it, but she wilted like a trumpet lily on the vine without rain. He could see her becoming smaller and sinking into herself. He wondered if she would just melt away and vanish like the shimmering fog into the air.

How would he survive without her? Without their only child? John held onto hope to encourage Josie. He gave her a pep talk every day. He held her when she sobbed or awoke from the nightmares that consumed her nights. While they lay intertwined in the bed, John flashed memories of Emma.

Emma was late for a meal when she was a young teenager, and John searched the barn for her. Hearing boisterous laughter coming from the bunk house, he opened the door.

Sitting at a round table with a cigar in her mouth was Emma. "Five card stud, boys," she called out. John froze in place, watching his wisp of a girl toss her cards on the table, wrap her arms around a pile of cash, and drag it into her lap.

"Read 'em and weep!" she crowed. John had tapped her on her shoulder, and her eyes widened. "Am I late for supper?"

John never told Josie the reason they both missed their dinner that night. But, he knew the cowboys were grateful to him for forbidding her to play poker again. The men didn't want to lose any more paychecks. Emma astonished him then, and she would bewilder him again. He willed it so, in spite of what everybody else thought.

When anyone from town expressed sorrow for his loss, John corrected them and assured them Emma would return. His ability to focus on tasks at hand had boded well for him in the past. But, now, he was afraid he, too, would succumb to the same debilitating grief as Josie.

At first, Josie had erupted, full of anger and denial. Then, she planned and fought and believed they would just ride a few miles on the ranch and find Emma camping as she had since she was young. Emma, stoking the fire with Honey-Boy tied to a tumbleweed beside her, would look up with surprise.

"What are you two doing here? I'm not ready to come home." He had heard those words from his daughter many times. He prayed he would listen to them again.

But it had been nine months. Nine months. The gestation time for a cow or a human to live in the world.

That same number of months flew by when he and Josie were waiting for Emma to be born. They had much to keep them occupied on the ranch. Josie rode her horse and worked as usual until one afternoon, she told him it was time to go to the hospital. His jaw dropped. Not already. It couldn't be.

Nine months of someone being out of your life passed much more slowly. It seemed like years. When he rose from the bed, he moved in slow motion every morning. He would laugh if it weren't tragic. But instead, his system turned into a snail's pace.

When he created family videos to show at Christmas parties, he liked to use freeze frames or slow motion on specific aspects of the ranch or people. Now, he was stuck in one of those photos, and someone from the constellations might observe him as if at a turtle's pace.

Alone that morning, John sat on his horse in a valley, watching a herd of Axis deer chewing plants. The days, still chilly in the early spring, created shimmers across the expanse, making the air rise with colored waves.

He thought his lungs might collapse from holding his breath to keep from crying. He began to sing, "You are my sunshine, my only sunshine…." *Join in, Emma.* The deer looked strangely at him for a split second and sprinted out of sight. No wonder they were called Ghost Deer. Here one minute and gone the next. *Just like you, my daughter.*

When he walked into the house a few hours later, his limbs seemed stretched like a rubber band and snapped back into place, leaving him limp and out of whack. *One foot in front of the other,* he kept telling himself. You are the support system for Josie and Emma.

John never considered his wife a burden during all their years together. Yet, now he carried her on his back, weighing him down more than her hundred pounds. She once was an anchor. Was she now a rock? How much longer could they hope? How much longer would Josie believe their daughter was still alive?

He blinked and looked at his tiny wife standing in front of him. She snapped her fingers.

"Earth to husband," she said.

"I'm here, Josie."

"Are you? I'm not sure either of us is here anymore. I want to fly over the cliffs near the Rio. I had a dream about caves there."

She pushed off his chest as if to make a getaway, but he wrapped both arms around her and held her close. John kissed the top of her head before losing his grip, and she dashed for her phone.

Josie called the pilot. Her voice sounded energized, and she paced the floor, waving her hands in animated movements.

They were off on another wild goose chase.

They flew that afternoon as close to the mountains as they could safely. But unfortunately, they did not see any caves, and Josie imploded into herself again.

CHAPTER 32

KAI

Kai loaded a pack with his fishing line and jerky to stay away from camp for most of the day. He counted the sharp hooked spines he had gathered from a cactus to anchor his bait.

Emma had told him they were from fishhook barrel cacti. She said they leaned to the south, and people often called them "compass cactus." Kai collected its flowers to eat and ground the tiny black seeds to add to salads.

He walked down the corridor and squatted beside his grandfather. Chatpa handed him a cup of hot broth. They sat silently, sipping the liquid.

"The men don't need my help with the horses, so I will fish today instead. Will you check on Emma later?"

"Are you afraid she will try to leave again?"

"She has not in a while, but I know she wants to go to her home."

"This is her home now."

"I hope she understands."

The older man nodded his head. Neither of them voiced that Emma was unlike other women.

Kai used a tiny blade of bone to dig into the fresh soil next to the stream. The rich bank provided ample worms and grubs; usually, an armadillo had been there before him and completed most of the digging.

He wrapped the wiggly creatures in a sack and began his walk. Kai hiked until he was near Topo waterfall. He would fish in the pool underneath the shower of water.

Kai's casting produced, and he scaled and sliced the fish before placing them in a bag with leaves and moss to keep them cool. Kai lay back on the bank and dozed.

He heard gravel falling from a cliff above the pool. An animal tried to traverse the span from the top of the fall to the flat land below. It skidded and plummeted. Kai was sorry he did not have his bow with him. He could have fish and an elk, perhaps.

Kai stood against the large oak and peeped around to see his prey. It was Emma.

Her feet flew out from beneath her, and she slid halfway down the steep incline. He could see her examining her hands. Kai could not see the blood from a distance, but her palms must be raw from the length of the rocky surface she traveled.

Emma did not give up. She stood again and reached for a small sapling on the path to steady her. He watched as she saw the waterfall. Emma's eyes widened, and she stood still to marvel over the beauty. Kai looked back at the cascade as if seeing it for the first time. It was splendid. The rock formed a bonnet for the stream to enter and fall a distance of many trees high. It was stunning as it splashed into the deep green of the pool, causing a ripple of waves to the banks.

Kai looked back at Emma. She did not linger long with her worship of the water. She was on her way again, glancing every few steps behind her.

Kai tied his pack with fish around his waist. He waited until Emma was out of sight around the tall cliff and followed. Should he allow her to leave? Did she have supplies with her this time? He could offer her the fish and then walk back home.

It was easy to maintain distance between them. The desert was vast, with brush and cacti to slide behind. Emma had quit looking over her shoulder. It was getting dark, and she kept a relentless pace. Not until dark descended on them did Emma slow and stop her movements. Kai could barely make out the mass on the ground where she stretched out. He, too, lay down. He wanted to rest before she started her journey again.

Kai was so close to her that it was surprising she could not hear him. The moon did not offer any relief from the darkness, and he could imagine her breathing as she slept.

She had laid beside him every night when he was healing. He told her he now knew her breathing as well as his own. She had a slight whistle sound between her teeth in a deep dream. She twisted from side to side and often slapped him with an arm or elbow.

Kai did not mind. He told Emma that he enjoyed the closeness of their bodies. He loved to hear her stories when she was not too tired from helping with the horses or sick children. She told him about her parents and the place they lived. He tried to picture the people and places in his mind as her words washed over him.

She described salty meat and spicy beans wrapped in flour tortillas. Some nights, she attempted dishes at Chatpa's with their supplies in the camp. She made a pancake and used venison to create a taco for him. She laughed and said it was not the same, but close. He thought it was delicious.

Emma's laugh was as enjoyable. It was appealing and loud as if it came from her belly. She threw her head back and closed her eyes. He always watched her in admiration. When Emma was happy, his chest swelled as if he somehow filled her with joy. He wanted to feel that pride again and again.

Kai loved to watch Emma with the horses. She was gentle and talked to them as though they could understand what she told them. Emma stroked their faces and braided their manes. She used a stick to clean mud out of their hooves and told him animals could develop a sickness if they did not keep them clean. Kai saw Emma frown as she listened to him tell her which herbs were poisonous and which were safe. She said they looked the same until he showed her the bloom or leaf shape difference. Emma grinned and pumped her fist in the air when she recognized what he described.

He remembered one day when Emma balanced on boulders to cross the creek, and she slipped and pitched toward him. He outstretched his arms and caught her as they fell into the cold water. Her arms were still around his neck when her head plunged under the rushing stream. When he pulled her to his chest, she sprayed him with the gulp of water in her mouth. Her laugh echoed through the trees. Little boys on the bank laughed with her, and Kai joined in. He could still remember her body as he pulled her up and carried her. Their faces were close together, and she rested her head on his shoulder. Their eyes locked on each other, and both seemed to take a sharp intake of breath simultaneously.

When he placed Emma on level ground, she had squeezed out her dress with her hands, heavy and dripping with water, tossed her hair, and walked back to Chatpa's. He stood watching her and realized nothing had changed between them.

Now, he felt rather than heard her move again. The sky was lightening. They advanced.

It did not take long for the night to become day and the scorching sun to make his cheeks burn as he strode behind her. She walked with a slight limp. He saw she wore the boots she had when they found her. Her dress was dirty from the dust of the place she slept, and her hair freed from braids over her shoulders. Still, she looked beautiful to him.

Emma was determined, brave, and persistent. She never gave up. Whatever she attempted, she did it to her best ability. He had seen that in her from the beginning. He did not like her working like a man with the horses and going on hunts, but she insisted.

"You have old-fashioned ways, Kai. Men and women are not in separate roles in the real world."

He was unsure what she meant by the *real world*, but he listened to her and learned what she shared with him. When Emma saw Chesma act stupid, she told Kai that in most groups, there were always some bad apples, like Chesma and his followers. Chatpa had instructed those men to be gracious to their fellow members like families should. But, Chesma didn't obey anyone, even Chatpa.

Sometimes, Kai talked to Chatpa about Emma's strengths and was delighted to hear him say she reminded him of his wife, Anna. Chatpa's parents had chosen Anna to be his wife, and she was, like Emma, a fighter. But she worked with Chatpa and gave him advice and guidance about leading the tribe.

Anna died when Kai was twelve. Yet, he could still shut his eyes tightly and see her brown eyes staring into his as she tucked his blanket around him. Kai lived with them after his parents died.

His father drowned trying to save his mother when she fell into the river. The water was too powerful for them. His mother had never learned to swim and slipped when she collected berries along the edge.

It took a long time for Kai's nightmares to subside. Finally, Chatpa told him his parents were trying to reach out to him from the Great Beyond to let him know they were safe with the ancestors. They were not in the watery graves of the mighty old river as in his dreams.

Kai was not dreaming now. Emma sank to the ground and cried out in pain.

He rushed to her side.

CHAPTER 33

JOSIE

Josie collapsed on her bed. She should declare to everyone she had given up the search. But instead, Josie investigated long after the sheriff warned them that there was little hope of finding Emma alive. When the sheriff first made his pronouncement, her eyes widened, and she ordered him out of her house. But she knew he just followed protocol, and she was the one who did not.

Josie still grasped at any flicker of a probing idea. She enlisted detectives to search Dallas for sex-trafficking operatives. The helicopter bills ran into the tens of thousands. She paid substantial sums of money to run full-page ads in the major newspapers in the state and beyond. The *New York Times* had never posted a missing person poster in their publication, but they did for the price she paid. When Josie opened the newspaper and saw her daughter's glorious eyes and radiant smile, she dropped the paper and dissolved into sobs.

Now, Josie had a directory of students from A&M in her lap. She combed through the entire senior class and called all 518.

"Were you in any of my daughter's classes? Did you know she is missing? We need anyone with information about her to step forward."

No leads. None of these young people could add any clues. A few had been in classes with Emma. One was her suitemate, Norma. Josie impulsively invited her to come to the ranch. She reasoned that someone who lived in close quarters with Emma for four years would bring a different perspective to their search.

Norma said she would do whatever she could to help. So, Josie chartered a plane to pick Norma up in Abilene and fly her to El Paso. There, Norma boarded the helicopter for the ranch. When Emma's friend landed in their front pasture, Josie ran to her and embraced her as if she were Emma herself.

The girl's eyes darted to one side when they walked back to the house with Josie's arm wrapped around her shoulder and her hand clasped tightly around her forearm. Norma stared at a ranch hand in the door of the stable.

"Jeff, is that you?"

"You know one of our ranch hands?"

"He was in our class at A&M. Emma had a crush on him."

Jeff walked toward them, and Norma hushed.

"What are you doing here?" he asked.

"I asked her to come help in the search for Emma. I didn't know you and Emma were close," Josie said.

He blushed, a deep red moving from his throat to his cheeks.

"I gave her name as a reference for you to hire me, Mrs. Rosales."

A slight memory from that statement seemed to float into Josie's mind.

"Ah. I seem to remember that. Why don't you join us for supper tonight? It will be nice to be with Emma's friends."

"Well, okay. I guess I can."

He seemed uncomfortable with the request and shuffled back toward the barn.

Josie raised her shoulders and eyebrows.

"Maybe he doesn't think we will be delightful company?"

Norma giggled. Josie showed her to a guest room next to Emma's bedroom. "Freshen up and relax. We'll have supper at six."

"What do I wear?" Norma asked.

"Whatever you'd like. We're not formal here." Josie pointed at Norma's feet. "You can wear your boots." It was Texas, after all. Texans approved boots for all occasions, even formals.

Josie pulled the door behind her and patted it, saying, "I think something good will come from this."

When Josie and John greeted Norma in the dining room, it was six by the clock that chimed from across the hall. A door opened then, and a short woman with a braid to her waist walked into the room. She carried a large platter of food. The smells made everyone breathe deeply and smile.

Before she could examine the food, Josie saw Jeff. He held a cowboy hat, and John pointed to a rack by the door. Jeff back-tracked and hung it on a hook.

"Well, aren't we fortunate to have Emma's friends with us tonight?" Josie sat at one end and her husband at the other of the rough-hewn table that could seat twelve. Norma and Jeff chose seats in the middle on benches flanking the long table and glanced awkwardly at each other.

Josie introduced the woman carrying the food as Flora. She brought mammoth-sized dishes to the table, far more than four people could eat. Warm corn tortillas piled high, steaming chopped brisket, pico de gallo in bowls, sour cream, cheese, fresh tomatoes, and a pot of pinto beans dotted the table. Tall glasses of iced tea with limes completed the meal. Josie looked over the dishes and nodded approvingly.

"Shall we?" she said as she passed the dishes to her guests and husband.

There was small talk about ranch work, Norma's job in Abilene until she could apply to vet school, and Jeff's duties on The Thorn. When tres leche cake arrived for dessert, Josie's mood changed abruptly.

"Please tell me about your interactions with my daughter and if you can venture a guess where she is."

Norma and Jeff looked at each other. Josie knew her mood had changed like a thunderstorm passing over the desert. She had waited as long as she could before spewing the questions at them.

"I haven't seen Emma since she came home after graduation," Norma began. "We texted. I called the ranch two weeks after she arrived home because she was supposed to meet me at the Sandhill Dance Hall. Flora told me she had gone camping and hadn't returned. I checked my phone to see if she had left me any messages, but she hadn't."

"What about you, Jeff? You gave her name as a reference to secure this internship at The Thorn. Did she recommend you because she knew you from classes at A&M?"

"I think Emma thought we could be more than friends. At first, she was glad to see me here at the ranch, but I bragged to the other ranch hands that I...well, I made remarks I shouldn't have, and Emma was angry with me."

Josie's eyes widened, and she pressed her lips tightly together. Jeff abandoned the deliciously moist cake with his fork suspended mid-air as his mind seemed to scramble to right the situation.

"Are you saying you took advantage of my daughter?" John murmured.

"Oh, no, sir. I mean, there was nothing physical between us. She might have had…we might have thought of beginning a relationship, but she was quick to drop those intentions when I disappointed her with my stupid behavior."

At least he's honest, Josie thought.

"When did you last see her?"

"The morning she rode off on her horse. I haven't seen or heard from her since."

Josie's eyes squinted, and her nostrils flared. "Are you the one who had a screaming match with her in front of the shed? Pedro told us about an employee he couldn't identify putting his hands on Emma. Did you tell her she would be very sorry?"

Norma and Jeff were squirming in their seats under the narrowed, watchful eyes of Josie.

"I didn't mean anything by that. We were both mad," Jeff stammered.

Josie tossed her napkin on the table.

"Norma, get some sleep. We'll return you to Abilene in the morning. John will transport you to the airport at nine. Thank you for being a good friend to Emma. She was…she *is* very fond of you. Jeff, your internship has ended. Your last check will be in your mailbox by noon tomorrow."

John shrugged his shoulders at them as he and Josie left the room. Josie clenched and unclenched her fists as he tried to hold her hand. She paced the floor in their bedroom. He changed out of his clothes while she ranted.

"The nerve of that boy. What do you think he did to make Emma angry? Do you think Jeff's the reason she left? Do you think he had anything to do with her disappearance? Was Jeff the last one other than Flora to see her? You don't think he harmed her, do you?"

John looked dizzy from her barrage of questions.

"Try to calm down, Josie. He seems like a nice kid. I don't think he would hurt her. And, if he did, I don't think he would stick around here."

Josie turned on him. "Don't you? Why don't we see what the sheriff thinks? I'll call him right now. He may want to talk with this boy before he leaves the ranch."

She spun around, stepped into her walk-in closet, and pulled her cell phone out of her pocket. Josie had hatched another plan. She was revitalized.

Nobody would harm her daughter and live to talk about it.

CHAPTER 34

EMMA

Emma squinted at him like he was a mirage. Kai had reached her within a few seconds after she fell. He scooped her up and laid her head on his lap.

"What happened?" he asked.

"Kai? What are you doing here?"

"I saw you trying to run again and followed you."

Emma shook her head.

"Guess it's a good thing. A rattlesnake bit me." She held up her dress and showed him the fang marks on her leg.

He looked frightened. "Terrible poison. Let me show you what I would do."

"I need your bone knife. I will cut the wound, and you suck out the poison."

He shook his head slowly. "I don't understand."

"The venom is entering my bloodstream, and I want you to take it in your mouth and spit it out."

She grabbed her bag of water and took a deep swallow. Then she spat it out on the ground. Emma looked into Kai's eyes and saw that he understood.

"I'm going to lie still and hope the poison doesn't travel to my heart. Here's what's going to happen. The symptoms of shock are clammy skin and confusion, and I may pass out. Do you understand, Kai? I may go into a deep sleep, but leave me here on the ground. Don't move me. Do you have any herbs with you?"

He reached into his knapsack and brought out the skinned fish with moss and leaves covering it.

Emma's face grew numb.

"Here we go, Kai. I cut, and you suck my blood and spit it out."

Emma raised the bone. It was as sharp as a surgical instrument. She sliced her leg between the fang marks and screamed as Kai leaned over and took a big gulp. He turned to the side and spat, and Emma could see red stains on the sand. Then he spit a second time.

"Not the latest method, but we certainly can't get me to a doctor in time. Wrap that fish around my cut, place the moss and leaves over the wound, and sit with me."

Emma looked down at her soiled dress and noticed fang marks on the hide. A sense of relief swept through her. When snakes bite through clothing, an entire dose of venom rarely reaches the bloodstream.

She lay back, and Kai reached for her hand. Emma felt lightheaded and nauseous. Her vision blurred as she saw Kai lean over her. A drop of her blood still stained his lip. Then, all went dark.

IN THE LATE AFTERNOON, Emma stirred. She had been salivating and wiped her face free of drool. Kai sat cross-legged with her head in his lap.

"Are you still here, Kai?" Emma mumbled.

"Of course. Are you better?"

"Maybe. I think the worst has passed. One day, I can sell fish packs as treatments for snakebite."

"What?"

"Never mind. I'm still a little delirious."

She rolled off his lap and to her knees. Then, slowly, she placed one foot under her leg and stood. Emma put her hand on his shoulder to steady herself.

"Guess we better go back," Emma muttered. She knew she was in no shape to travel any farther than she already had. "Better yet, come with me when I am stronger. Let me show you the modern world. Aren't you curious?"

"Leave my tribe?" He frowned at her. "Why don't you stay and not run again, Emma?"

"No promises."

Emma leaned against Kai and hobbled back toward the cliffs. She did not hear any helicopters or sounds of horses. It was quiet in the desert.

It looked like miles to the edge of the caverns and cliffs. She looked up at them. They were majestic in their pink glory. The pale stone glistened in the distance, and the dark green of the pines on the sides of the mountains were perfect disguises for the wild game and cave dwellers.

There were small openings on this side, but the larger ones were opposite. *That's why they've gone undetected for many years,* Emma thought.

It was ingenious the way The People chose where to place their dwellings. The tall rock walls concealed the pasture, stream, and people who lived there. It looked like any other mountain from the "front" side of the range.

Emma took deep breaths and tried to believe the poison was no longer a deadly threat to her body. Kai had removed the venom quickly, and her clothing protected her from a large percentage of the strike. Still, she looked cautiously around the cacti and boulders where snakes liked to lie on the sun-warmed stones.

Her arms and hands were still numb. Maybe it was from Kai's strong clutch. He guided her like they were going for a stroll down a hospital corridor. Emma had failed to escape again; she was losing hope.

The skies darkened, and Emma felt Kai quicken their pace. She knew he wanted to get her home to a dry bed and herb tinctures and wraps that he and Chatpa would produce.

It amazed her the skill those two possessed and the cures they could wring from the earth. When Emma thought she could not take another step, they entered the side pasture and began a slow incline to their cave.

When she stopped for the fifth time, Kai lifted her in his arms and climbed the rest of the way. Chatpa sat outside his dwelling when they arrived. When he saw Kai carrying Emma, he jumped to his feet and beckoned them to come inside. Kai gently lay Emma on her bed of hides, and she lost consciousness a second time.

She didn't know how much time had passed, but lightning and thunder woke her. There was a roaring fire in Chatpa's cave, and she perspired profusely.

"Hot, Kai, too hot," she mumbled.

"Chatpa thinks you can sweat out the danger."

Emma looked at her wrapped leg and smelled a pungent odor radiating from it. The two men had concocted a salve for her. She believed it was as close as they could come to modern medicine.

Chatpa brought a steaming cup to her lips.

"Drink, Emma. It will make you better."

Emma drained the hot liquid. Chatpa smiled at her and nodded his approval.

Kai piled wood on the fire and more hides on top of her.

"You're going to smother me."

His response was to lie down beside her. She knew he must be exhausted; he hadn't slept in many hours. But he did not close his eyes until she did.

Emma dreamed of a dragon instead of a snake biting her leg. It took her leg from her body and flew into the air, spewing fire as it climbed. She looked down at where her leg had been, and it was a horse's leg, slender and hooved.

Emma remembered thinking she could *run like the wind with the horse's leg. She could run all the way home.*

Kai told her she muttered in her sleep, and he rearranged her hides and let the fire burn out. Her skin no longer felt clammy, and Kai removed most of the coverings. She thought she would have a better night's sleep without the weight of many skins.

Emma knew Kai never left her side. And, Chatpa must have told Essie about the injury because the next time Emma awoke, there was something for her to eat and a woven ribbon for her hair.

Emma's weakness lasted a few days. She tried to stand and found her legs were too shaky. She scooted against the rock wall to eat and talk to Kai. As she had told him stories of the ranch, he told her of dreams the people had shared with him and his interpretation of them.

One woman dreamed about three trees on the banks of the river. They grew strong and healthy and bore much fruit. Kai's interpretation was that she would bear three sons. They would grow into men and care for their mother in her old age. She was delighted with his account of her dream and brought him duck eggs for his breakfast.

"Did the dream come true?" Emma slurred.

"It did," Kai whispered back to her.

"What other dreams have The People told you?"

Kai tilted his head toward her.

"One dreamed his maize grew taller than the cliffs. He could not reach the corn, and his family starved. He had to cut down all the stalks so they could harvest. I told him he was concerned about the rains destroying the crops and worried because his wife had given birth to another child, their sixth. He was scared about feeding all of them."

Emma leaned close to him and shared her dream. "A dragon breathing fire stole my leg and gave me a horse's leg. What do you think that means?"

Kai studied her face and said, "You want to go home. Not even monsters can stop you. You will find another leg, another way to go where you want. Emma, you are a runner, and I am afraid you will always be." His eyes looked troubled, and his expression drooped.

She nodded. "That's what my interpretation was. I want to run like a stallion and make it back to my ranch."

Emma wondered if she could interpret dreams as well. She had decoded that one. She remembered her grandmother, Valeria, reading Bible stories to her when she was a little girl. Didn't Joseph interpret dreams for the Pharaoh? And that was after they rescued him from the pit his brothers had thrown him in and sold him as an enslaved person.

She was undoubtedly in a pit or would have been if Kai had not rescued her. Or had he? Her mind tumbled, and her stomach pitched.

He and Chatpa possessed the gifts of healing and dream interpretations. She admitted they were pretty remarkable. But, wait, was she delusional? She studied psychology in college and remembered the Stockholm syndrome, where a small percentage of hostages develop a psychological bond with their captors.

Kai and Chatpa were kind men. If Kai had not won the competition, a man like Chesma might have already forced her into marital relations.

Emma shivered. Kai loved her.

CHAPTER 35

EMMA

Chatpa didn't look well when Emma came out of her room after the snakebite incident. She saw he held a skin wrapped around his shoulders and pinched tightly under his chin. His skin looked as white as his hair.

"Chatpa? Are you sick?" Emma squatted beside him.

"I stayed up too late three nights ago talking with the elders. One of the men introduced me to the new wives they brought back."

Emma's skin crawled. Before she disguised herself to leave the camp, she had heard Chesma bragging about an excursion across the border.

"How does he enter a village without being detected? How does he meet women?"

"Chesma is crafty. He travels late at night and leaves the horses on the outskirts. I do not know where he entertains the women."

"How many?"

"They returned with three."

Emma walked out of the opening. She looked for Kai and spotted him examining the horses. She steadied herself on the ledge and walked down the steep path.

"Where are the recruits?" Emma's voice sounded harsh, and Kai looked up in surprise.

"You mean the wives?" Kai corrected her terminology.

"I mean the women Chesma charmed into joining his cult."

"I do not condone his methods of convincing women to join us, but some of our people believe it is the only way to preserve our numbers."

Was that the real reason they want me to stay? Maybe they aren't afraid of intruders but want me to increase the tribe's numbers? Emma's eyes narrowed, and she snorted.

"Which men collected them?"

"Lolo, Chesma, and Kewil."

Emma swung around and ignored his protests as she scurried back the way she'd come.

She knew where Lolo and Kewil lived. They shared a common area near Kai's home.

A hide covered the doorway, and she flung it back. The room was dark. Two young women sat on the floor. They cowered when she burst into the room.

"Are you okay? Are you hurt?"

One girl sprang to her feet and began chattering. Her halting English was easy enough to understand.

"We did not realize the conditions here would be this rough."

"Chesma probably put his own spin on where you would be living."

"Spin?"

"The men want you to be their wives."

"Yes, our village is impoverished, and we wanted better for ourselves. Not sure this is an improvement." She looked around the cave and its primitive conditions. "We are very sick."

"What do you mean?

"We have the bad flu."

"Was your diagnosis Covid? Were you tested?"

"The clinic did not have any tests, and they called it 'the flu.'"

Now, Emma squinted at the girls and had a sinking sensation in her gut. "I'll get some herbs to treat you. Wait here."

Emma marveled about the men entering and exiting a town without discovery. They saw dwellings and knew where people resided or found a way to meet people in an outdoor square or festival where no one questioned how they dressed.

She hurried up to the roof and examined the jars of dried plants. Finally, she reached for a small vial of a brown liquid. Kai soaked herbs for fever and chest congestion. She thought it might help with the flu if that is what the girls had. *Please don't be Covid.*

She entered the cave and told the girls to drink the concoction she had brought. They obeyed her. She stoked the fire and spread out a hide on the floor.

"Sleep here and see if you feel better. I'll talk to the men about your conditions when they return. They're probably hunting to please you with meat from their kill."

The women said nothing but nodded.

Emma left and saw Kai waiting at the end of the corridor.

He walked toward her.

Emma spit out her words. "They're sick, Kai. They've brought illness into the camp."

He looked at her and nodded. "We will heal them."

"I already gave them a liquid. You can check on the women later."

Emma whirled around and left him standing there. She was furious—with their situation, with her situation. What could she do about it?

She marched back down to Chatpa's. Now, he lay on his back, his hands folded on his chest, and was still.

Back to the roof she went. She poured another portion of the dark liquid and climbed back down the ladder. When she arrived back at Chatpa's, his breathing was noticeably shallower.

Emma sat behind Chatpa and propped his head against her chest. He opened his mouth to accept the medicine, and she laid his head back on the ground.

Had Chatpa caught the flu or Covid from the men who brought the women into the camp? Chatpa and the elders were at greater risk because of their advanced ages and frailty. Her heartbeat accelerated. Emma was concerned about the sick women, but severe cold or flu could turn deadly among The People.

She and Kai would have to work together to treat Chatpa and make more medicines.

When Kai checked on Chatpa, Emma mapped out a course of action for him.

"Let's go upstairs and work to create enough medicine for the camp. I have a bad feeling."

Kai stared at her and agreed. They climbed to the rooftop and began chopping and soaking the dried plants. She knew it was fortunate they had picked such a tremendous number of herbs the spring before.

"Have you ever had a severe sickness in the camp?"

"Not since I was young. Chatpa said we lost several members from illness when I was a child, but I don't remember."

"Go to Lolo and Kewil and tell them not to have relations with these women. We need to isolate them where they are. Get Chesma to bring his new woman to join the other two. We must keep them together and away from anyone else until this illness passes."

Kai left to find the men and instruct them about preventing the sickness spreading to the rest of the camp. Emma knew he would tell the young men they would have to lodge together as the women would do until he could see if they, too, were sick.

Emma did not know who would become ill or to what extent. For now, they would pass around the medicine and restrict anyone from visiting with each other. Emma told Kai it might be a while before the symptoms appeared. It could be a long wait for the disease to strike.

With the quarantines in effect, Kai and Emma worked to stay ahead of the demand for medicine. They experimented with different combinations of herbs to stretch the supply they held in the storehouse.

Her fingers were raw from stripping the dried herbs from the stems. Some had thorns and cut like razors. Kai stored a jug of what looked like corn moonshine. He used it to add to their herbal mixtures. Emma remembered her father's old remedy of honey, lemon juice, and bourbon for coughs. It did work to quieten her throat, so she hoped this mixture would.

Kai returned to Chatpa's while Emma remained on the roof measuring out the amounts of the remedies. Then, she heard Kai calling to her from the ladder below.

"Emma, come quick. Chatpa is asking for you."

She scurried down the incline and broke into a run in the dark corridor. Kai made it back before her and cradled Chatpa when she flew through the doorway.

"He is weak. He wants to talk to you."

Emma took Chatpa's hand and knelt beside him. Kai backed from the room to grant them privacy. He behaved as though this was a sanctified moment between Emma and his grandfather.

Emma, too, sensed a spiritual time in the room, forehead to forehead with this man.

"Emma." His voice was barely a whisper.

"I'm here, Chatpa."

"I am going to meet my ancestors."

"No, you will get better," she lied to him.

"They are here to escort me, little one." He waved his hand toward the wall.

Emma put her ear to his mouth. She did not want to miss a single word.

"I dreamed about you and Kai. You will be together in this land. You will bear his children, my great-grandchildren."

She did not correct him or deny his claims. Chatpa tried desperately to take deep breaths, but he drew short ones.

Her knees were numb from kneeling, but she could not adjust her position for fear of missing anything he said.

"You will learn to love this man. He will be good to you. You will be partners on your life's journey."

"You need to rest, Chatpa."

His head made slight shakes.

"Listen to me, my child. Believe that your marriage will be one most would covet. Like mine and Anna's."

She had never heard him use his wife's name. *Anna.* There was much more to his story that she wanted to know.

Flashes of her parents were in her mind—her mother's gentle hands, cool to her fevered forehead, her father leading a pony around a ring when her chubby little legs could not reach the stirrups, and the two of them belting out their favorite song in the middle of the desert. Would her parents be able to live their lives not knowing what happened to her?

She closed her eyes to pray until she realized Chatpa no longer breathed.

Emma backed toward the door with her eyes on his physical body. Her mind swirled with conflicting thoughts. He was her captor, yes. But also a kind and generous man who raised his grandson as his own. She struggled to square the two. Was it just Stockholm syndrome that made her think that? Or was this feeling—this grief that had rocked her as she watched him fade away—real?

Emma marveled at Chatpa's inner strength as he had watched his tribe grow and recede, his ability to interpret dreams and heal others with his passion for the earth and plants that grew on it. He had led his tribe in a peaceful existence here on her family's land, *his* land.

Chatpa was as impressive in death as he was in life. She stared at his high cheekbones, powerful jaw, and full head of white hair. She had not known him very long, but he felt like family to her now that he was gone. Tears slid down her cheeks, and she swiped them away with the loose sleeves of her garment.

Kai stood with his head bowed just outside the door. She slipped her hand in his and looked into his eyes, eyes like his grandfather's.

"Chatpa has gone to meet your ancestors," she whispered.

Kai sighed. He squeezed her hand and ducked back inside the cave. She watched as he sat cross-legged beside his grandfather and chanted.

Emma did not fully understand what Chatpa's death would mean to the tribe and her life. The news of his leaving the physical world passed through the tribe like a wildfire that escapes its trenches and spills into the dry forest.

The elders met before Chatpa's body grew cold. There was little discussion as to who would take over the leadership of this tribe. Kai was the obvious choice. Only one man opposed him.

Chesma had been jealous of Kai since they were children and most recently competed for Emma to be his wife. He had acted sullen for days following his defeat. Finally, Chesma tried to make his case to the elders that he was the superior hunter and would be a better leader. They listened patiently to him but then handed the spirit stick to Kai.

The stick was an elaborately carved rod about five feet long. It reminded Emma of the walking sticks she used when her family visited national parks and hiked into the mountains.

Kai held the possession lightly, balancing it between his two hands. He treated it as a reverent object. Now, he would step forward to guide his people, but Emma thought he probably just wanted to crawl under his hides and sleep away the shock of losing his protector.

Emma had not shared what Chatpa predicted for their future as he lay dying. She did not want to sully Chatpa's memory by telling Kai that he was wrong. They would not be living together on this land and having children together.

But the last spoken words from someone were hallowed. Chatpa's whispers were still in Emma's head. It was as though she had heard a priest whispering to her from behind a confessional screen mixed with a fortune teller stroking a crystal ball.

What did she believe to be true? What would happen if she never left this place?

She looked at Kai, holding the stick, and her eyes misted. He loved Chatpa like a father. Now he was utterly alone. True, the tribe was significant, but each member had created their own families with wives and children. The members thought Kai had done the same with Emma.

Although she knew Kai did not consider himself primed for being The People's leader, he was the best person for the job. He loved his people and wanted the best for them. Chatpa had taught him well. He would rise to the occasion and take on the responsibility, like putting on a familiar warm jacket. He was unaware his gentle training had prepared him well for the task. But first, he must bury his grandfather.

Emma was solemn. Before leaving the cave, Kai told her about the funeral and how they would proceed. The People's tradition was to build a bed from tree branches to carry their dead. Then, lifted by four robust men, they would walk him around the pasture with the remainder of his people following behind him.

Under the elders' watchful eyes, the chosen men constructed the bed, which looked like a stretcher paramedics used in war to transport patients. It bore two long limbs for the sides, handles, and planks to hold his body.

Kai dressed Chatpa in a delicate white hide coat. Before she died, his wife, Anna, had sewn bits of quartz and shells into the skin with ribbons, creating flowers on his lapel. It was a work of art that would hang in a museum if someone from the outside world found it.

On Chatpa's silver hair sat a wreath with colorful feathers of every hue and a turquoise chain around his neck. Once, Emma had asked Chatpa about his necklaces. He told her traders came through his land many years ago and traded jewelry and trinkets for animal furs and hides. The People had handed this particular necklace down for several generations.

Four young men entered the cave and carefully lifted Chatpa onto the bed. Then, they raised it and turned to go.

Emma held Kai's coat for him to wear. He shrugged his shoulders and reached his arms into the sleeves. It was not as intricately elaborate as Chatpa's but was still as impressive as any she had seen in Santa Fe shops.

Kai nodded at her, and she followed. When they reached the meadow, he reached for her hand and brought her to his side.

Emma and Kai walked in the front of the processional. Kai flung water with a green branch to each side as they walked, much as a priest would swing incense or sprinkle holy water. They slowly made a processional around the pasture and up a hill to a flat area decorated with white stones and painted symbols. Emma knew this was a revered place. A fire burned, and the heat assaulted her face. It was a blazing bonfire, tall with timber and melting coals. A large, fringed arrow, shot deep into the ground, denoted honor to a worthy man.

The men carrying Chatpa sat the bed on the ground. She and Kai stood beside him. Every member not consumed by the sickness walked past Chatpa, one by one, just as a funeral procession at home would view someone in a casket. Each person spoke to him as they passed or left a tiny rock, piece of food, or possession on his bed.

Kai leaned down to take the priceless necklace from around Chatpa's neck when all the people had passed. Emma reached for the chain and placed it over his head. The coronation was complete. He was now the leader.

Quietly, The People left the hill. Only she, Kai, and the four young men remained. The men lifted Chatpa into the blaze and stepped back, lowering their heads and closing their eyes. She and Kai followed suit.

No one wanted to see the body they had loved catch fire, but they stayed close in case ancestors drew near enough to see. It did not take long for the glorious coat and his frail body to become ashes. Some floated high into the air, and the rest dropped into the coals.

Kai and the men sang chants that were eerily beautiful and haunting. Then, when the flames devoured the wooden bed and it dropped into the massive blaze, the tribe members turned and walked back down the hill. It was a touching moment, and Emma realized as the men departed that she had not once thought of the smoke as a signal to bring rescuers to her aid.

That night as she and Kai remained on the hill, she held his hand as they lay beside each other.

When she first arrived and realized this group of people was living life as if it were the sixteenth century, she had wanted to share what existed elsewhere.

Emma had wanted to lead them to the contemporary world and showcase them to archeologists and researchers. She had wanted to share cell phones, television, and flush toilets with them.

But, the more she became enchanted by their way of life, the more she realized she might be the one who needed rehabilitation.

When she wanted a new western shirt to wear to a rodeo or a pretty dress to wear to a fraternity or sorority function, she just shopped online, and, a few days later, it arrived in the mailbox.

Feeding herself was as easy as driving her car to a fast-food drive-thru and ordering from a vast menu of hamburgers, fried chicken, or barbeque sandwiches. Did she ever once think what a feat that was?

Now, she watched people who grew their food and stalked animals to feed themselves and their families. Her own family hunted for sport—a beautiful antler rack to hang over the mantel or a trophy fish to mount in her father's office. But those same items in Kai's world would sustain life or create a weapon or utensil.

It slowly dawned on Emma that the innocence and unencumbered life here on the outskirts of her ranch was one to be admired, not mocked. Emma had thought of The People's way of life as "simple," but survival is quite complex, and this society had developed systems to sustain civilization for millennia. She looked at this tribe with new respect.

She lay her head on Kai's chest and fell asleep thinking of Chatpa running toward his ancestors in a place where the Great Spirit welcomed him with open arms.

CHAPTER 36

JOSIE

Josie gained a new mission—to convict Jeff Bower for her daughter's disappearance. Finally, another cause gave her reason to arise from her bed every morning.

John tried to talk to her about the lack of evidence against Jeff. But she ignored his arguments as he lingered at the breakfast table.

"It's been a while since we enjoyed breakfast together," John said.

A newspaper lay beside her plate. She perused her horoscope every morning. She had never read such predictions before Emma's disappearance. Josie now jumped to conclusions about their life and search for Emma based on a paragraph in a publication.

"Listen to this," she said with excitement. "Today's horoscope says, 'Be patient and persistent!'"

Flora grinned at the two of them and poured steaming black coffee into her mug.

"Thank you, Flora. I feel like having huevos rancheros."

Flora nodded her approval and enthusiastically broke eggs into a bowl. The smells of the eggs, fresh vegetables, tortillas, beans, and cheese filled the room in a few minutes.

"My mouth is watering. I didn't realize how hungry I am." Josie grinned.

John smiled at her. "I'm happy to see you eat. You've had me worried."

Josie waved her hand to him, saying, "I'm fine." But she knew he had cause to worry. Their last year had been detrimental to their health, the ranch, and their marriage.

She had once believed nothing could affect their union. When she saw John walking a bull toward her at the rodeo, she knew he was the one. Her mother had told her the same thing had happened to her. Every Rosales woman was "hit with lightning" when they saw their husband-to-be for the first time.

Josie had hoped Emma would have the chance to fall in love and continue the tradition here on The Thorn. Suddenly, the eggs that tasted delicious, with the yolks dripping their yellow goodness over pan-fried potatoes, stuck in her throat.

Emma was never out of her thoughts, but sometimes her craving for her daughter hit her as suddenly as if the ceiling fell on her head.

Josie swallowed and hoped the egg mixture would not return how it had traveled. She took a long swig of coffee and then golden orange juice.

She clapped her hands and said, "I'm ready for the day. What about you? Want to ride into town and visit with the sheriff?"

"I think the sheriff is tired of our visits. Didn't he say last time that he'll call us if his leads go anywhere?" John quizzed her.

"Won't hurt to keep a fire under his feet. He was supposed to tell me what Jeff's parents had to say about their son's involvement with our daughter."

John stood and picked his hat off the rack at the back door.

JOSIE PUSHED THE SHERIFF'S office door; it swung on its hinges. A bell attached to the knob rang to inform everyone that a visitor had arrived. The office was in a small concrete block building just off Main. A printed sign and bars on two windows showed the intent of the building. Those barred windows were holding cells.

Josie hoped the sheriff would tell her Jeff remained in one of them. But, before she could tell the receptionist who they wanted to see, a side door flew open, and a tall woman stalked out. She still talked over her shoulder to whoever was inside the room.

"Unless you have a warrant or cause to talk to my boy again, I'd better not see you within fifty miles of his place."

The woman wore faded blue jeans, a plaid shirt, and a leather vest. Cowboy boots that looked like they'd seen too many rodeos completed the outfit. Her hair was so bleached it looked transparent.

The sheriff followed her out of the room, looking sheepishly afraid of her. His eyelids blinked rapidly when he saw Josie and John standing in the waiting room. He shuffled up to Josie and turned his head away from the formidable woman to speak.

"Mrs. Rosales, this isn't the best time for you to be here." He used his head to point toward the woman walking toward them.

"Did you say *Rosales*? Are you the ones trying to railroad my son? You've got a lot of nerve."

Josie looked up at the woman, who towered six inches above her. She felt her blood boil at the remarks from this less-than-stellar woman.

"I would not be the one throwing accusations around if I were you," Josie said through gritted teeth. John appeared at her elbow and gripped it. He tried to steer Josie away, but she stood her ground, toe to toe with the angry creature.

"The truth is, your daughter wanted my son. She invited him to join her on your ranch to work. They were in love."

Josie held her hand up in the air at that statement as if she asked for permission to speak.

"I beg your pardon, but my daughter was not in love with Jeff, and he said he had a recommendation from her to secure a position at The Thorn. He lied then, and he's lying now. Several witnesses will testify they heard him bragging about following her to our ranch when he discovered Emma was a Rosales. He intended to seduce her, but she was smart enough to see through his actions. I only wish I'd sent him packing earlier."

"Look, Miss High and Mighty, you aren't convicting my boy for something he didn't do. You need to tell that sheriff you're not filing any charges. You don't want to get yourself into trouble you can't get out of."

Josie could feel her blood pressure spike. Her face flushed, and her eyes narrowed. "Are you threatening me? Sheriff, maybe Mama here wants to cool her heels in a cell with her sorry excuse for a son."

A crowd watched the spectacle playing out before them. Two scrappy mama bears fighting over their cubs.

Before Josie could see what was coming, the blonde swung her shoulder back and clocked Josie right on the nose. Blood sprayed everywhere. It splattered John's starched white shirt, Jeff's mother's leather vest, and the front of Josie's denim jacket.

Josie staggered backward from the force. The sensation was like a hot iron poker thrust up her nostrils. But then, the sheriff stepped between them. She had never seen the bulky sheriff move that fast. He placed handcuffs on the blonde bear before Josie touched her nose.

"You crazy…" The sheriff's remark lingered in the air.

A deputy scampered from around the corner with a bag of ice. Obviously, this wasn't the first time an altercation had happened in the office.

The woman screamed obscenities at Josie as they dragged her through the door.

Then, silence. Everyone was stunned.

John dabbed at the blood on Josie's face with his cloth handkerchief while she held the ice on her already swelling nose. "Come on, we'll take you to see Dr. Maben before she leaves for the day. Your nose looks broken."

"I've always wanted a nose job," Josie said, her voice muffled. The ice numbed her searing pain and reduced it to a throb. She had to breathe through her mouth.

The sheriff looked down at the ground when he spoke.

"I'm sorry that happened. That woman's been ranting for a while about the injustices by this department concerning her son. Guess she just blew."

Josie fumed. "Well, she better blow into another county. Don't think she'll survive the jury in this one."

He nodded affirmation and opened the door for them.

Dr. Maben's office was just down the sidewalk, but they drove in the truck. John said he did not want the town gossiping about Josie Rosales' encounter. They would say it was the first time anyone bested her.

A nurse standing by the front desk took one look at all the dried blood on Josie's face and directed them to a private room. Dr. Maben entered soon after they did.

"Did a horse kick you?" she asked as she examined her nose.

"It sure felt like it, Doc."

"Looks like we may have to do some internal cleanup, but you'll be fine. You won't look good for a while. Expect black, blue, then purple and green bruises. Come back to see me when you get through the color wheel and land on yellow. We may send you to El Paso to reconstruct, but I will clean and tape you for now."

Josie sank back against the examination bench. The paper crunched under her and sounded like her nose when she touched it.

"I swear, John, that whole family's bad news. Emma dodged a bullet when she turned that boy down." Too late, Josie thought better of her choice of words.

"Just sit still," John murmured.

"Ow. That hurts," Josie complained when Dr. Maben stuck a long cotton-tipped stick up her nose.

"Sorry. One more look, and I'll get you out of here quickly." Dr. Maben held Josie's face in one hand while she probed with the other.

The ride home was quiet. Josie had used up all her energy in the sheriff's office, and the pain medicine the doctor gave her mellowed her out. She dozed until they turned into the entrance to The Thorn.

Flora met them at the front door. She threw her arms around Josie's waist and wailed.

"What happened? Did you have a car accident? You let Josie get hurt?" She lifted the dishcloth hanging on her shoulder and slapped John with it.

"Flora, stop," he complained.

Josie's stomach pitched, and she dashed toward the powder room. She could hear John and Flora whispering outside the door as they listened to her retch. When Josie flushed the toilet, she opened the door. She wanted to splash water on her face but didn't want to disturb the packing in her nose.

"Just let me go to my bed," she drawled groggily.

"Let me help you," Flora and John said in unison.

The sheets, freshly washed, were cool to Josie's back. She did not bother to shower.

For years, Flora changed their sheets once or twice a week, but now Flora changed them every morning when they left the bedroom. Josie knew it was because they were rank after her sleepless nights. Neither woman mentioned the change of laundry schedule.

As Josie began to doze, she heard Flora chastising John.

"Well?" Flora said.

"A woman in the town attacked her."

"What? Attacked our Josephine?" Flora's eyes narrowed, and her nostrils flared. "Who would dare?"

"The mother of Emma's friend, Jeff."

"Oh, Dios! The whole family must be loco. Pedro thinks he was the last one, except me, to see Emma."

"Sure looks that way. I think I'll sleep in a guest room so I won't disturb her. Josie needs her rest. It's been a pretty terrible day."

Josie nodded as if she were part of their conversation. But then, the meds took control, and she faded away.

CHAPTER 37

EMMA

Emma and Kai awoke with a faint covering of cold dew on their skins, and they shivered. Millions of stars glowed in the sky, and Emma told Kai that Chatpa was now among them. His lips spread into a sad smile as he looked overhead.

"I like to think that. Chatpa was such a fine leader here on this land. I hope he guides the ancestors among the stars and is successful in the Great Hunting Grounds. He told me stories about what he thought it would be like."

"How did he describe it?" Emma asked, thinking of her ideas of heaven.

"The plains in the Great Beyond are endless, with all the wild game necessary to hunt every day. The rivers are so pure you can catch fish as large as yourself. There is a feast every night, and the elders sit around the fire and discuss their lives before."

Emma nodded. "It sounds like a wonderful place. I believe you will see him, your parents, and all your ancestors someday."

He looked wistful. "I have dreams of it."

Kai used a stick to stir the remaining coals to warm their hands, and he opened a large knapsack to collect ashes. In the piles of burned dust, he found the stones and shells from Chatpa's splendid coat and added them into the mix in his sack.

Then they walked to the rooftop of the commune. Kai mumbled a few words and let the ashes fly. A strong wind caught the gray particles into what looked like a mini-tornado. Emma's emotions seemed to rise into the wind with Chatpa's remains.

"How did you sleep?" he asked.

She wanted to say "like the dead," but that would have been inappropriate.

"I'm rested. We must get back to the task of healing."

"I am going to meet with the elders. Why don't you join me?"

"Do you think that's wise?"

He shrugged, then led her down the path to a large open room on the ground level. Men sat in a loosely formed circle.

When Kai and Emma walked into the room, they all jumped. The glances shot toward Emma were not kind, and although their language was familiar to Emma's ears now, she did not need an interpreter to understand they were not happy about her presence. No other women were among them.

Kai made gestures with his hands and pointed to Emma. He looked brave and robust before a group of mostly older men. Then, finally, they all sat again. Emma took a spot on the ground to the right of Kai.

"Chatpa was a great man for many years. He taught and guided me to ensure I took his place when he left this world. I am ready to keep his wishes. This is a new day for our tribe. Our first act should be to release Emma to return to her home."

Emma's mouth dropped, and she almost needed her hand to close it. She shivered uncontrollably.

A few nodded their approval; others shook their heads

aggressively. Some flung their heads so quickly that the feathers in their headbands slapped them across their faces.

The tone of their voices was unmistakably angry and confused. The snatches of conversation Emma understood were "intruders," "danger," and "against ancestors' wishes."

Kai ended the meeting by passing around a jug. Emma thought it must be the moonshine-like concoction he made from corn. She figured if Kai couldn't get them to cooperate sober, he'd give them something to relax those tempers. She grinned but dropped her chin to her chest, so no one noticed.

They walked away from the meeting, and she wondered if she would ever feel more like a partner to a man as she did right now. It was a heady moment.

When they entered Chatpa's home, Kai gripped her forearms with his hands and pulled her close. After releasing her from his hug, he touched her lips. Emma pulled him toward her.

They sank onto her bed of hides and kissed until she blushed. *Will Kai truly let me go? Do I want him to?*

"Kai, thank you for asking the elders to let me go home. Will you come with me?" Emma's impulsive inquiry caused her heart to seize.

He looked at her for a long time as if he were fighting a battle with his conscience.

Emma did not want to give her love to someone while she was a captive. She would depart, and then, what? It wasn't like Kai was a college kid living in a nearby town. He was from an uncontacted tribe. His existence was not just miles away but centuries away from hers. How would those two worlds ever meld?

She could not envision him in her life, nor her staying in his. But, now, she could not imagine life without him.

CHAPTER 38

JOSIE

The house phone rang, and when Josie answered it, the caller hung up. Their beautiful cast-iron gate, complete with The Thorn brand, was spray-painted with graffiti. Someone shot a cow that wandered too close to the fence on the road.

Josie raged. She knew who harassed them. It had to be Jeff's mother. By the following day, John installed game cameras on posts near the gate, hoping to catch a person in the act of destruction. It was as if the perpetrators knew when the cameras were active. The vandalism ceased.

"The little punk knows the ranch from working here," Josie complained. "He knows the shortcuts on and off the property. He probably shared those details with his crazy mother."

Josie's nose, still taped, doubled in size. The doctor in El Paso scheduled reconstructive surgery for the next week. The idea of Jeff's mother being able to steer her away from her daughter's disappearance and Jeff's prosecution, even for a short time through surgery, infuriated Josie. If they could prove that Jeff harassed her family, it would strengthen their case against him.

The sheriff informed her that they had released Jeff's mother on bail. People got away with murder, literally. She prayed she was wrong and Jeff had not been violent with Emma. He could be an obnoxious jerk, but she hoped he had not crossed the line to insanity.

Standing by the kitchen counter, Josie filled a glass of water and tossed back her antibiotics and a pain reliever. She was tired of sleeping on her back. Her usual position of being on her stomach with her face squashed in the down feather pillow did not work with a metal bar and tape across her throbbing nose.

Josie wanted to scream. Slugging her might have been a tactic Jeff's family used to dilute Josie's determination to see Jeff pay. His mother could have considered her detention necessary for the cause. Jeff's mother had an arrest sheet a mile long. This assault was not the first time she used her fists instead of her brain. Brain? Josie was not sure she possessed one or self-control either.

Josie walked into the study and lay her head back on the tall leather office chair. Sometimes, the pulsing of her nose stopped when she propped her head against something.

John poked his face in the door. "You feeling okay?"

She nodded without opening her eyes. "What time do we fly to El Paso tomorrow?"

"The plane will be at the airport at eight. It should give us plenty of time to get to your appointment. I wish you didn't have to go through this, honey."

She reached for his hand and squeezed it.

"Me, too. Did you hear anything today from the sheriff's office?"

She asked him every day, and the answers were usually negative. This uncertainty and waiting was their life now.

For a year, they searched the ranch, held meetings with private investigators and sheriff's deputies, wrote letters to law enforcement state officials, and finally submitted to interviews by national and state reporters.

Every night, they had sat in front of the television watching the filmed interviews until Josie's interview with Carter Blue, a reporter with WLAN from El Paso, aired.

Carter stood at the ranch gates and stuck a microphone in Josie's face. She looked startled and then mad. He had ambushed her when she stepped outside the entrance to collect mail from their box. Her hair blew around her face and slapped her eyes, making them water.

"Mrs. Rosales, our sources tell us that you refuse to believe your daughter is most certainly dead. After all these months, don't you think it's time to face the facts in this case?" His voice had a nasal twang that indicated to Josie he was not from Texas but the eastern seaboard.

Josie pasted on her face the same condescending smile that the reporter wore.

"Mr. Blue, is it? You obviously don't have children because you would know that a parent never gives up searching for a lost child. You are inventing a story rather than reporting on one. Now, get off my property before I have you removed."

John clicked the remote, and the screen went black.

"I guess I looked as crazy as I sounded?" Josie turned to her husband.

John patted her shoulder and walked down the hall toward the kitchen. She could hear him fixing a sandwich, his knife scraping the bottom of the glass mayonnaise jar.

Their days were full of cattle, horses, crops, and shredding pastures until Emma disappeared. Back then, they saw each other only in the early morning and at nightfall.

But, now, Josie and John did chores sporadically and bumped into each other in the hallways. They had learned more about each other's habits in twelve months than in the previous twenty-five years.

Some good, some not so good. Josie became irritated when John flossed his teeth or passed gas while watching television. He told her she spoke loudly on the telephone—like holding a megaphone shouting orders.

They needed Emma to come home. Their twenty-fifth wedding anniversary was just a few months away, and Josie feared John had planned a trip. Out of the question. She could not go anywhere. They had not celebrated birthdays or Christmas except to wrap Emma's presents.

Josie did not want Emma returning home and thinking they did not remember her on holidays. Inside a brightly colored Christmas present lay a new pair of boots, burnished mahogany with intricate tooling, and a beautiful belt the same color, with a wide silver buckle. Her last birthday present was a new colt born on Emma's twenty-third birthday. They called him "Safe Return" and "Ree" for short.

Flora had baked a chocolate cake, and Josie took a big breath and blew out the candle as she became Emma's substitute wish-maker. Her slice tasted salty instead of sweet because her tears dripped on the icing.

Josie whirled the desk chair around and walked out the door toward the barn. Maybe seeing Emma's horse would lift her spirits. Inside a wide stall, the tiny replica of his mother nursed. They looked like twins, only in different sizes.

Each was a speckled gray with black markings and a star-shaped spot on its forehead. Ree was from excellent stock and would be a fine horse for Emma.

Josie loved to watch Emma ride in the ring. She sat lightly on the saddle but in full command of the grand creature below her. Even as a child, Emma was not afraid of the enormous animals. They bucked her off, and she climbed right back on. Once, her reins snapped, and the bit fell out of the horse's mouth. She had clung to the horse with her arms wrapped around his neck as he barreled at top speed back to the barn.

Emma was tough but sensitive, too. She took gentle care of the barn cats and baby goats. When she was a teenager, Emma set up an empty stall as her vet's office and treated her pets. Josie was proud of the woman Emma had become. She longed to watch her in future episodes of her life—falling in love, getting married, having their grandchild. Josie prayed, *Please, God. Let Emma have those times ahead of her.*

The colt turned from eating and eyed Josie at the stall door. Then, he came to her and waited until she nuzzled his nose.

"No worries, little one. Your Emma will be back before your next birthday, her next birthday."

Life was very different now. Usually braggadocious and loud, the ranch hands whispered and looked away when she was near them. Everyone tiptoed around her. They seemed cautious of whether she would be magnanimous or shrill.

Was she such a chameleon, adapting to this situation without grace? Josie did not have those answers. The Thorn was not a happy place now. Only a year ago, it was full of laughter and hard work. The ranch hands' competition where Emma won most of her events was a distant memory. They postponed this year's event, not canceled, until Emma's return. The same with the Fourth of July party and barbeques and rodeos. Everything was wrong, frozen in time, suspended like insects in amber.

Josie's shoulders slumped, and she dragged her feet when she walked back toward the house. Seeing the horse did not have the effect she had hoped it would. Ree was in the same waiting stage they all were. He would not meet his owner until Emma came back.

Josie plopped on the giant swing on the front porch. It looked more like a twin bed than a swing with fat posts made from tightly wound grapevines and a mattress.

When Emma was in high school, Josie had a carpenter design the rustic porch furniture. Emma spent hours lying on it as it moved back and forth. She read books there while eating snacks and watching the horses run in the front pasture.

Now Josie lay her head down on the broad pillow. Could she still smell Emma's shampoo, or was that just her imagination? Josie thought all liquid was out of her body and she could not produce another drop. But that notion was wrong.

The tears flowed down her face, soaking the bandage taped to her cheeks. Finally, the crying stopped up her damaged nostrils, and she gasped air through her mouth. But she did not get up. Instead, she pretended Emma lay beside her.

Squeezing her eyes tight, she talked to her daughter.

"We ate your favorite chocolate pie last night. I cut the slices extra-large just as you would have. We've changed nothing in your room. I was going to update it since you are a young woman, not a child. But I wasn't sure you'd want me to eliminate all the trophies and ribbons you've won. I used to think I could read your mind and decide what you would choose for yourself. Now, I question everything, like I've forgotten what you like or don't like. I haven't failed to remember you, Emma. I never could."

Her sobs began again, and she pulled herself abruptly off the swing. It slammed into the side of the house as it banged back and forth.

Flora must have heard the noise against the house and hurried to the front door, where Josie stood dazed.

"I thought someone was breaking into the house."

Josie noticed that when the ranch experienced destructive behavior, it spooked Flora. Yet, Josie was confident this staunch defender still protected her and John.

They supported each other more intensely now because they could not help Emma.

CHAPTER 39

EMMA

Kai and Emma ran back and forth to the roof, where they secured their herbal remedies. Finally, they set up a storehouse of medicines in Kai's home. It saved them minutes each day, and they needed extra time. Every second counted.

This illness did not behave like the regular flu. Instead, the effects were faster and more intense—high fevers, shortness of breath, and sudden death. The older adults of the tribe were the first to come down with the disease, but it spread to younger ones, even children. Emma was at a loss. She needed much more powerful drugs than their herbal remedies.

"Kai, if you let me have a horse, I will ride to my ranch and bring back medicine for the tribe. It may be our only hope."

His eyes drooped, and his feet shuffled.

"We have discussed this before. I have to wait until the elders agree to release you. Otherwise, The People will not permit me to lead after that."

"You may not have a choice. This tribe is dropping like stones. We don't know how to treat this illness. It's like nothing I've experienced before."

"Your ranch medicine man may not have the answers, either." But, because Kai studied her arguments and hesitated, she knew he seriously considered going against the elders and letting her go.

While she wanted an opportunity to leave, Emma feared if she left, there would be no tribe members alive when she returned.

Emma maintained a compassionate heart for The People even if she was a captive. She would do her best to save them. It would take prayer, a lot of work, and luck.

Emma had been called an animal empath by her fellow college students when she felt she understood the pets' feelings and emotions. Now, she couldn't look in the eyes of The People suffering without experiencing their fear. Their worry penetrated her core and crushed her bright, hot hope of escaping.

Emma enlisted the women that Chesma brought in to be wives. They came into the camp sick, but they had recovered. She would teach them enough nursing skills to assist.

Emma regretted not learning more Spanish. She could string a few sentences together, but she was not fluent. Her mother tried speaking Spanish to her when she was little, but her father only spoke English, so she gravitated to it. Now, she was sorry she was not more compliant. The Spanish language was in her blood but not on her tongue. She could not roll her 'r' like her mother. As a result, her use of a second language was clumsy and broken.

She looked at the eyes watching her, awaiting instruction.

"Habla Ingles?" Emma asked the women.

"Un poco."

"Okay, we both know a little of each other's language. We'll make this work. Are you being treated well?" Emma asked.

They shrugged their shoulders in unison to say, "Well enough under the circumstances."

One of the women wore tight jeans and an oversized white shirt. Her flashing brown eyes watched Emma closely.

Finally, she spoke. "My name is Angela. These are my friends. We will help you with the sick."

Emma was glad to hear at least one of the young women spoke English. The others looked at her with blank expressions, and she did not know if they understood her translation. But they all had an immediate crisis, and they would pull together to put out the fire of disease that threatened their camp.

Emma showed how much of the liquid they were to administer unless it was a child, then she showed a smaller amount. She gave them broth to feed the sick and told them about isolating the patient from the rest of the household. When she thought they understood enough, she introduced them to Kai, and he made their assignments and walked them to where his people lay in distress.

They tended to the sick every day and watched the death numbers multiply. Emma had once asked Kai how many lived in the caves. He thought there were sixty. Now, she guessed there were thirty left. Emma and Kai fell asleep as quickly as they lay down. She wondered if they were making any difference at all.

The smoke from the cremation hill always seemed present. Kai attended the funerals, but she could not. She was depleted and seeing the grief-stricken faces of the people mourning their dead would be too much for her to bear.

Walking through the dark corridor, Emma sensed rather than saw a person coming toward her. She moved to one side to allow passage. The woman bumped into Emma, and she heard her voice say she was sorry.

"Are you well?" It was a common phrase but used these days to inquire about that person's and their family's health.

"Yes, my household has not caught the sickness."

Emma let out a relieved sigh. She had meant to check on her friends in the camp, but Emma allowed no time for chitchat or visiting if someone's family was not sick.

The young woman grasped Emma's hands and squeezed. "You are one of us. You are helping our people survive."

Emma's face flushed. Did she think of herself as one of them? Was she helping at all? Would they all survive? They seemed to have no immunity against the deadly virus, and Emma did not know how better to serve them without modern medicine.

Where had she been going? Oh, yes. An elder had passed away, and his widow was sick. Groto. She lived in the hall beyond this one.

Emma's steps were surer with the trails and passageways. This entire cliff was a maze of caves and houses built into the side of the cliff with clay and rock. Sometimes, she caught her breath when she stood in the pasture and looked back at the ridge. It was indeed a masterpiece of ingenuity. No one had ever found The People in the five generations of Rosales on The Thorn; their homes were very concealed.

These innovators took the area left to them by their ancestors and improved it. Once, maybe only rough caves sheltered them, but today, a series of open balconies and homes that looked like stucco condos protruded from a granite mountain. It was outstanding work.

With no machinery, they'd created a sanctuary for more than sixty people. She marveled at the structures, the gardens, and the horse pens. They were the pioneers of this land, before her own family. She had an epiphany when she observed the entire operation.

Emma whispered when she reached Groto's entrance. All the elders had secured the best accommodations. Some had balconies and indoor plumbing—really just an outhouse at the far end of the home. She wondered about the construction of a drop from the hole in the floor.

"Groto?" Emma spied a mound in the corner. She gently lifted the fur and leaned back. Groto burned with fever. Blisters covered her mouth, and she squinted her eyes as if she were in pain. When she opened one eye and saw Emma, she moaned.

Emma reached into her sack and poured water down Groto's throat. She gulped greedily, and a bony hand clutched Emma's wrist.

"Oma grata. Oma grata. Help me," she said.

"Lie back and rest. I'll warm broth for you."

The firepit looked like she had not used it in her husband's absence. Emma could not remember when he died; there were too many deaths.

She found a pot and stacked wood on the cold ashes. Emma had become a pro at creating flame from flint and dried leaves. At campouts on The Thorn, she cheated and used a propane starter. Now, Emma could get a nice blaze going without modern conveniences within a few minutes. The older woman felt the warmth from where she lay and rolled over to face the flames.

Emma poured broth into a cup and held it to the woman's lips. *How many more like Groto are alone and suffering in these caves?* Their small group of misfit doctors was not enough to care for so many.

Emma had experienced this sense of helplessness once before while working at an animal shelter during college. Just when she thought they had cared for all the dogs and cats, the door opened, and more poured in. The unending stream of abandoned animals overwhelmed her. Emma took dogs and cats home every time she visited.

It became a family joke about Emma's animals taking over, but at least she knew somebody fed them. She couldn't save them all, though; it was a crushing weight on her chest.

She felt the same now.

CHAPTER 40

JOSIE

The American and Texas flags on either side of the judge's bench rippled from the air conditioning vent in the ceiling. Deputies mingled with court reporters, and the massive door in the back of the room creaked open and slammed shut with a loud clap when people entered and left. After what seemed like hours to Josie, Jeff Bower finally stood in front of the courtroom and answered questions from the district attorney.

No, he did not have any knowledge of Emma's whereabouts. No, he did not harm her. Yes, he made some stupid statements about acquiring the ranch by marrying her, but that's all the comments were, just bragging in front of his fellow ranch hands. No, he did not think working on the ranch would provide him a way to force his interest on her. But, on the other hand, he did like her and wanted to get to know her better.

This inquisition was not a trial but a method of determining if there was enough evidence to proceed with a case. The questions and answers lasted for an hour. Josie's head swam, and she wanted to yell at Jeff with her own questions. But instead, she glared at the woman and man seated behind Jeff's defense table.

With everyone still wearing masks because of Covid, Josie didn't know if her anger translated adequately, with only her eyes being visible. Jeff's mother might have broken her nose, but not her spirit. Josie's stomach was in knots. John squeezed her hand, and their lawyer cross-examined Jeff.

The day dragged on. Finally, the district attorney said she would take the testimony under advisement and return to make a decision.

Josie, John, and Valeria, Josie's mother, walked across the street to a café. They ordered the lunch special—chicken fried steak with mashed potatoes, white gravy, and green beans. Josie drained a large glass of iced sweet tea and then dug into her steak. She had declared when leaving the courtroom that she wasn't hungry. Her stomach disagreed.

Josie cleaned her plate to the amusement of Valeria. Her mother had been quiet since their return from Europe and remained in her casita most of the time. Josie knew Valeria, like Flora, blamed herself for Emma's disappearance. She and John blamed themselves, too. Emma would not have gone on the camping trip if they hadn't taken the vacation. Wouldn't she? Were any of them at fault? Anyone except Jeff? Josie still believed he was guilty. Her husband was not sure. *Jeff does not seem the type to harm someone*, John said. *His mother was*, Josie said. *Like mother, like son.*

Her cell phone vibrated on the table. Their lawyer summoned them to the courtroom. There was a decision.

Seated back on the hard oak seats, they waited for the district attorney to re-enter the chamber. She did not look happy.

"I reviewed the testimony of everyone today. I'm sorry for the parents who lost a daughter and for the parents who have a son accused of her disappearance." She looked at Josie and her family.

"You are pillars of this community and employers of most in this county. However, with no more evidence than we have here today, only the actions of a foolish young man boasting to others, we cannot prosecute this case."

Josie grasped the thigh of her husband. Her mother grabbed Josie's hand and pulled it to her cheek—stunned.

To make matters worse, Jeff's mother jumped to her feet and yelled, "We beat you high and mighty Rosales! Didn't think that would happen, did you?"

Josie's skin flashed ice-cold and numb. She could taste metallic bile in the back of her throat.

The district attorney told Jeff's mother to be quiet, but she waved her hand dismissively and stood to leave. When she passed Josie, she whispered, "Look in your backyard to find your daughter. Jeff had nothing to do with it." She wrapped her arm around her son's shoulders. At least Jeff had the decency to look ashamed of his mother's actions.

Josie held her husband's arm like they were processing in a wedding. Finally, they made it to the parking lot. John opened Josie's door and one for her mother.

When he backed out of the space, Josie sighed deeply. Another dead end.

"Can you believe that boy has gotten away with this?" Josie whispered.

Her mother, Valeria, said, "How could this have happened?"

Josie did not know if she meant the hearing, Emma's disappearance, or both. Nobody spoke on the long ride home. She was tired of the long silences in helicopters and trucks and at meals.

Josie hung her dress in the closet and sat at her dressing table. She plunged her fingers into thick, almond-scented cream and smeared it on her face, then used tissues to wipe the remainder. Wearing makeup was almost foreign to her now, and she did not appreciate the additional time to remove it.

Now what? They were running out of ideas to find their daughter. Helicopter searches and hundreds of riders combing the property had not worked, and now, the court had not assisted them.

Josie stared at her reflection in the mirror.

"I'm sorry, hija. I let you down." Josie apologized to an absent daughter.

She walked down the hall to Emma's room, lay on the bed, and pulled a blanket around her shoulders. John called her name. Spices roasted in the kitchen. The central air blew directly on her face. She felt and heard nothing.

Josie had run out of time, out of hope, out of dreams. Had she been so arrogant to insist Emma follow in her footsteps and run the ranch as the Rosales women had for generations?

Emma had mentioned how nice it would be to go to vet school and have a veterinary practice in a small town. Did Josie squash that dream? Maybe the last one she had? Josie drowned in regrets.

Her words, actions, and thoughts rammed into her brain and caused her to spin. Her vision blurred. What kind of mother was she? Had she thought the ranch was more important than her child's desires?

What possessed the women in her family to force tradition on each who came after them?

Did she ever have a choice? Would she have chosen differently if she had?

CHAPTER 41

EMMA

Emma held the baby's hand and mopped his forehead. Watching the elderly take their last breaths was one thing, but children were even more heartbreaking. She swept the tiny boy's damp hair out of his eyes and encouraged him to sip water.

Emma's friend Essie stood in the corner, watching her. She bit her fist and tried to be brave for her son. But Emma could see the cracks in her expression. She seemed to pray to her gods to allow her child to live.

Adriel developed a racking cough. It was disconcerting to hear such a small body emit deep, raggedy sounds.

Emma had been walking home from nursing an entire family. Her feet were dragging in the corridor, and she stubbed her toe on a rock in her path. Essie ran up to her and grabbed her arm.

"Come, Emma! Come!" She yanked and pulled her. They hurried down the dark pathway.

When they arrived at Essie's home, she released Emma's arm and rushed to her son's side, where the baby lay in a twisted pile of damp blankets.

Emma flung her pack down and looked into Adriel's eyes. He looked dazed and confused.

"Adriel, it's Emma. You aren't feeling well, are you?" The child's eyes dilated, and he could not lift his head. He sipped water as if he drank from a straw.

His father, Leto, walked in the door and saw Emma kneeling in his bedroom.

"What is the matter? Is Adriel worse?" He picked up his son and held him against his chest. "He is on fire."

Emma nodded and pulled the last of the liquid medicine from her pack.

"Let's see if this will help with his fever." Adriel swallowed some of the liquid; the rest ran down the corners of his mouth and onto his chest. The thin shirt he wore stained with a deep rusty color.

Emma reached out her arms, and Leto handed Adriel to her. She peeled the cloth over his head and showed Essie how to bathe his reddened skin. Anything to cool him.

Emma whispered to them she would return, but to continue the bathing and getting water into his minute body.

Emma leaned against the rock wall when she left their cave. How much longer could she care for these people in this epidemic? Working in animal clinics did not equip her to deal with sickness on this scale. Until now, she treated one animal at a time. This disease was a feat for which she was not prepared.

She ducked into her cave and found Kai stirring soup over the fire.

"Emma? I wondered where you were." She told him about Adriel, and he shook his head. "Our young people are dying, too. How can we survive this?"

She looked at the deep lines around his nose and mouth that had not been there before. Kai carried the weight of this entire tribe on his back. It would have been doable without this plague. Now, she wasn't sure of the outcome for him or the tribe.

They sat without speaking, sipping hot liquid. Each seemed to play the day's events repeatedly in their minds. It was unspeakable. And, yet, they had to continue fighting the disease as well as they could. There had been a few successes. The newly arrived women had survived and assisted them with nursing duties, but maybe they produced more antibodies since they were from the outside world.

Kai's people had been isolated for their entire lives, and their bodies were vulnerable to diseases. No one here had ever taken a vaccination. But, their prowess at herbalism had strong preventative and supportive capabilities, even in the case of critical illness, until now.

Emma was at her wit's end. She could only imagine Kai's emotions. He kept them private, but she could tell they were eating at him like termites in a wood post from the inside out. That was why his stomach ached, and he had anxious feelings. While they concocted medicines, he described his condition to her.

She could diagnose anxiety and stress. Maybe even a stomach ulcer.

"We have to make more medicine tomorrow. I gave Adriel my last dose."

"We are running out of the plants. I don't know what to do."

"Kai, take me home, and we will bring back medicine."

"You said it was far away."

"We can do it. I know we can. It may be our only way to save The People."

Emma did not want to think about her most authentic concern—Kai and her catching the disease and being unable to save themselves or the remaining tribe members.

That night, Emma dreamed about a fire that consumed her

family home and spread throughout the ranch. It devoured everything in its path: the trees, barns, every structure.

Was that a sign she would not return home again? Or that all these outstanding people would perish?

In the morning, she and Kai climbed to the roof. She wanted to inventory what herbs remained and how they could make more medicine. It discouraged them they had run through a year's supply of dried plants in such a short time. It did not bode well for the coming days.

They scraped together the remaining herbs and diluted them as best they could. Then, they began their rounds separately, as if on a hospital rotation. She went one way and he another. They would compare notes when they met again.

Emma began her day by going to Essie's, checking on her son. His fever still raged, and he lay limp in his mother's arms. His eyes rolled back in his head.

Essie rocked him back and forth.

"He is no better. What else can we do?" Essie asked when she saw Emma enter the room.

"I don't know. Adriel is very sick."

Emma looked up at the splendid wall paintings above Essie's head. To be in such spectacular surroundings and suffer. It was a juxtaposition of monumental comparisons.

"Go." Essie stared at Emma, her voice guttural.

"What?"

"Get away from my child. You are not helping; you are hurting us. Maybe you are poisoning us."

Tears sprang to Emma's eyes. "I know you are frightened, but that is not true. I would never sabotage you."

"Our people did not have this misery until you came. You

must be the source of this sickness." Her dark eyes looked stormy. Emma saw loathing in Essie's expression for the first time since she met her.

"I'm your friend. Don't send me away." Emma's voice croaked.

"You are no friend of mine."

Emma stumbled down the corridor with Essie's words ringing in her ears. She pushed past a few people, ran into the pasture, and to the stream. Emma knelt and splashed cold water into her face.

Then, she startled when a hand gripped her shoulder. Kai. Emma shielded her face with her hand to look up at him.

"Are you all right?"

Emma explained the reason for deserting her duties. She told him of Essie's pronouncement that she blamed her for the sickness. Emma cried and said they were running out of medicine and she didn't know what to do. Kai offered her a hand and lifted her to her unsteady feet.

"This is a terrible time for our tribe. It is not your fault."

As the words left his mouth, Emma saw a blur from the corner of her eye. Leto bolted toward them. Face distorted, he shoved Emma with both hands. She fell to the ground and caught herself before her head banged against the rocks. Emma looked up in disbelief and saw Kai standing behind Leto, restraining him with an arm around his chest.

Leto leaned toward Emma, pointing at her, and speaking their tribe's language. Kai turned Leto to face him as they shouted angrily at each other. Emma scrambled to her feet and dusted off her dress. Her throat was raw from swallowing salty tears.

Kai gripped Leto's shoulders with their heads lowered together. The anger on Leto's face turned to sorrow, and now Kai consoled him.

Leto lowered his eyes and did not look in Emma's direction again. Instead, his chin rested on his chest, and he wandered up the path toward the caves.

"What did he say about Adriel?"

"He died."

Emma slumped against Kai's stiff body. She had no words—poor little boy. Emma's chest tightened, and every breath hurt. She grieved for all the souls she could not help, especially Adriel. A child she birthed not long ago. But, to have Essie blame her was too much.

"Please, let me go to my cave."

Kai placed his hand on her shoulder and guided her up the hill. Emma moved to her bed and pulled the hide over her head.

"Want me to cook for you?" asked Kai.

"No," Emma muttered from beneath the heavy covering. She wanted to vomit and did not think she could swallow if she tried.

All she could think about was the funeral tomorrow for a tiny body. A body her mother and father would have to watch go into the flames and exist no more. It was unbearable. Emma wanted to sleep to block out the images of Adriel's limp form in his father's arms.

Kai didn't disturb her. She didn't know if he went to his cave.

Emma heard drums beating the following day and knew the processional walked to the high hill for the cremation.

Kai sat in the dark, watching her.

"We need to get ready for the funeral," she said.

"I will go, but you must stay here."

"What? I need to be with Essie and Leto."

"They asked that you not come."

"I know they're angry, but they'll realize I'm not to blame. Won't they?" She was dizzy from worry.

Kai pulled her toward him. He nuzzled her hair and whispered in her ear. "It was not your fault. They are angry at the gods, but you are here, so they blame you."

She jerked out of his grasp and lay back down on the bed, turning her back to him. Her sobs were primarily silent, but her shoulders shook with helplessness coursing through her body.

Kai slipped outside without disturbing her. Emma cried herself to sleep with a stuffy nose and a pounding headache.

The next thing she knew, Kai was back.

"Come in here, Emma." He grabbed hides, wrapped one around her, and led her into Chatpa's private space. The room felt damp and had a musty odor, like old houses where no one lived.

"Let's not light the fire and call attention to your presence here."

"What's happening? Why are you hiding me?"

"Essie and Leto are talking to the elders and blaming your inability to heal in the camp. They say you intentionally kill our members as revenge for making you stay here. They are not in their right minds. I am meeting with them tonight. You stay here and do not leave this room until I come for you."

What about all the patients? Who cared for them?

Emma lay down again. She did not want to think anymore.

She was comfortable in this old cave. Emma wanted to believe Chatpa's spirit lingered here. His soul would watch over her. She could rest.

Someone shook her. Startled, she sat up. "Who is it?"

"It is me."

She heard Kai's voice, but he sounded far away.

"Did you tell them I had nothing to do with the sickness?"

"I told them."

"And what did they say?"

"They will consider my arguments."

Emma breathed a sigh of relief. "Kai, no one wants me here except you. Please let me leave."

Kai said he would return to his home, but she was to stay in Chatpa's room. He didn't say "until things blow over," Emma thought, but that is what he meant.

Emma shivered in the night. Before dawn, she pulled a hide around her and padded in her bare feet to Kai's cave. He snored softly. She curled up next to him. At least she would not be cold.

The morning was still gray with just the undertones of pink on the horizon when someone grabbed Emma's arm. A man snatched her to her feet before her mind comprehended that other people were in the cave. Fire from torches smoked in the small space, and Emma's eyes watered. Her heart pounded in her chest.

Kai struggled to get to his feet.

"What are you doing in my home?" he yelled into the group. There could not have been more than six or seven people, but they filled the space and made it seem like a crowd of one hundred to Emma.

"You are a good provider, Kai, but you are blind to what the ancestors tell you. This woman has caused scales on your eyes. It is time to rid ourselves of this outsider. Then, the ancestors will ask the gods to remove the sickness before anyone else dies."

Emma squinted to see the man speaking. It was Leto. Fresh from mourning his son and encouraged by the man accompanying him, Chesma, he had turned his grief into revenge. Chesma held Kai's arms to restrain him while Leto and the others led Emma down the path to the pasture and up a nearby hill.

"Don't do this, Leto. I tried to help Adriel. I cared for him." The panic in her voice sounded ragged.

"No more. Do not mention my son, whose soul has not yet left this place."

A tall tree near the top of the hill was their destination. They used ropes made of cornhusks and hide strips to bind her to the trunk. Emma sobbed uncontrollably until she lost her breath and began to hiccup.

"We will make a sacrifice of you to the gods. They will know we are ridding our tribe of the outsider who brought sickness to our camp. Your slow death is required to free ourselves of the misery you brought to our tribe. You will stay here until we drain life from your body. Unless the wild creatures claim you."

Emma's back ached from the rugged tree bark. They wrapped her torso so tightly that she took tiny breaths to fill her lungs. Her arms were snug against her body, and her bare feet were exposed to the ants and creepy crawlies on the ground. She closed her eyes and moaned.

When she opened her eyes, they felt scorched and gritty. Her face burned. Chesma's influence had already affected the tribe since Chatpa's death.

Throughout the day, members of the tribe came by to stand and look at her. *Look at the healer,* they seemed to say; *how far she has fallen.* She pleaded with familiar faces to release her.

"Don't do this. I will leave. Just untie me. Please..." Emma did not recognize the hoarse sounds coming from her own throat. A wave of nausea gripped her empty stomach until dry heaves caused her throat to burn. Emma could smell her own sweat, sour like fermentation. Did they tie Kai up, too? Why had he not come to rescue her? The first day dragged as if it were more than twenty-four hours. Ants stung her feet. She couldn't see them, but she knew there were blisters from the bites.

Emma tried to calm her thoughts and meditate, but she could never quiet her mind even when she took a yoga class in college, much less now.

That night, coyotes howled just beyond the woods where she sat. If she fell asleep, one of them could test her ability to harm them by darting toward her, closer and closer, until he could smell her fear. Then he would strike. Maybe he would tear a leg away from her body. The blood would signal the pack. They had the strength to pull her from the tree.

Dear God. She had thought a snake bite was the worst that could happen to her. Her eyes darted from side to side.

Thirsty. She was so thirsty. Emma imagined lying in the cool water of the stream and swallowing huge gulps.

By the second day, the tribe members quit walking up the hill to see her. Her lips swelled, and her skin must have been the color of the lobsters in traps off the coast of Maine.

Emma remembered holidays to the rocky shoreline during the hot Texas summers. She thought of the beaches of Florida and the dazzling blue water with sand, so white it was blinding. Emma still had a shell collection in her room.

Her room! In her mind, she walked into her bedroom at the ranch. She looked at every object—a Faith Hill poster on the wall across from her dresser and a book on the nightstand with a corner turned down where she stopped reading.

In her head, she heard her mother calling her for supper. She walked down the hall and into the dining room. Her mother and father sat waiting, and she perched on a bench. There was Flora. She brought a lasagna into the room on a large brass tray. Lasagna! Was Flora cooking Italian dishes now? Emma piled a plate with lettuce, fresh tomatoes, green onions, and peppers from the garden. She dolloped a big spoonful of ranch dressing into the middle and stirred it around with her fork before digging in.

"Emma, slow down," her mother warned. "There's plenty of food. You don't have to eat fast." Plenty of food. You won't starve. Is that what her stomach told her? Was she starving? It was dark again. Her arms and legs were numb but stung like needles stuck in them. Was her circulation completely cut off? Dehydrated, she had not released her bowels or kidneys in two days. *That's not good.*

Her lids swelled until she could only see through tiny slits. She heard a noise. *Please, no. Go away, coyotes.* She tried to move her feet to scare them. Her heart slammed against her rib cage.

"It's me, Emma."

Relief flooded her body. Kai was here.

"Help me," she mumbled. There was no room in her mouth for words.

Kai used a bone knife to cut through the bonds. She cried out when he pulled them away from her arms. The strips stuck in her skin and showed red welts. His knife gnawed against the ties. When the last one broke, so did she. Emma slumped to the ground. She could not stand.

Kai scooped her up in his arms like a child and climbed the path to her cave.

CHAPTER 42

JOHN

John sat on the bed beside Josie, causing her to roll toward his body weight. She opened her eyes.

Josie was still in Emma's room. Yesterday's ordeal with the district attorney did not go as they'd hoped. Now they were out of options. A year had passed since they reported Emma missing. Everyone gave up hope they would ever see her again—everyone except Josie.

Josie sat up, threw her arms around his waist, and placed her head on his shoulder. Would she accept Emma's death? He held her tightly until she stopped shaking, and her sobs quieted.

"Do we have a funeral? Do I clean out her room? How are we supposed to know what to do next?"

"I don't know. But we will do it together." His voice cracked.

At first, John had not allowed himself to think past the searches and wild goose chases. He was at a loss like his wife. Then, John tried to be the steady one, protective and strong. Now, he was afraid he, too, would break wide open.

John had known other ranchers who lost a child. Then, after the funerals and meals taken to their houses, the neighbors returned to their own lives. What did the families do when they were alone? Did they ever truly heal?

He had bumped into Ted Black in town the week before. Ted's son had died in a tractor accident two years earlier, but he still looked like the walking dead. His skin was pale under his tan, and his eyes hollow. He barely spoke; he just nodded at passers-by. John shook his hand but could not think of anything to say that would not scratch at the scab of his son's absence or his own daughter's. What a club for them both to belong to.

Now, all John could do was cling to his wife. She needed him, and he needed her. Josie said she felt at the bottom of the sea and could not breathe. He planned to drag her to the surface with him. They would survive. At least he hoped they would.

He squeezed Josie closer to his chest and then pushed her back to see her face.

"We have to be the people Emma wanted us to be. She would not want us to give up on each other or this ranch we love. So, let's just get back to running this place and heal our hearts. Can you do that with me, Josie?"

She shook her head slowly from side to side. "I don't know."

He pulled her to her feet and said, "Wash your face, get dressed, and meet me downstairs. We're going to buy some cattle."

She smiled wearily at him because he knew her well. She loved a livestock sale with the intenseness of bidding against other people and the smell of manure, popcorn, and sweat. Josie had gone to sales with her father, and Emma had gone with hers.

Would every memory of theirs always include Emma? Would that prevent them from moving forward? Josie staggered to their bathroom and threw cold water into her eyes. She walked into her closet and pulled on jeans, a plaid shirt, and cowboy boots. One step at a time. John watched her with a weak smile on his face.

When they parked the truck and walked into the sales arena, John knew the cattle auction was what Josie needed. It never changed and was a constant in their lives. Buying and selling animals. The joy and sorrow of it. Having and losing. Flip sides of the same coin.

Josie sat near the front while John went to the concession stand. She told him she rarely thought she was hungry these days until she smelled the food. He waved a chili hot dog with pungent white onions and orange cheese melted on the top under her nose.

John laughed when he heard her stomach growl. She smiled at him and reached for the meal. Three bites, and it was gone. She swigged a Diet Coke while waving her paddle in the air.

"Look at that group. What do you think? Love that heifer." She questioned John but waved the paddle before he could reply. He studied her. She had caught his attention years ago and carried it still. He loved her with a passion that frightened him. It was bad enough to lose their precious child, but if he lost Josie, his reason for living would leave with her.

Josie had watched her parents' relationship for years and probably wanted her husband to be more of a partner than her father was with her mother. But, for her to feel that way, he would have to exert himself, be more in charge. Then, she would trust he could make the same decisions as her, that they worked as a team.

John swore that day he would be the man she desired and needed him to be.

He raised his own paddle.

CHAPTER 43

KAI

Emma moaned. Kai laid her on the hides in Chatpa's back bed-room space. It was far from the front entrance, and if someone looked inside the opening, they would not see her.

When Kai asked Emma about being tied to the post, she could not remember what had happened. She tried to sit but could not. Her lower extremities seemed frozen, and her arms did not work. Kai held water for her to sip, but she could not swallow.

It was dark and damp within the rock walls. Emma shivered—there was no fire to warm her. Then, she slept again.

Kai dressed her wounds as if he was moving a limp cornhusk doll. She did not respond to touch.

He left her alone and walked back to his—*their* cave. The young elders searched for him and found him later that morning.

"How did you escape your guard, Kai? Where is Emma?"

They demanded he return her to them. If they found her, they would finish the slow death they planned for her. The elders led by Chesma wished to rid themselves of the bad blood Emma had brought into the camp, the reason many were sick and dying.

Kai struggled to keep his voice calm when he wanted to shout.

"The People have never treated anyone in this manner. Emma and I need to attend to the sick. Get away and let me help our people."

The men parted and allowed Kai to leave the cave. He walked to the roof to prepare more medicine if anything was left.

Leto followed him and told him the elders thought it best if they gave his leadership position to someone not married to a "bad woman who was trying to poison them." If he wanted to remain a respected leader, he would renounce Emma and turn her over to them. Kai said he would meet with the elders later. Now, he just wanted to treat them.

Each day, the tribe lost several members, and the sickness showed no sign of relenting. Kai feared not only for The People but also for Emma.

After administering medicine and performing final chants over more of the members, he walked into the open pasture, where he saw the elders gathered. They sat on the ground around a fire. The smoke mingled with the constant fumes from the cremation site above the pasture.

Sitting beside them, Kai asked questions of the men.

"My family, I understand you are not happy with my leadership. What is it you propose?"

His fingers stroked the necklace on his breastbone.

Chesma spoke first. "Our tribe has been here since the ancients. We have never experienced such devastation in all those years since. Now, our tribe looks like it will not survive. Who do you think is to blame?"

Kai's narrowed eyes never left Chesma's face. "No one is to blame. Some of you are married to women who came here already sick. Do you think they could have infected our tribe?"

Chesma's face contorted. He instigated the trip across the river and claimed one of the young women as his wife.

"They are well now. You are trying to point a finger away from one we know to have bad medicine."

"You know nothing. Chatpa was the finest leader our tribe has ever had. He welcomed Emma into our family. He would not have made a poor decision. Do you not trust in his wisdom?"

Kai knew Chesma could not dispute the leadership of Chatpa. No one gathered around the fire wanted to refute such a great leader. But Chesma seemed determined to make a case against Kai and Emma.

"Your tribe has lost confidence in you, Kai. You can step down and allow someone else to lead. Emma is in danger from the angry ancestors and us. I predict she will not live much longer."

Kai jumped to his feet and stalked away from the group at that declaration.

He sneaked back into Chatpa's to check on Emma. It looked as if she had not moved. He reached his hand to her face—her skin blazed with fever.

Had his own people wished this illness on his wife? She had worked beside him to cure them of this sickness, and now she writhed under a hide. He held her head and forced her to swallow the last of the brown liquid. It ran out of her mouth and down the front of her chest.

"Emma, can you hear me?" No answer.

He stood near the door to Chatpa's home and saw through an opening into the field below. The elders departed. Night had fallen, and no one was visible. He lifted Emma into his arms and walked the path he had brought her home the day before.

As rocks shifted under his feet, he held her close to his chest and carefully shuffled along the path.

Reaching the water's edge, he peeled her clothes away and lay her on the damp grass. Then he dropped his own. Kai had never been intimate with Emma and had never seen her naked. It was too dark to see her now. But he held her against his bare skin and walked into the water.

It startled her when the cold water surrounded them both. Shivering, Kai knelt to his knees and held her body under the water with her head against his neck. Emma had told him about cold water baths reducing temperatures. Kai stayed there for what seemed like hours.

Then he rose and took her back to the bank. Pulling her hide dress over her head was more difficult than removing it because her wet skin clung to the tanned leather and resisted.

Kai pulled on his pants and picked her up once more. He was out of breath when he entered Chatpa's.

Emma's breathing seemed shallow, but her skin was cooler to the touch. Although he wanted to stay with her, he could not allow himself in case the others returned. He walked back to his cave, his long hair dripping down his back.

Kai lay down to dream about Emma outliving the sickness.

"Please, Chatpa, speak to our ancestors and do not allow Emma to die."

His eyes flew open to see three men standing over him.

"Where is she?"

"Who?"

"Your wife."

"She is not here."

"We can see that."

"Please stand, Kai."

Kai could barely draw a breath. He stood before them, towering over the three men in height and breadth. The shortest one reached for Kai's necklace, but he could not seize the symbol and ducked his head.

"We are here to remove you from the leadership of this tribe." His voice sounded small and embarrassed.

"Who is to replace me?" Kai asked.

"The elders selected Chesma."

The choice did not surprise Kai. Feeling sad but not defeated, he removed the heavy strand around his neck and placed it in the man's waiting hand. They nodded to him and left the room.

He did not protest his removal as leader. He had more important things to do than fight over such a detail. Emma was in mortal danger, as were many others.

Looking from side to side in the corridor, he made his way to Chatpa's. Kneeling beside Emma, he whispered, "Are you better?" No answer.

Her mouth was open, and her skin parched. All Kai had was water to soothe her lips and throat.

He lay beside her and wept.

CHAPTER 44

JOSIE

Josie's eyes watered when she saw a dress laying on her bed. The bodice of the dress was crème with elaborate embroidery of turquoise, hot pink, lime green, and sky blue covering its surface.

Vines of pale green and dark green leaves encircled the colorful flowers and gave depth to the creation. Josie's hand flew to her mouth. She did not own such a superb outfit. She dressed casually at the ranch, usually in blue jeans and denim shirts. Even when they hosted events, she exchanged her denim shirt for a white one and added fancy boots—nothing like this.

On the last auction day, she and John decided on the ride home to mourn their daughter. To accept her death and to celebrate her life. It was time. Emma was not coming home.

Josie told John she remembered the funeral she and Emma attended for Edward Black, a rancher friend's son who died in an accident. Leaving the funeral home, Emma told her mother, "If something happens to me, I don't want everyone wearing black and crying and singing sad hymns. I want colors and a barbeque and dancing. If we believe there's a better place than this Earth, why don't we behave as we believe?"

Josie remembered thinking how wise her young daughter was. She had patted Emma's hand and said they didn't have to worry about that for a long time. But unfortunately, that time had crept into their lives like a sneaky fox searching for eggs in the hen house. Josie was not ready, but she had no choice.

Her daughter's funeral would be a true celebration. Few children instructed their parents about their final arrangements. Josie had not realized at the time what a gift Emma had given her. She did not have to wonder about what Emma wanted; she knew.

Josie immediately dropped to her knees on a plush white rug, grasped her hands together in prayer, and thanked God for the years they had with their daughter.

"I'm not ungrateful, just sad. And not knowing what happened to Emma is painful. Help me try to understand and be a better person."

Without her rosary, her prayers seemed childish and awkward in her ears. It had been a year since she prayed for anything other than Emma's return. She hadn't prayed as much as begged. Then, her pleas turned to anger and rants before falling back to quiet sobs and promises she knew she could not keep.

Would her oaths to God be like giving up chocolate or wine for Lent? How many days could she last before she succumbed to temptation? *This time will be different*, she told herself. If Emma returned, she would give up anything, even the ranch. No one who knew her would believe that promise or threat.

If her mother, Valeria, heard she would give up the property, she would shake Josie by gripping her forearms and say, "Come to your senses, girl. The Rosales women who came before you lost babies and husbands, but they never gave up the land. The acreage is your heritage and your legacy. Without it, the Rosales family would cease to exist on this Earth."

Would Josie and Emma turn into a vapor and leave a contrail in the sky to signify the only evidence they had been on this planet?

Josie pulled herself off the floor, holding onto the bedpost.

She chose a pair of strappy gold sandals to wear with her dress instead of the standard cowboy boots. She wanted to make Emma proud. She imagined Emma peeking into her closet and seeing her mother dressed up.

"Oh, Mama. You look gorgeous." Even before Emma could pronounce more significant words like "gorgeous," she would try, and they'd laugh when she said "srog" for "frog" or "babbit" for "rabbit."

Josie had loved listening to her daughter's slight lisp, especially when she lost her baby teeth and could stick her tongue through the gap. Then, the oversized adult teeth looked too long before Emma's face matured. They seemed as large as horses' teeth, but Josie never told her she was anything except beautiful, and she was, in Josie's eyes.

"Every crow thinks theirs is the blackest," her mother would say. *Yes, mother, every parent thinks their child is the smartest, prettiest, or most handsome.* And they were all correct.

Every child was worthy of being loved and having their parents as their biggest fans. Josie hoped Emma had always felt their love, admiration, and pride. But unfortunately, today would be the most challenging day of their lives. She wished she could confide in Emma and ask, "Is this what you wanted? Did we do okay?"

Josie stared out the window that overlooked the rolling hills of the backyard. It looked like a garden party with long tables and linen cloths blowing in the wind—silver punch bowls and coffee services with platters of sandwiches, fruit, and cheese trays. Crystal plates glistened, and light bounced off the gleaming silverware.

Tall stands of roses and peonies created an aisle through rows of chairs. An altar was at the end of the walkway, and a priest stood there studying a program. Josie heard the strands of a violin and harp, soft and dreamy tunes.

John stepped behind her at the window and encircled her with his arms. She leaned back and tucked her head under his chin. They watched the catering staff rushing from table to table, adjusting and organizing for the reception after the service.

She suddenly stiffened.

"What's the matter?" he asked.

"It looks like a wedding. This gathering is what our girl would have had for her marriage ceremony." Josie shivered.

"We celebrate our Emma today, Josie. It looks like a celebration of a life well-lived, just cut too short."

She nodded, and a bittersweet smile tugged at her lips. "Instead of my helping her dress in a wedding gown and you walking her down the aisle, we will say prayers she's at rest."

Josie and John hugged each other. Then they walked into their separate closets to dress. Josie wanted everything to be perfect. It was the last public display of their affection for their only child.

Josie pulled the beautiful dress John had ordered over her head, slipped sandals on her bare feet, and John buttoned the pearls on the back of her dress. When she turned around to face him, she drew in a breath, noting how handsome he looked in his white flowing shirt and dark pants.

He whistled low.

"You're prettier today than the first time I saw you."

"I'm afraid your eyesight is failing."

"Only 20/20 for looking at you."

Josie reached out her hand to her husband, and they walked out the door to greet their guests.

CHAPTER 45

KAI

Should he have listened earlier to Emma's pleas to go home? Now, his tribe had turned their backs on him, and she was hurt and ill. Kai slept in fits and starts for several nights while Emma made little whimpering noises, so he knew she suffered. Was it too late to help her now? He would remove her from this madness. With a firm decision made in his mind, Kai began to gather his possessions.

In Chatpa's living area, Kai moved a wood stump next to the wall and reached as far as possible. Lifting containers from the shelf, he placed them on the floor and sat next to them to look inside.

One by one, he opened the tops. The first one contained silver coins. Surprised, Kai wondered what they were. He had seen nothing like these. There were numbers on the bottom of each one: 1865, 1847.

The second bowl held beautiful jewelry. Had it belonged to his grandmother? It did not look like the necklaces brought from across the river or strung by the women in camp. Instead, these were impressive pieces with large green and red stones, swirls of gold metal holding them in place.

Who had worn these?

Kai knew the legend of his great-grandmother. The story told was of a white woman who traveled a long way to live among his people. She wore long dresses, with her hair piled on top of her head. Was she the owner of the important-looking jewelry?

Next, he found a paper image of a woman with a full skirt and the same necklace around her neck. Was this the woman who came to dwell with them? It was a small black-and-white picture, but he thought Chatpa had her eyes.

Under the photo lay a large drawing of a great span of land. It showed rivers and caverns. There was fancy writing on it and a big circle stamped with words. Kai could not read the mysterious markings, but he would ask Emma if she could when she awoke.

The last jar held a dried mixture. Why did Chatpa store what looked to be valuable medicine here in his cave? Most of the tribe's herbal stock existed on the roof. He sniffed the potent mixture. Then, uncertain of what it contained but hoping for a miracle, he mixed a small amount in water and fed it to Emma.

Kai hoped it was not to be smoked in a pipe but taken by mouth. She was groggy and could not hold her head up. He propped her and let her sip.

Kai sat watching her for a long time. She seemed to sleep peacefully after the medicine, and he returned to his search. There were many jars full of the most exquisite finds.

There was a ring with large clear stones. He knew Chatpa had worn a ring on a chain around his neck for many years after his wife died. These items were a mystery that he could not solve without his grandfather.

"Where am I?" Emma sat up straight and looked around with blank eyes.

"At Chatpa's." Kai rushed to her side.

"Who's Chatpa?" Emma whispered, but her words were distinct.

"You are dreaming. Go back to sleep." Kai worried about the medicine he had given her, but it was their only hope.

She slumped, and Kai caught her before her head hit the hard ground.

Was she any better? He could not tell. It was apparent she had visions.

"Just sleep. Everything will be all right." Of course, he didn't know that for sure, but he intended to save her from his people.

Kai dumped all the jewelry and silver into a small hide and folded the sides over each other. He placed the medicine jar on top of his bundle.

Kai heard drums and walked out to the ledge where he could see into the meadow. People gathered there—not as many as they once had because most of the tribe were sick or had died.

Standing there in front of the crowd was Chesma. He held his arms up and threw his head back, looking into the sky. His chants were echoing off the canyon walls. Kai's stomach pitched. How had he allowed his legacy, his grandfather's pride, to pass to such an arrogant man as Chesma? He may lead the tribe, but a small one it would be. Their numbers dwindled each day. He could see ashes flying in the air, and the smell of cedar and sage smoke was a constant now.

Wearily, he sat and watched the spectacle before him. The wind blew the words toward him and then away as he listened. Kai snorted about Chesma protecting the tribe from evil spirits that claimed their families. What protection did Chesma possess? Kai would respect him if he could take this sickness away, but he knew Chesma could not. Few survived once they had the disease.

Kai stroked Emma's hair. He split his time between caring for her and visiting all the other sick patients.

He did not know if Emma knew he was there or who he was. She was delirious and often mentioned things Kai did not understand, like "truck" and "two-step."

She smiled at him or toward him and said she would ride tomorrow. Honey-Boy was waiting for her.

He realized she relived her journey to his people, but she never arrived. Emma was lost in the desert. She needed to make a fire. She ran out of beef jerky. He hoped the sickness had not taken her mind completely.

Listening to her, he was afraid. This Emma was not the fierce woman who ran away repeatedly and never gave up. She was not the gentlewoman who nursed him when she had shot him. Emma could ride a horse and use a bow like a man. He marveled at her and prayed to his gods that she would return whole. Kai bargained with the universe.

When he closed his eyes that night, he could see his and Emma's children in his mind. Tanned from the sun, they raced each other across the pasture. They swam in the river and climbed trees. He taught them to hunt and fish, and she taught them how to speak English and ride horses.

They had his dark hair and her fierce determination. They were stunning; they were genuine to him. Seeing his and Emma's children soothed him and gave him hope for the future.

Kai dozed off with the visions in his mind and dreamed the same thoughts from when he was awake. He had already seen the children. His ancestors had sent a glimpse of them, foreshadowing what was to come.

Then Emma shrieked. He feared others in the caves down the

hall had heard her. It was a bloodcurdling scream. He had never heard her sound that frightened.

Two tribe members, each with one of her arms, dragged her out of the cave.

Kai rushed forward and pushed them. They dropped Emma's arms, and she crumbled to the floor. She twisted from side to side, yet not quite awake.

"What are you doing?" he demanded.

"We are taking her. Her evil spirit needs to leave this place."

Kai's face burned with rage, and he clenched his fists. "She is not evil. Who told you to do this?"

One man puffed out his chest and said, "Chesma, our new leader. He said the deaths will end when she is gone."

He pointed at Emma but simultaneously acted as though he feared her. The other member shaded his eyes. Kai was confident Chesma had instructed them to shield themselves from Emma's malicious powers.

"You tell Chesma that he can come himself if he wants Emma. He will have to beat me to take her."

They crept out of the cave. Not long after the men left, Chesma appeared in the doorway.

"You offered your leader a challenge?" He sneered.

"Our tribe is less than half of what it once numbered. You should concern yourself with assisting with the sickness, not trying to attack Emma for something she did not do."

"She is to blame," he insisted.

"If you continue to cause the tribe to think she is, I will leave you without a healer. No one is trained except me. Me and Emma."

Chesma hesitated but exclaimed, "We don't need her kind of medicine." He hurried out the door as if to race away from a wicked power.

Kai had no other recourse. It was time to leave.

CHAPTER 46

JOSIE

Josie's lower back ached from standing for hours, and the smile that stretched tightly across her face felt like a grimace as hundreds shook her hand and whispered their condolences.

The guests obeyed the dress code of the ceremony and wore pastels and bright hues. As a result, the audience looked like a myriad of color and light, *just as Emma had wanted.*

Josie remembered when Emma was a young girl, she had held her tiny finger where her name appeared in the family Bible, and next to her, she said her husband and children would be there. That would not happen now, and the Bible's space beside Emma would always be vacant. Josie would have to use today's date as Emma's death date. She looked down at her mother seated beside her.

Valeria wiped her face with an antique lacy handkerchief. Was it the same one Emma would have carried in her bridal bouquet?

Josie clutched the turquoise and silver beads around her neck. The musicians had begun playing. She had given them a list of Emma's favorite songs, or what she thought might still be.

The line approaching them dwindled.

"May we sit now?" she asked John. He nodded and extended

one arm to her and a hand to help her mother to her feet. They walked to a table under a live oak tree.

"What do we do now, querida?" Her mother wrung the handkerchief in her hands. "Who will inherit The Thorn? Maybe a cousin?"

Josie knew her mother's grief about Emma intermingled with the responsibility of the massive property. They had never experienced this type of loss before. They had never considered who would claim the ranch besides a Rosales daughter.

Josie spoke in hushed tones. "I don't know, Mama. Let's not worry about that today. Instead, I must think about our precious Emma and how remarkable she truly was."

A tear fell onto her brightly colored dress and left a stain. Would she ever be able to wear this beautiful outfit again, or would it forever be her daughter's funeral dress? There would be many more blemishes on the luscious fabric today. This was just the first.

Josie reached for her mother's hand and gripped it as they watched neighboring ranchers, politicians, the sheriff's staff, and high school and college friends pile their plates at the buffet tables. She focused on the people clustering together like a flock of birds, glorious in their plumage and youth.

Despite the solemn nature of the day, the young men and women flirted, laughed, ate voluminous amounts of food, and drank beers. They were a joy to see. But, of course, Emma would have been the center of their attention. Emma would have called out their requests for the musicians and grabbed a boy's arm to two-step her around the dance floor.

Josie smiled and could almost see her daughter's mane of dark hair among the light ones in the group. One girl saw her watching them and put a finger to her lips to silence her friends. She used her head to point at Josie. Then, in reverence, they all quieted.

Josie rose from her seat and walked toward the group. They looked sheepishly at her as she approached.

"Today is a day to celebrate Emma. She would want you to laugh loudly, dance, eat, and share wonderful memories of your time with her. Please don't think I want you to be quiet. Thank you for being friends with Emma. We're glad you're here."

The men and women nodded at her. Some shared memories with her that made her laugh out loud.

A petite dark-haired girl with glorious blue eyes said, "Remember when Emma taught us to swim in the creek? We were afraid of the bullfrogs and turtles, but Emma relocated all of them, and we didn't worry."

Josie smiled. Their girl had been exceptional. Everyone who had known her agreed.

The crowd lingered until the air cooled, and the first hues of pink and orange sherbet colored the sky. The Thorn was a long way from anywhere else. Everyone had to travel several hours to reach the ranch house. Now, they loaded their cars and drove down the long road between rows of live oaks to depart the property.

Josie, John, and Valeria walked wearily toward the house when the last of the guests' red taillights blinked out in the distance.

It was a monumental day. Josie and John had finally accepted their daughter would not be coming home. They did not know what had happened to her, only that she was gone. It would have to be enough. Their days would no longer revolve around finding their child but would return to the ranch's activities.

Josie could not face the platters of food from the reception, now lukewarm from sitting outside. The caterers had brought them into the kitchen and loaded the leftovers into plastic cartons. Josie tossed them all into the garbage container.

She had hugged Flora earlier and told her and Pedro to go to their casita to rest. Her tiny mother slept in her own home. So, now Josie walked to the refrigerator and reached for butter, eggs, and a block of sharp cheddar cheese. She pulled a large cast-iron skillet from the rack hanging over a massive butcher's block.

The ignitor's *click-click-click* on the gas stove sent flames around the base of the skillet with a swoosh. Butter melted in the hot pan, and she cracked eggs into a bowl and whisked them with salt and pepper. Then she poured them into the butter and whipped the bright yellow yolks until soft mounds of scrambled eggs filled the pan. Into another skillet, she dropped thick slices of bread to create toast.

Josie placed hand-painted dishes beside the stovetop and heaped eggs covered with cheese and toast on the plates. Large glasses of freshly squeezed orange juice completed the supper.

"Come and get it," she called out to her husband.

Just two of us now.

CHAPTER 47

KAI

Kai prepared to leave his home, the only one he had ever known. He had grown up in the caves, exploring from the time he walked. Kai was never afraid of the darkness or the jagged edges of the granite. He cut himself, tripped, fell, and slid down the rocky paths, but he continued to discover areas of the caves.

By the time he was a teenager, he could race through the corridors with his eyes shut.

"Kai, watch where you are going!" they would shout at him.

He would nod and take off running again. He loved to go to the underground lake. At first, it was eerie, but then he hollowed out a fallen tree and made a canoe and paddle. He used a bone hook to catch large fish in the chilly waters. Did they fall from the stream above the waterfall into the lake? He always wondered how they had arrived there in the cave's water.

His childhood was every boy's dream. He was proud when Chatpa presented him with his first pony. The petite horse was brown with a black mane. Kai named him Lapa. Lapa followed him around the pasture like he begged to go on a ride. His grandfather walked beside the horse until Kai could grip the horse with his knees. Then, Chatpa would run and pull the horse, watching Kai bump up and down on its back.

When Kai bounced off the horse's tail end, Chatpa laughed. Kai was mad at first, but his grandfather's chortle was contagious, and Kai rolled on the ground, holding his stomach and joining the hysterics.

Finally, Kai would grab a handful of mane in his left hand and fling his leg over the back of the horse. They would ride until Lapa needed to drink in the stream.

Kai practiced for hours until he could lie back flat on the horse, and they moved as one. His grandfather said his grandson and the horse were a sight.

Soon, Kai rounded up wild horses in the land surrounding the mountains. He was the fastest rider and reached the skittish herds first. The whoops and hollers kept the horses running in the right direction as the tribal members led them down into the caverns where they could trap them. Kai prided himself on training the horses to allow riders on their backs and not run away when given a chance.

Kai remembered days in the pastures picking herbs with Chatpa and taking them to the roof where they processed and dried them. Chatpa held up each flower and stalk and told him the name. Then, he asked Kai to repeat it until he could recite them all. Chatpa showed him the measurements of how to turn them into medicines.

"Garlic is for fever; winter cherry, if a woman cannot conceive; peppermint for stomachaches; and goldenseal for infection."

Kai did not know how Chatpa was that wise or patient. When Kai had difficulty remembering his parents, Chatpa mentioned his father carving a stick or his mother holding his hand as they walked. Then, Kai had a flash of that specific memory, almost as if Chatpa called it into his mind just for him. Chatpa was responsible for being both mother and father to him after his parents and his grandmother Anna died. Kai was grateful for his tutelage.

Now, Kai walked the entire compound, down the river to the Topo waterfall, remembering fishing trips and gathering vegetables. He looked back at the magnificent mountain with the homes of his people, many vacant from the deaths of their occupants.

He walked to the mound where they cremated Chatpa. First, he knelt and paid his respects to his grandfather. Then, looking past the still-burning site, Kai saw one of the wood body carriers leaning against a tree. He picked up the ends of the bed-like implement and dragged it up the hill.

Kai walked back to Chatpa's cave to check on Emma. She twisted in the hides, and he pulled them back. She was drenched and hot to the touch. It was time.

He picked up the hide filled with his and Chatpa's possessions. Then, he piled dozens of leathers on the wooden frame. He packed a bag with pouches for water and dried venison. Finally, he mixed a jug of the medicine found on the shelf with water and gave Emma a drink before closing the top.

Kai pulled the saddle Emma brought with her out of the corner. He dragged her baggy dress off her shivering body, placed a shirt over her head, and pulled tight pants up her legs.

He was out of breath from the effort. Kai had never dressed or undressed someone before Emma. He thought he remembered Chatpa saying the clothes came from beyond the river.

Kai lifted Emma onto the stretcher and surrounded her with their food, water, medicine, and other belongings.

He spoke as he looked around the room. "We are going now, Chatpa. One day, I will see you again."

Kai picked up the ends of the bed, and they plodded down the mountain.

Emma was not heavy, but the items surrounding her and the bed were already causing Kai's shoulders and forearms to ache. His determination to save Emma from his tribe kept him moving. Reaching the bottom of the hill, he realized he needed a horse to travel far into the desert. He pulled Emma into the shade of the mountain and jogged back the distance they had already covered.

His legs stung, and his lungs burned. The days were now sweltering before noon, and the bright skies did not offer a chance of rain. Even the cacti looked droopy and needed a drink.

Kai did not want to leave Emma alone too long, so he pushed his endurance and climbed the mountain.

When he reached the pasture, he broke into a run and made it to the horse pen.

"What are you doing, Kai?" A voice behind him broke his concentration.

"Riding my horse." He turned back to the enormous creature beside him and tried to breathe steadily.

"Where is your wife?" Chesma had to look up to see Kai's face, but his confidence was not lacking, and he stood like a bantam rooster spreading its feathers for attention.

"Stay away from me. You don't want to see me angry."

Chesma spit and just missed Kai's foot.

"If I call the elders, they will keep you from being near her."

"Not brave enough to stop me yourself?" He remembered the embarrassment and fury in Chesma's face when Kai bested him to win the competition to impress Emma.

Chesma held up his palms, and Kai leaped onto his horse. Kai reached out with his foot and struck Chesma with his heel. Chesma dropped to the ground. When Kai galloped out of the cavern, he looked back to see Chesma still sitting.

Kai wanted to place distance between them. He did not want the elders to ride after him and find Emma in her weakened condition. They might decide to overpower him and leave her in the desert to die.

He did not slow the horse until he saw Emma's bed in the shadows. He jumped down and pulled out the rawhide ties he had brought. Kai had planned to raise Emma's bed off the ground at night to protect her from wild animals. Now he needed them to pull her.

Kai lifted her saddle and placed it on his horse's back. Initially, his horse shimmied away from the foreign object, but he finally allowed Kai to secure the long strips to both sides of the saddle and the bed.

He was glad Emma had shown him how to secure a saddle to a horse. It would be slow-moving, but the horses sometimes had to pull pallets like this when they hauled large game animals after a hunt. Kai worried most about the bed's deep tracks in the sandy soil.

He climbed into the saddle and tried to become accustomed to the feeling of such bulk under him. Kai had never ridden on such a seat before. He became conscious of holding onto the horn in front of him.

The horse took only ten steps before Kai looked back to see how Emma fared. She had not roused since the journey began, and the only time before that was with her terror and screams.

Kai worried about her. Would he have to bury her to keep animals from finding her body? Kai chanted softly to himself, sending a blessing to her from the ancestors. Then, he remembered Chatpa's explanation of why The People differed from others and were blessed to have survived for that long in hiding.

Chatpa said their origin story was an emergence from the great tunnel generations ago. Now, Kai was far away from that enchanted passageway and home.

When the daylight rapidly evaporated, he looked for a place to spend their first night. He passed a couple of places he didn't really like, but it looked like there were no better choices.

Then, he spied a small cave opening on the hill. He pulled the horse as closely as he could to the cavity. It dismayed him to look back and see the deep trenches the bed had dug in the sand. It would not take an expert to follow them.

Kai freed the ties and removed the saddle from his horse. He allowed him to graze. He would have to find a river soon for the horse to drink. Tomorrow would be twice as long as today. He patted Emma and then walked to the opening to look inside.

It probably had been a coyote den. There was no headroom, but it was about twice the size of Emma's bed, and it was cooler than remaining in the outdoors' heat. Kai pulled and pushed the bed, first placing Emma's feet into the cave. That left her head near fresh air. He did not trust the walls; he wanted to pull Emma quickly outside if they collapsed. Kai opened the container of dried meat and ate a strip. Then, he drank water.

He held the pouch of medicine to Emma's lips. She did not open her teeth, but he drizzled it into her mouth until she gagged. Maybe some of it went into her body. Kai crawled into the cave and lay beside her—both of their faces sticking outside.

He looked for the stars about which his grandfather had told stories. There was the Great Sky Road, and there was the North

Star. One was a swirl of stars and one so dazzling it could lead someone to a destination.

Kai wished Emma would open her eyes to see the enormous heavens. When he was a little boy, Kai told Chatpa he feared the sky, which might swallow him like the mighty river near their caves.

"We look to the skies for comfort, not fear, little one. We count our ancestors among the stars, who look down on us each night and watch over us, keeping us strong. Your mother and father are there. Look up and tell them your dreams. They will do what they can to accommodate you."

After Chatpa's comforting explanation of the blue above, Kai believed the stars were there to remind him of the people who had cared for him and would greet him when he passed into the other life. He fell asleep physically exhausted and not sure he was mentally capable of handling what might happen next.

THEIR DAYS IN THE desert looked the same. Kai rose before dawn and dragged Emma's bed to his horse. Tying her securely, they would begin another leg of their journey. When the sun was too hot overhead and Emma's skin reddened, he found a place to stay until the cool of the evening or the following day.

Just when Kai thought he would have to pour water into his cupped hands to allow the horse to drink, he saw a swampy area with trees growing in a stream. Then, it rained.

Rain was rare in the desert; surely a sign from the gods. So Kai opened all his skin bags and let the water fill them while he sat beside Emma in the sporadic shower and let the water wash over them. Then, he climbed back into the saddle, and they were on their way again.

Two days, then three passed. Kai looked around at the unfamiliar landscape. He had never been this far from his home. Even the tribe members who traveled across the mighty river and visited villages only stayed one night.

Kai was the first of The People to be this far into the desert. That fact did not make him feel significant but smaller.

Chatpa told the elders stories about evil traders and thieves. Many cheated his tribe members or stole their horses. Would he find those waiting for him in this place? He was away from all he recognized and all who knew him. Yet, here he was with no end in sight to his journey. Had he acted in haste? Kai needed to put as much distance between his people and him and Emma. He could not take the chance they would find and destroy her or them both.

He peered over his shoulder as he did hundreds of times each day. Emma had not gotten worse, but she was no better. How long could a sickness last before you lived through it or succumbed? Everything Chatpa had taught him about treating illness or making medicine from plants seemed useless.

Kai could not save the one person he wanted—his wife. Well, *wife* in name only. They had not been husband and wife physically, but he thought of her as his partner. When did that happen? Kai remembered sitting with Chatpa the day of the competition to win Emma's respect. The other men wanted her. They had seen no one quite like her before.

Although she was a captive, she did not bow to them. They knew Emma was a challenge. She showed that when she used a bow and arrows to defeat them or rode a horse as well as they did.

Then, she began helping Chatpa and Kai nurse the sick animals and assist women in birthing babies. She was a natural. The people seemed to respect her—until they didn't.

On the day of the competition, Chatpa had asked about Kai's intentions.

"Will you compete for this girl who stays with me?" Chatpa questioned.

"Probably not." Kai tried to deny his interest in her.

"What if your parents and the ancestors sent her to you to be your wife?"

Kai cocked his head to one side and looked at his grandfather. "What makes you think that?"

"She is the most capable woman I've ever met. She could be your equal in all ways. Imagine the children you could have together."

"That is just you dreaming."

"She is the only one to come to us speaking the language of your great-grandmother."

That gave Kai pause. Why would this English language still linger among his people? Why did his mother want him to learn the language if not for this?

Chatpa had wandered down to the field to watch the proceedings while Kai sat in his cave thinking about Chatpa's reasoning. Before they had completed many events, Kai joined the competition.

Emma had left Chatpa's side and returned to the cave by then. She did not know he had won the challenge until he arrived back at Chatpa's.

Was it excitement on her face when Kai told her he had won the competition or just relief? She had gotten to know him from his daily visits to his grandfather and their healing work together. Maybe she thought he was the lesser of the unknown evils out there.

In his mind, he could imagine Emma in her natural habitat. He knew the names of people in the barn and her friends from school. When Kai closed his eyes, and Emma told him stories, they had transported him to another land. She drew words she used in the sand and told him what they meant. He copied her words and learned how to read them from her drawing.

They could have been happy in his home. He truly believed she would have accepted him as her husband. But then the sickness arrived at camp. He did not know if his people would survive the deadly disease. It had swept through every household, almost every family.

Kai dreaded the day he, too, would become sick. Then, who would care for him and Emma? They could die here in the desert.

Kai led his horse to the stream to drink. It was cooler there by the water. The rain had drenched their clothes, chilling their skins and allowing them to lie on the ground without the sun baking them like the cracked clay.

He ate a strip of dried meat. There were only a few remaining in his bag. He mixed Emma's medicine and pried open her gritted teeth, then poured it down her throat. She moaned.

What would happen if he lost her? Would he return to camp and hope for forgiveness from his tribe? Or had he cut ties with them forever?

Kai's head hurt, and he was alone and fearful. But, a rush of excitement filled his chest, too. He wanted to see the modern world. He remembered Emma's stories about riding in cars, not on horses, and watching stories play before your eyes on what she described as a box filled with daydreams.

Kai leaned close to Emma. "I will tell you a story. Listen to my voice and come back to me. I need you to get well."

She stirred slightly but did not open her eyes. The few times she seemed awake in the past few days, she stared in front of her, unseeing. Her eyes were flat, with no life behind them.

"Chatpa told me my great-grandmother was traveling with her family when they became ill, and died. My great-grandfather was one of the hunters who found her trying to dig graves. The sight of her, Elisabeth, took my great-grandfather's mind."

Kai looked to the sky as he continued. "She was young, but he was a great provider and handsome. She fell in love with him, and they became husband and wife. Their firstborn was Chatpa. He was the best of both of them. They called him Chatpa, which means 'Rising Owl.' My great-grandfather saw a white owl the night Chatpa was born and said it came to welcome his son into this world. They had a happy life in the caves and are among the ancestors who watch over us. I want us to be like them, Emma. I want you to grow to love me and for us to be happy."

He stroked her cheek and thought he saw a dreamy smile on her face.

CHAPTER 48

JOSIE

Josie undressed slowly. She stroked the outfit's beautiful fabric. It was too exquisite to remain hidden in a plastic bag in her closet. But Josie did not think she could wear it again.

This day permeated the fabric and threads. Her loss stayed in the fibers as if she had woven grief and sorrow into the design. *But, dear Lord*, she was exhausted. Not just physically but mentally and spiritually. Their hope for the future had changed in a way they'd never imagined.

The past year's anxiety, rage, sadness, and worry weighed her spirit so heavily that she did not know if she could ever feel frivolous again. No more shopping trips to Dallas. No Broadway plays in New York. No vacations at the beach or late-night baking brownies and heaping them with homemade ice cream. There was no more teaching Emma to apply makeup, buy college clothes, or pick out a horse. *No, no, no.*

Josie believed John when he said they would return to their lives. Back to lives without Emma? She still could not comprehend such a thing. Existence, perhaps, but not the life she had dreamed of when she first held her daughter in her arms.

Josie had considered a home birth. They were far from the nearest hospital, and she knew a good midwife in the area. Josie liked the idea of her baby being born on the ranch she would inherit one day.

The closer she got to her due date, the more anxious she became. Something did not feel right. They drove to El Paso and stayed in the hospital, and an experienced physician told them the baby had its umbilical cord wrapped around its neck. Could the midwife have saved the infant if they had been on the ranch?

When Josie gave a final push and John stood behind her head, the doctor lifted a mucus-covered, squalling infant into the air.

"Is she okay?" John croaked.

"Perfect," the doctor declared. And perfect she was—a head full of black hair, ten fingers, ten toes.

Josie's rough edges melted away for that moment. She was no longer the daughter of the ranch owners. Instead, she was the mother of her own daughter. Josie caught her breath when they handed the baby to her.

John leaned over to glimpse the child they had created, but Josie cradled her against her breast for a first look all her own.

"Well, who does she look like?" John said. "You said we'd name her when we saw who she looks like."

"She looks like herself," Josie declared, although she could see the shape of her mother's eyes and her own nose. Maybe her husband's ears?

"Josie, is she an Emma or a Victoria?" He named off their top two choices for a girl. One was Josie's grandmother's sister's name, and the other his grandmother's. She hated to be selfish, but Victoria sounded pretty formal for a girl who would grow up riding horses and camping outside.

"She's definitely an Emma," Josie declared.

Only a tinge of disappointment passed over his face before it quickly disappeared. "Emma it is, then."

Josie knew John would follow her lead, as he did in most matters.

Emma's pucker seemed like a smile when Josie whispered her name in her ear. It was as if she already knew what she would be called and just waited for her parents to discover it for themselves.

Emma seemed a wise soul from the beginning. Walking her into their home for the first time, Josie and John beamed at each other, and Josie squeezed Emma more tightly.

"You're on The Thorn, niñita. This is your home, where you will spend your life and your children's lives and see your grandchildren grow up here."

Emma looked around wide-eyed and seemed to take in the whole place. She was born on Texas soil, that was all that mattered. Josie knew a few ranchers' daughters who had moved to Alabama or Mississippi, and when they were ready to have their babies, their fathers sent boxes of Texas dirt to place under their hospital beds to ensure the babies would be born on the earth of Texas. Texans were serious about their birthrights.

Josie had held Emma up in the wide window and turned her from side to side.

"As far as you can see and farther still, Emma. This is your ranch."

Now Josie shook her head, trying to dislodge the poignant memories. It was not unusual to think of a child's birth when you relinquished her to the universe and gave up hope of a future with her. After the year they'd had and the exhausting funeral, Josie felt twice her age.

She limped toward the bed and found John already there. He lifted the covers, and she burrowed herself next to him. He was muscular and had the scent of a spicy after-shave. She lay her head on his chest, and her eyelids drooped.

They held each other until their bodies were saturated with each other's warmth.

Then, Josie rolled to a cool spot on her side of the bed without being conscious of moving.

CHAPTER 49

KAI

Kai's mouth was so dry, his tongue stuck to the roof of his mouth. When he looked over his shoulder at Emma, her face looked so swollen, she was unlike the girl he knew. She had blisters on her lips, and her eyelids were fluttering.

Extreme heat caused the desert to shimmer and created mirages of water ahead of them. With no breeze, the air was suffocatingly still. Rattlesnakes slithered away from his horse's hooves, and prairie dogs darted out of their way.

Kai's eyes searched in front of him for water while he sat sideways on the horse to keep watch over Emma at the same time. The desert dust had coated them both and seemed to add another layer of clothing to their bodies. Even his horse dragged his feet. Kai stopped at a cottonwood tree and peeled the bark to feed his steed.

Kai thought his ears were ringing. What was that sound? Rustling leaves? There were no trees here, only scraggly cacti and dried mesquites.

His horse lifted his head and snorted. Then, the animal turned abruptly to the right. Kai feared the quick action would throw Emma from her bed. The wooden frame tilted and jerked but righted itself when the horse straightened.

Kai allowed the horse free rein. He realized the noise rever-
berating in his ears was the roaring of a mighty river just over the
next hill. "Good, good," he said while patting the horse. The horse
lurched forward and made it to the water. Kai jumped off his back
and pulled the ties from the horse's back, or he might have pulled
Emma into the current with him. Instead, the horse stood in the
wide river and drank.

Kai fell to his knees and leaned down. His belly filled quickly.
Then, he lifted his sack, filled it, and took it to Emma. He splashed
her face until she grimaced.

"We're going in the river, Emma. I want to cool your skin and
wash the dust off us."

He placed his arms under Emma and lifted her easily. She
seemed frail next to his body, not the robust, healthy woman who
had challenged him and the tribe. Her head fell back over his
forearm and bobbled.

Kai carefully walked over slick rocks and sat in the water near
the bank. It was shallow there, and he stretched out his legs and
lowered Emma in front of him. Kai propped her against his chest,
and the stream splashed over their legs. He cupped one hand,
washed her arm on one side and repeated the gesture on the other.
Then, he swiveled to one side and held her head back until her
hair was drenched and the dust floated on the clear water's surface.
They stayed there until darkness surrounded them.

Kai pulled Emma to the grassy bank. They lay beside each
other, and with clothes drenched, they slept.

The next morning, Kai used a bone hook and a tiny piece of
dried beef to fish. It did not take long, and he had a sizable catch.
Building a fire was more difficult. He dripped onto the flint, and
the flame extinguished each time he struck it.

Kai had given up trying when it smoked, and a tiny spark ignited. He dropped dried grass and twigs into the flame. While the fire grew, he filleted the fish. Kai used two wet sticks to hold it, then held the warm flesh to Emma's lips. She licked the fish, and he squeezed it into her throat when she opened her mouth.

At first, she gagged, then she swallowed. Kai thought he had tasted nothing that good. He led his horse to a tree growing in the stream and tied the reins to a branch. Then, he carried Emma to lie in the shade of a small tree with roots snaking along the ground.

Kai worried. Emma's skin looked raw, and she shivered and moaned most of the time. Kai thought he'd protected her from death by the tribe, but now he wondered if he saved her so she could die in the desert.

His horse looked happy to eat the tall grasses by the river and drink more water than they had found in several days. Maybe they should stay there. But Kai feared Emma's condition would worsen, and he was out of medicine.

As he contemplated their limited options, he heard horse hooves in the distance.

Kai scrambled to hide his horse and pull Emma's bed into the tall river grasses as best he could. Maybe the riders would not come in their direction, and they would be safe, but he peeked around the tree's trunk and saw Mawa and Cloyta riding directly toward him.

The tribe did not give up easily. Once, that would have been a source of pride for him. Not now. They certainly did not come with good intentions.

He sprang from the tree and held his hands in the air. They ran their horses up to him, slinging dust and gravel against his legs.

"Why are you here?" he exclaimed. The men jumped from their

horses, ignored Kai, and strode to the water. They drank greedily, dipped leather sacks into the rushing water, and poured it over their heads.

Then they turned back to Kai.

"I asked you why you are here." Kai stared defiantly at the two.

"Do you think we wanted to come this far to find you? Our leader said we are few now, and members are still dying. Your wife is to blame because she is still alive in this world, and you left us without a healer."

They looked around and did not notice where she lay in the weeds.

"Emma is not to blame. Return to help the tribe."

"We will not leave until her soul has departed this place."

"Will you kill me, your great hunter's favored child?"

The men looked at each other with dismay. They had admired Chatpa and followed his lead.

Now, Chesma asked them to kill Chapta's grandson's wife. They were uncertain of the ramifications of such an act, and Kai knew they hesitated, so he presented them with a dilemma.

"If you return to camp and tell them you found me alone, they will believe Emma has died, and her soul is not here. Chatpa and the ancestors will reward you."

The men muttered to each other. "Let us see her body."

"Not possible," Kai said. "You cannot see someone who has departed."

"What do you think Chatpa would have done, Kai? Allow the tribe to die without destroying the cause?"

"Chatpa loved my wife. He would send a curse to you and your families from beyond if you harmed her. Do you want to risk his wrath?"

The men shook their heads. Kai realized they had ridden farther away from their camp than they had been in their lives. They had not known what they would encounter. Still, Kai knew because of Chesma's hold on them, they would do his will.

"How did you find me?" Kai asked, already knowing the answer to his question.

"You left a deep trail behind you. You were easy to track."

Of course, they had followed the wood bed digging into the sand as he pulled Emma behind the horse.

"All this way, and we have nothing to show for it?" One man argued with another.

"Give me something to take back to Chesma, Kai, to show we found you without your wife," Mawa said.

Kai pulled one of Chatpa's necklaces over his head and handed it to him. Mawa stretched its length between his two outstretched hands. The entire tribe knew this string, and it was holy to them.

Kai watched Mawa's expression as he seemed to worship the piece. Suddenly, Kai heard a crunching noise behind him, and he turned to see Cloyta with Emma's limp body over one shoulder. He walked with her toward the river.

Kai moved to pass Mawa when a crushing blow landed around his chest. Kai's eyes bulged when he saw Cloyta dump Emma into the water and hold her head under the surface.

Mawa pinned Kai's arms against his side. His attacker was hefty, but Kai kicked his foot back and caught Mawa with a thud.

Kai's feet left skid marks as he raced to the river. He leaned down and grabbed a rock as he slid down the bank. He ran into the rushing water and toward Emma. Her dark hair floated on the surface like a lily pad. Cloyta was so intent on holding her underwater that he did not see Kai lunge at him.

Kai threw his arm back over his shoulder and brought the stone down with a vicious impact on Cloyta's head. His eyes rolled back, and his last glance at Kai was fleeting. His body fell backward into the deep water and floated downstream with the swift current.

Kai wouldn't think about Cloyta or Mawa. His focus was on Emma. She, too, floated in the dark water. Kai swung her body over and lifted her into his arms. She squeezed her eyes shut and gasped for a breath. He did not know if she had been under the water too long.

He knew this brutality harmed her already diminished condition. Her breath was warm but slight against his chest. Kai slipped and recovered on the smooth stones beneath his feet. When he reached the muddy shoreline, he laid her on the ground and swept her heavy hair out of her face—still breathing. Kai had to place his ear against her nose to hear, staring at her chest as it heaved. Muddy water rolled out of her mouth and down her chin.

"I will start a fire to dry you."

When he stood, he saw Mawa limping toward his horse. It would be a painful ride home. Kai was furious with the two men. They were following orders from Chesma but had disregarded his time as leader and Chatpa's memory to harm Emma.

By the time he nursed a fire to a warming flame, Emma quaked. Although soaked and cold, her fever remained high, and her skin glowed.

Kai placed a hide as close to the flames as possible without it or Emma catching on fire. She seemed to relax when the warmth reached her skin.

"We have to travel tonight. Others may wish to harm you after those two. So, we will ride by the moon's light."

He straightened her bed and wrapped her tightly in a hide. Next, Kai filled up every sack with water for the journey ahead.

They left the campsite when a colossal harvest moon rose in the sky. It was as if someone led them by the path of a bright star. The moon's glow cast shadows from cacti that looked like men standing in the desert watching them pass.

How many days had they been traveling? Kai lost count, but the dwindling food supply showed him it was longer than anticipated. The night became a challenge and the desert an obstacle course, but the horse kept plodding along. Finally, Kai stopped to give Emma a drink of water, although her hair still dripped and she was a sodden bulge in the hide blanket.

Far in the distance, Kai saw light shining. Not from the moon or sun but from the earth itself. He did not want to show fear but he was unsure about this new territory. A haziness on the horizon became brighter. The stories Emma had told him tightened his belly.

"We are here, Emma. We must be. I wish you were awake to tell me if this is true."

A grove of briar bushes created a hiding place to conceal Emma's bed. Then he lifted her onto his weary horse's neck and catapulted beside her.

He laid his hands on her back to hold her in place, and they rode again. He could now see tall poles with lights beaming from the top. Not fire as they used in the caves, but an unnatural glow.

He halted the horse and stared. Beneath the lights was the feature he sought. From Emma's stories, she had described them precisely as he now saw them with his own eyes.

The gates of The Thorn.

CHAPTER 50

JOSIE

*B*am, *bam, bam!* The noise in the night's stillness startled Josie awake. John still slept. He snored loudly and often alarm clocks and blaring music did not rouse him.

"Oh, my goodness. Did the dogs get out?" Sometimes, they sneaked past Flora when she left the kitchen door cracked. Belle, a large yellow lab, and her sister Star, a smaller black lab, liked to jump onto the wide porch swing. Josie did not want them sleeping outside because of the threat of coyotes.

When the pets sneaked away to explore at night, Josie would find them both in a pile on the mattress in the morning. The force of each dog's hundred pounds caused the swing to bang into the side of the house and sounded like someone hammered a fist on the door.

Josie grabbed a robe from the end of the bed and slippers from underneath. She was groggy and promised herself no treats to those scoundrels when she reached them and dragged them back into the house.

She steadied herself on the door frame as she stepped outside. It was still dark, and a layer of dew made the floor tiles slick. As she had expected, the swing still moved back and forth, and there was a mound resting on top.

"Come here, Belle. Here, Star," she called to them. They didn't bark or leap from the swing. "You bad dogs. Come inside."

Josie walked to the swing to grab the dogs' collars and pull them off the swaying bed. She jumped back when her eyes adjusted to the darkness. There were no dogs.

A person lay there. She leaned down to see who slept on their swing. A strained cry escaped her throat.

Her daughter, Emma, curled up on the platform.

Josie's screams awakened John and half the ranch hands.

"Emma! It's Emma!" she cried repeatedly. Her mother, Valeria, hobbled from the casita behind the main house and joined a dozen ranch hands standing at the edge of the porch. Everyone stared at Josie who now sat beside her sleeping child.

"Wake up, honey. Emma, wake up." There was no response to her pleas.

"Oh, dear Lord. She's burning up with fever." She looked up and saw Henry, a ranch hand, standing before her.

"Go to town as fast as you can and bring Dr. Maben. Tell her Emma's home, and she's sick."

He nodded once and took off in a run to the nearest pickup truck. Slinging gravel behind him, the vehicle roared down the driveway toward the road. Josie could hear the winding of the motor as he held the accelerator to the floor. In moments, all she saw were the red tail lights.

John appeared at her elbow. "Is it really her? Is it Emma?" he cried.

"Yes, it's her. She won't wake up. Please take her to her room." Josie took charge and handed out orders. She had slipped back into her familiar leadership role.

"Mama, please ask Flora to bring a bowl of ice water and bath cloths to Emma's room. I need ibuprofen."

Josie took the stairs two at a time behind her husband, with Emma in his arms. As soon as John laid her on the bed, Josie stripped the nasty clothes from Emma's back, holding her with one arm to prop her up and using the other to peel the damp clothes off.

"What's she wearing? Are these hide pants?" John shook his head and turned his back to shield his eyes as his wife held their naked daughter in her arms.

"Why won't she wake up? Do you think she's in a coma?" Josie exclaimed.

Flora appeared and rushed to the bedside, sloshing water from a large bowl with cubes of ice floating in the liquid. She dipped thick white cloths into the water, squeezed them almost dry, and handed them to Josie. She placed one on Emma's forehead and the other on her neck and chest.

"How can this be?" Flora muttered. "How did she get here? Who found her?"

Josie shook her head in bewilderment.

"I don't know. Emma was on the porch swing. I thought it was the dogs."

Josie saw John with a bottle of ibuprofen and a glass of water in his hands.

"I hope we don't choke her trying to get these tablets down her throat."

Josie pried Emma's mouth open, just as she did a stubborn horse to check his teeth. She tossed one tablet into her mouth and poured water in after it. She watched as Emma took a big gulp involuntarily and followed the procedure with the second dose.

"Flora, please look in her bathroom and find a holder for all this hair. It looks like a rat's nest."

Josie gathered up the long, tangled mess and used a ponytail holder Flora handed her to get the hair out of Emma's eyes and off her neck.

She peppered Emma's face with kisses and whispers. "Where have you been? We missed you. You came back to us. You came back to us!"

John stood with his hand on Josie's shoulder. Josie sat next to Emma, with her mother and Flora perched at the foot of the mattress. Their family was complete. They were back together.

Josie examined her daughter more closely. Emma's eyes looked swollen shut. Blisters covered her lips, and her body had lost its curves. She looked like a skeletal version of her former self. When Josie had stripped off her daughter's clothes, she gasped because she could see Emma's rib bones through her skin. She could have counted each one.

Josie did not know how long they all stared at Emma. Then, suddenly, in the doorway appeared Dr. Maben. The ranch hand must have flown the truck like a jet plane to get to town and back this quickly.

"She's here? She's really here?" Dr. Maben dropped her bag on the bed and began examining Emma. She ran her hands over her body and drew out her stethoscope to listen to her lungs and heart. She shook her head when she took her temperature.

"She's dehydrated and has a temp of 103. Time to get this one to a hospital."

John was already calling on his cell phone.

"A helicopter will be here in a few minutes. Where are we going?"

"San Antonio," Dr. Maben replied.

Flora returned from Emma's closet. She had stuffed a small suitcase and sat on top of the luggage to close the zippered top.

"Don't worry about packing for us. We'll buy whatever we need in San Antonio," Josie told Flora, her heart thudding with fear.

She turned to her mother.

"I'll call when we know something." Her frail little mother, Valeria, cried softly, and Flora's stern face seemed to melt with tears flowing down her creased cheeks.

Dr. Maben asked if the cowboy who had delivered her to the ranch could take her back to town and said that she would make hospital arrangements before the helicopter landed in San Antonio.

Henry stood by the truck and looked sheepishly at the doctor when she joined him.

"I'd appreciate you driving a few miles under the sonic boom this time," she told him as she climbed back into the truck.

"Yes, ma'am." He grinned at her and jumped into the driver's seat.

They heard blades slicing the wind with distinctive sounds nearing the pasture.

"Grab her suitcase and let's go," John told Josie.

He lifted Emma again into his arms, and a motorized gator picked them up as they stepped off the porch. They drove to the hovering aircraft, and he handed Emma to the waiting medic and followed her in.

John gave Josie his hand and pulled her inside. The helicopter immediately rose, hovered, and then took off.

Josie looked out the window and saw a circle of ranch hands in front of the house. It was the same formation as a candlelight vigil for Emma months ago. All those rugged old cowboys removed their hats, held them over their hearts, and bowed their heads to pray. Josie turned her head to join them, praying for her daughter lying beside her. Emma was alive, but only barely.

THE REST OF THE day and the week blurred. Josie could not remember doctors' names, there were so many—as numerous as the tubes running in and out of Emma's thin body, as the electrodes and wires. Her daughter had not gained consciousness. The doctors seemed baffled.

"It may be a virus because of the high fever. Her first Covid test was negative, but we'll do another one. She has varying symptoms."

"Her organs could be shutting down."

"She's completely dehydrated; we cannot find a vein for an infusion."

Over and over, the news was not good.

Please, God. Don't let us find her to lose her again, Josie prayed. She prayed by Emma's bedside. She prayed in the hospital chapel.

She and John began a routine. He reserved a room in a hotel across the street from the hospital, and they alternated spending the night there. One of them stayed with Emma at all times.

The other walked to the cafeteria for a bowl of soup or coffee. Then, one crossed the street to a hotel room with a bed and shower. Finally, that person returned fresher and ready to take on more wait time.

Josie Ubered to a nearby Walmart and bought underwear, T-shirts, and blue jeans. They washed them with liquid detergent in the hotel sink and hung them in the shower stall to dry.

It was like a tag-team match—or handing off a baton in a relay race. Josie and John were entirely in sync and acted like one human. Josie never felt closer to him than she did when they did not touch but passed in the doorway after an overnight watch. Josie slept in the hotel room but still listened for a phone ringing.

She prayed for John's call to announce Emma had woken up. The nights were miserable on Emma's hospital room's narrow, stiff love-seat. Lights hummed on, and a nurse entered to take Emma's vitals several times each shift. Then, just as Josie dozed off, the lights popped on, rousing her from any hope of rest. Not that she complained. She would never lament again if Emma survived this.

"Please wake up, Emma. Please tell us what happened to you," she repeated like a mantra.

The doctors seemed perplexed. They could not understand why Emma had not regained consciousness. A week passed, then two.

Josie fielded calls from the ranch and decided on the daily activities, but her heart was not involved. Instead, she poured her entire consciousness into one still body in a mechanical hospital bed. She lived for the doctors' rounds, morning and night, when one of them might give them the news they yearned to hear.

"Your daughter is better."

"Your daughter is awake."

"Your daughter will make a full recovery."

But, as another week passed with only slight improvement, the doctors looked like they were avoiding Josie's eyes and murmured instead of sounding confident. Then, finally, they began meeting in the hall and conferring with each other out of Josie's earshot. When they did speak to her, they asked questions for which she had no answers.

"Mrs. Rosales, has your daughter been out of the country?"

"We don't know where she has been for a year."

"Then, we will bring in an infectious disease physician to check for unusual foreign diseases."

Josie buried her face in her hands. What had someone done to their girl? Where had they taken her?

The infectious disease expert did not name what could be devouring Emma's body. He just went straight to work, pumping her full of antibiotics, every kind imaginable. He flushed her system and cleansed her blood. He had her scanned and prodded and biopsied and tested.

Finally, they saw improvement when the doctor said he had done all he could for her. They could not tell if it was the intense treatments, her body giving its last fight, or the hourly prayers. Josie did not care. She was grateful for any change instead of hearing the opposite every day.

Josie crossed the street and entered the hospital as she had done dozens of times. John hugged her, stretched his arms over his head, and moaned. She knew his back ached. Hers did every other night on that hard divan. Then, he kissed her, and he was gone. He walked to the hotel for a shower and breakfast.

Josie walked to her daughter's bed and kissed her cheek. Emma scrunched her forehead and moaned. "Kai?"

"Emma! Are you waking up? Can you hear me?"

One eye and then the other, Emma peeked up. Her eyes moved from side to side.

"Look at me. Can you see me?"

Emma nodded slowly.

Josie whirled around and ran to the door.

"Nurse, come here. Get a doctor! Emma's waking up!"

She flew back to the bed and perched beside Emma. Suddenly, the room filled with frantic movements. Physicians and nurses crowded into the small space. They checked her vitals. Specialists spoke to her, listened to her heart, and pinched her toes. Then, they asked if she could see them, feel them, and talk to them.

Emma swallowed as if the effort was painful. She touched her tongue to her chapped, blistered lips.

Josie grabbed a small plastic cup from the bedside table and held the straw to her daughter's mouth. Emma took a tiny sip. Some of the water ran down the sides of her chin.

"Welcome back, Emma. Everyone in this room has been waiting to meet you," Dr. Williams, the head of Emma's team, spoke to her.

Emma's eyes followed him and then peered at her mother leaning over her, blocking her view of the others circling the bed.

Josie's voice cracked, and she cried, "Oh, querida. I'm thrilled you're awake. We love you, Emma. We've missed you!"

Everyone in the room clapped. Emma seemed to wince from the sudden racket.

Dr. Williams quickly cleared the staff around the bed, thanking his team for all they had accomplished. However, he did not rest on his laurels but discussed the next steps with Josie with a blunt but kind diagnosis.

"We will continue the regimen of moving her body, so it doesn't atrophy, but she will need long-term physical therapy to walk again. After the weeks here, she won't be able to stand independently."

Josie gasped, not comprehending an image of her vital young daughter unable to walk.

"We'll help her. She will regain her strength. Just as it took her a long time to wake up, she will need a long time to recover. But this is an excellent first step." He patted Josie's arm and walked to the door.

"We can never thank you enough, Dr. Williams," Josie said.

"Seeing Emma awake is thanks enough."

Alone in the room with Emma, Josie realized John did not know the news yet. She quickly punched his number on her cell phone.

As soon as he answered, Josie announced, "Our girl is back. Emma's awake."

He did not speak. A gurgle sounded, and then he whispered, "Thank God. I'm on my way."

Josie held Emma's hand as John rushed into the room. He had showered, and his hair was still damp. The breeze he stirred as he ran to the bed was of Ivory soap and generic hotel shampoo.

Josie stood and moved for him to sit by their daughter. He leaned down and kissed Emma and lay his hand on the side of her face.

"Hello, beautiful. What a spectacular day this is!"

Emma's mouth attempted a smile, then a cracked whisper.

"Hi, Papa."

Josie turned from making a phone call to her mother and Flora at the ranch in time to hear the minute speech from Emma. Two words. The only words they had heard from their daughter in more than a year. Tears trickled down her and her husband's faces, but this time they were of joy, not grief. Josie had believed she had no moisture left in her body, but she did. Her sobs became jagged, and she hiccupped and blew her nose. It was an ugly cry, but she did not care.

They had little time with Emma alone before the parade of doctors and nurses began again. As before, the room continued to be active, twenty-four/seven.

Soon, they were trying to help Emma sit on the side of the bed. She was wobbly like her head was too large for its stem. Her bones seemed like gelatin and collapsed under their weight, which was minimal. Josie knew she could lift her daughter into her arms and run with her; Emma looked as light as a feather.

They placed slippers on her feet with rubber soles for traction and a walker in front of her. It took a nurse strolling behind her to catch her if she fell and another person to drag the drip pole. And Emma only made two steps before she had to return to the bed. Her legs were floppy and weak.

A wheelchair rolled her to physical therapy, and she sat in a whirlpool and adjusted her legs in the warm water. She still could not speak very well, so every time they could understand her was a gift.

Loose strands of her luxurious dark hair fell onto her pillow when they brushed it. Her skin lacked color, and her teeth looked too large for her mouth against sunken cheeks.

Josie spoon-fed her broth or Jell-O, then mashed potatoes or a milkshake.

"Vanilla or chocolate, Emma?"

"Ch-ch-chocolate," she stuttered.

"Of course, chocolate!" Her mother crowed as if her daughter had finished a marathon. Every step, every bite, every word was a trial.

Josie did not want to be impatient or expect too much, too soon. She'd hand-feed her daughter the rest of her life if need be. She could not express, even to herself, what having Emma back meant to their family. They had plenty of time to find out what had happened to her. Josie did not want to upset her with terrible memories. She wanted her to regain her strength before the hard questions began.

Emma's father was not as patient. He wanted to know where she had been and what had happened to her—if somebody had harmed her.

"Emma, where have you been?"

Emma looked at him with wide eyes and a puzzled expression. She tilted her head and stared at him as she focused.

She repeated the question. "Where?"

"Yes, where have you been?"

Emma shook her head as if she did not understand.

John did not continue his investigation, although Josie knew the suspense killed him, and he would use his bare hands to strangle the person who harmed his little girl. She saw rage roil in him, and he did not have an outlet for the feelings Josie knew stirred in his gut.

Josie reached for the lip balm on the tray next to Emma's bed and swiped her daughter's dry mouth. Then she placed ice chips from a mauve plastic pitcher onto her tongue. Emma puckered her mouth as they melted and closed her eyes. It seemed difficult for her to stay awake. Emma slept most of the day between physical therapy appointments, and every time Josie walked into the room and saw her daughter's eyes closed, her heart raced, thinking Emma had lapsed back into a coma and they would have to start over.

Josie and John continued their tag-team sitting with Emma. One of them read to her and asked her questions about the story. Emma spoke in halting sentences. Her facial expressions conveyed her emotions if a needle stung or she wearied from a challenging physical therapy session. When she tried to string more than a couple of words together, she shook her head in frustration.

"It's okay, baby. You're getting better every day," Josie told her.

Emma's doctors concurred, and her parents saw the results slowly taking place in their daughter. Color returned to her cheeks. Her sentences became paragraphs, her steps surer.

The day Emma used her walker to traverse the entire length of the corridor, a cheer went up at the nurses' station. Emma grinned as she once had for winning a rodeo prize. How long before she could ride a horse? Josie chastised herself over thoughts of pushing her daughter past her limits.

"When do you think Emma will remember where she's been?" Josie questioned Dr. Williams outside Emma's room on his nightly rounds.

"You can begin asking her, but I'm not sure she's ready to tell you. Emma's still confused about why she's in the hospital."

Josie observed this when talking to her daughter. Emma looked around like an answer to her questions was on her tongue, but she could not voice it.

Josie began by asking Emma about what she remembered. She started with the summer Emma left college.

"Emma, do you remember graduation from A&M?" She watched as it seemed Emma flipped through a Rolodex to retrieve that memory from a stack of cards.

"We wore black gowns," Emma finally said.

"Yes! Black gowns. What color was the braid around your neck?"

"Gold."

"Yes, gold, because you graduated with honors."

Emma smiled at her mother as if to say, *What a silly game we are playing.*

But Josie continued. "Where did Papa and I go after you came home to the ranch in the summer?"

"Europe."

"Exactly. Very good! Where did you go after we left?"

"Camping."

"On the ranch?"

Emma nodded.

"Where did you camp?"

Emma shrugged. Uncertainty was in her eyes.

"What happened to Honey-Boy?"

Emma bit her lip.

"He broke his leg. So I had to…shoot him." She seemed to struggle to remember that, and her eyes watered.

Josie tucked Emma's blanket around her legs and smiled. They had plenty of time to get answers.

CHAPTER 51

EMMA AND JOSIE

The day Emma returned to The Thorn from the hospital became a celebration.

When they knew Emma was coming home, Flora's husband, Pedro, dug a pit in the yard, filled it with large stones, and soaked them with water. He field-dressed a wild hog and wrapped it in herbs, spices, and banana leaves. It roasted overnight until they removed it from the pit, steaming and so tender the meat fell off the bones. Flora cooked beans, patted out homemade tortillas, and grilled corn.

When the car door opened in front of the entrance, they whiffed smoky aromas escaping into the surrounding air. Emma's mouth watered from the familiar smells she had missed. John removed the walker from the trunk and handed it to her. Emma grew stronger every day but still needed support to traverse more than a few steps at a time.

Josie beamed at her and declared, "We're home!"

Emma looked at the house in front of her. It seemed like a life-time had passed since she left here. Her memories were cloudy, like haze on the horizon. She loved the fog that settled in the valleys and over the water. That's how her mind felt, opaque and distant.

Her father placed his hand on her back and guided her toward the courtyard, where a massive copper sculpture by a famous artist in New Mexico loomed over them. A group of ranch hands lined the sidewalk to the front door. Emma ducked her head as each congratulated her and welcomed her home. They held their hats in their hands and tipped their heads toward her in a quick salute. She smiled and tried to remember their names. *Roger, Walt…is that Kim?*

Some had been with them for years, but she had difficulty placing their faces and names together.

Then, another step and she entered the house. The smells from the kitchen overwhelmed her senses. After months in a sterile hospital where only disinfectants and the metallic odor of blood were prevalent, home cooking seemed twice as powerful.

Flora rushed toward her, wiping her hands on a starched white apron. "It's good to see you back in this house!" She threw her brawny arms around Emma and almost lifted her off her feet. "Dios te bendiga!"

"It's wonderful to be home," Emma whispered. She looked at her once-familiar house as if seeing it for the first time. Emma's thoughts about where she had been were trapped in a big black box inside her memory.

Her walker bumped into the doorway facings, but she made her way to the large kitchen. Flora had outdone herself on the homecoming celebration dinner. On every counter, there were platters piled high with food—shredded pork, steaming tortillas, pinto beans in a cast iron pot, and two chocolate pies.

"Who's joining us?" Emma laughed. "This spread's enough to feed an army!"

"I wanted you to have all your favorites." Flora ducked her chin to her chest and smiled shyly. "Pedro roasted a pig."

"Thank you, Flora, and thank Pedro. It looks delicious."

She kept hobbling around the U-shaped house until she reached her room.

Josie followed behind her and asked, "Do you need any help? Do you want to shower before we eat?"

"Yes, please. I want to wash off this hospital odor." Unfortunately, she could still smell the medications seeping from her pores, and her breath tasted like sulfur.

"Use your shower seat, so you don't slip."

Emma nodded at her mother's directive and walked to her dresser to retrieve clothes.

Choosing gray sweatpants and a white T-shirt, she entered the bathroom. Emma had to pull out several drawers before remembering where she stored her toothbrush and hairdryer.

Had it been so long that she did not know her way around her own room? The shower stall was broad, and had only a large opening in the clear glass enclosure instead of a swinging door. Her mother had placed a shower chair inside the walls.

Hot water fogged the glass, and she filled her palm with luxurious shampoo. The aides never had untangled her hair or cleaned it thoroughly in her hospital bathroom. Now, she scrubbed her body and her hair for what felt like an hour. She had to rest between the shampoo and conditioner on the seat.

Emma dried with a plush towel and propped on the walker as she lifted one foot at a time to don her pants. Then, leaning against the counter, she pulled on her shirt and dried her hair. Holding the dryer made her arms tired; she left the bathroom with damp hair.

Emma joined her parents and grandmother at the dining room table.

"There she is," her father announced and jumped up to pull a chair out for her.

Emma inhaled a sigh of relief to sit down. She breathed as hard as if she had run a sprint instead of cleansing herself.

Everyone watched her expectantly, constantly worried, always wondering how she felt. She knew this because they asked her multiple times every hour.

Her father picked up his wineglass and held it in the air. "Let's toast the homecoming of our girl. Back where she belongs with her family. We're grateful."

Everyone lifted their goblets, and Emma held up her water glass to clink against theirs. She smiled and thanked them.

The feast began by passing around the platters heaped with food. Emma chose one small item from each platter, which over-filled her plate. She knew her appetite was not back to normal, and she could not eat half of what she had chosen. Still, Emma wanted to taste each of the foods. But, before eating more than a few bites, the rich foods hit her stomach with a vengeance. Emma had to excuse herself and wobble to the bathroom.

When she returned, she waved her hand at them to continue eating, but she just sat there, nibbled on a flour tortilla, and sipped her water, queasy. Again, the concern on their faces caused her to be sad, but she just smiled and listened to their chatter. Her parents made plans to catch up with their ranch duties and speak to the ranch managers the next day. Emma was interested but suddenly was so tired.

"May I lie down?"

"Oh, of course, querida. We've worn you out on your first day home. It'll take a while to build back your strength. Day by day."

Her mother sprang to her feet and walked with Emma down the hall. She pulled the coverlet back and asked if Emma wanted to change into her pajamas.

"No, I'm good. These are just like PJs," she said, pointing to her pants.

"Well, here's the book you were reading when you left. I'll leave it here on your nightstand and a glass of water."

Emma sat on the side of the bed, and her mother picked up her legs and swung them onto the mattress. She parked the walker where Emma could reach it.

Josie swept Emma's damp hair off her forehead and kissed her.

"Rest, my love. I'll be within yelling distance if you need me." Josie lingered, and Emma could tell her mother had plenty of questions. But unfortunately, she didn't have any answers.

Emma snuggled into the clean, crisp sheets. Her favorite pillow of down nestled under her slightly wet hair. Her bed was expansive compared to the one in the hospital room. Emma spread her legs out to find cool spots under the coverlet and dropped into a dreamless sleep.

THE NEXT MORNING, THE smell of food woke her. Coffee brewed, and bacon filled the house with its fatty fragrance. Emma moaned and rolled onto her side. She looked at the small clock on her bedside table—eight o'clock. Emma had slept for twelve hours. She pulled the walker toward her and lifted herself from the bed. After splashing water on her face, she padded slowly down the hall to the kitchen. Only Flora was still there. She was sure her parents had left the house hours ago, eager to return to ranching work.

"Come here." Flora waved her over. She pulled out a chair at the breakfast table. "Let's try something easier on your stomach today?"

Emma nodded, and Flora pulled a saucepan from the cabinet, filled it with water and a teaspoon of vinegar, and placed it on the stovetop. When the water simmered, Flora dropped two eggs into the swirling liquid. She slid them into a China dish in just a couple of minutes. Handing Emma a fork and napkin, Flora sat across from her. Emma took a small amount of the poached egg from her fork to her mouth. It was warm, salty, and delicious. Emma sopped her plate with a soft tortilla.

"Bien, bien," Flora said.

"How long was I missing?" Emma wanted to get honest answers to her questions.

Flora cocked her head to one side and stared at Emma. "Well, let's see. First, you were missing from the ranch for more than a year. Then, your mother found you on the porch swing and took you to the hospital. You've been there for two months."

Emma's mouth dropped open. A year. She had lost more than a year of her life. Where had she been? Listening to conversations with her parents and the doctors, it sounded like they didn't know. Dr. Williams said the high fever had burned Emma's memories from her mind.

"Will she ever remember?" Josie had questioned him.

"Maybe. Maybe not. The mind is interesting. It protects us from things that may harm us. Emma's memory from when she went camping on the ranch until she woke up in the hospital is a blank slate for her. She doesn't know what happened. I wouldn't push her. It won't do anything but frustrate her."

Josie told Emma the doctor's analysis when she asked her

mother why she could not remember. Did the sickness truly erase a year's worth of memories?

Emma heard a knock on the door and handed Flora her plate with yolk smears.

She knew her parents had scheduled a physical therapist at the ranch three days a week until she regained full use of her limbs.

"Hello." She opened the door to find a small woman wearing pink scrubs. "Let's go to the sunroom. It'll give us the space we need for our exercises."

The young woman agreed, and they entered the glassed porch. Natural light poured into the room, and it was bright and cheerful with chintz fabrics of blue and yellow.

The exercises seemed simple, but Emma wiped her face before a drop of moisture slid off the end of her nose. She remembered riding horses all day, mucking stables, and pulling wild game out of the woods by herself. Rarely winded during past strenuous activities, now she fretted about having difficulty tying her shoes.

The physical therapist applauded her efforts as Emma pushed herself to exhaustion. Her teeth clenched until she thought they'd chip. Emma was not easy on herself, but her body betrayed her. She wanted her life back, her strength and memories. Emma determined to work for all three.

After the therapist left, Emma remained on a chaise lounge to rest. She stared out the tall windows at the desert landscape. She loved the cacti in the rock gardens. When they bloomed with yellow blossoms, it was awe-inspiring. How could a plant adapt to the harsh South Texas climate and still have such lovely flowers? Only the infrequent rains gave them a drink of water. Moreover, the plants were native to the grounds in which they flourished. They were here before any settlers and would probably still be here if her family left.

Emma watched the ranch hands outside the windows digging up weeds and pulling at vines. It was a constant battle. Mother Nature ultimately won if you gave her half a chance.

Emma heard her mother searching for her and found her still looking out the windows. "Are you okay?"

"Yes, Mama. I don't understand why I'm tired all the time. What do you think happened to me?"

Her mother looked startled at the direct question. "We don't know, Emma. The doctors said we might never know. We have to be satisfied with having you back. That may have to be enough for you, as well."

Emma pursed her lips and wondered if she could stop worrying about where she had been and accept that her memories of the past year had disappeared for good.

"Tell me about the time I was gone, Mama. I want to know what happened here at the ranch."

Josie looked uncertain whether it was time to share with Emma, but she could no longer refuse her. She sat on the window seat, pulled her legs under her, and talked about being in Europe and receiving the message Emma was missing.

"Your father and I searched for a year. Finally, we offered a reward, and the ranch hands scoured the entire ranch. No one knew if you'd been in an accident or abducted."

Emma gasped. "You thought someone kidnapped me?" Emma's mind whirled. She imagined herself riding out on the ranch, camping, Honey-Boy beneath her saddle. Snatches of those memories rattled through her mind, but nothing else. "Tell me more."

Her mother continued and then stared at her hands in her lap.

"We didn't want to give up, Mija, but it had been more than a year." Josie shook her head. "In my heart, I could not conceive of it, but there had not been a sighting of you. So, we planned a celebration of your life. It was the day I found you on the swing!"

Emma's mouth dropped open. They had held a funeral for her.

"Remember one time when you told me what you wanted if you died?

Emma remembered her childish banter with her mother and her stipulations about her memorial service. At the time, she did not truly believe she would die at that age, or that her mother would ever need to follow the plan.

But Josie had followed the instructions. She had planned her only daughter's service as she thought she wanted it. Emma was stunned. She remembered reading Mark Twain in high school and loved the story about Huckleberry Finn attending his own funeral. If she had shown up a few hours earlier and been coherent, she'd have done the same thing.

Josie stood and held her hand out to her daughter. "Want to walk through the stables?"

Emma grasped her mother's fingers and stood. "You bet I do."

Strolling beside her mother made Emma feel like she was on a boat, rocking in the ocean with the smell of diesel fumes in the background.

But seeing the stalls with horses sticking their heads over the gates, Emma felt a tug of longing. She missed being on the back of one of these wonderful creatures, clutching their flanks with her knees and feeling their power. Emma loved riding and wondered how long it would be before she could climb on a horse and gallop through the tall grasses.

Emma's brow relaxed among the animals she loved dearly, and when Emma walked back to her room, she told her mother she would rest, so Josie left her alone.

Instead, Emma opened the laptop on her desk and searched her mind for her password. Much to her surprise, it popped into her head. Scrolling through an online Texas news magazine, she blinked rapidly. What was this?

Daily Star, San Antonio:
Thorn Heir Released from Hospital.

Today, Emma Rosales, heiress to the largest ranch in Texas, was released from a San Antonio hospital after spending two months in the long-term care facility. Rosales, age 23, disappeared more than a year ago. Her parents recently held a celebration of life for their daughter. But they later discovered her back home before being airlifted to the hospital. Sources tell us that the young Rosales woman is under a physical therapist's care and expected to recover fully.

Emma squinted at the comments under the article.

Kayohhay: *Where has she been for a year? What secrets is the heir-apparent keeping in south Texas?*

Limonade23: *Be kind. What are you implying?*

Bigdog45: *With that much property, she could have been anywhere on it, and they wouldn't find her.*

1989joe: *Do you wonder if she knows about the accusations toward her boyfriend and that her parents had him arrested?*

Emma slammed the top of the computer. Her boyfriend—arrested?

"Mama, rapido!" she called.

Josie rushed into Emma's room. "What's the matter?"

"Maybe you didn't share everything about the time I was gone? I just read a news article about arresting my boyfriend? What boyfriend?" Her words, full of anger, blew into the room.

"Calm down. I'll tell you what happened." Josie pulled up a chair and joined Emma at her desk.

Emma glared at the laptop like it was a rabid dog. "Well?"

"Some of the ranch hands told us about the day you overheard Jeff Bower bragging about being close to you so he could own this ranch. They said you slammed a pie into his face. We thought he might have gotten angry enough to hurt you."

Emma placed her head in her hands. "You thought he harmed me?"

Josie looked bashfully at Emma. "Pedro said someone he didn't recognize threatened you. I assumed it was Jeff. The district attorney examined him, but refused to prosecute for lack of evidence. Sorry, honey, but we were frantic and grasping at straws. We were desperate to find you or find out what happened to you. Unfortunately, his family has a violent streak, and we thought he might, as well."

"Oh, Mama. He's harmless. He hurt my feelings, but I was never afraid of him."

Josie lowered her eyes with an embarrassed look on her face. "I'm glad to know that, but we couldn't be sure, and you were not here for us to hear your side of the story. I'm afraid I wanted to punish someone for your disappearance."

"Is there anything else you haven't told me?"

"I don't know. I'll have to think about it."

"I know you were doing everything possible to find me, but that was pretty extreme."

JOSIE WENT INTO THE kitchen to make a sandwich for Emma and placed it on a tray with a glass of cold milk and a freshly baked chocolate chip cookie. She bumped her hip into Emma's room door and heard her say, "Come in."

Josie balanced the tray on one hand and forearm and opened the door with her other hand. Emma sat in bed, perched on several large pillows with the laptop open.

"I brought you a snack. Are you hungry?" She sat the tray on Emma's lap as she removed the computer.

"Yes, I'm starving." Emma took a big bite of the peanut butter and grape jelly sandwich. The thick mixture seemed stuck to the roof of her mouth, and she swigged a gulp of milk to wash it down. Josie smiled at her trying to swallow the sticky lump.

"Seriously, tell me everything that happened while I was gone. Leave nothing out."

Josie gave her a pat on her leg and said, "I will. I promise."

JOSIE WATCHED AS EMMA became frustrated with her slow progress. She said her body ignored her pleas and thwarted her every action. Josie could hear Emma's low rumbles of a pent-up scream throughout the day, especially after her therapy appointments. Finally, the PT met with Josie and John and said Emma had progressed, despite their daughter's beliefs. It was just slow going.

Josie passed Emma's bedroom, noticed the door open, and

Emma was not there. Josie circled through the living room and kitchen—no Emma. Panic rose in her chest, and she opened the door and hurried toward the stable.

"Has anyone seen Emma?" The hands shook their heads.

She spun around and jogged behind the barn. On the same stump where Emma had climbed onto a horse at age five was her daughter.

A small grey with saddle and bridle stood waiting, and Emma grasped the saddle's horn and pulled herself up from the stump. She used her hand to push her leg so her foot could find the stirrup.

Emma sweated profusely, and Josie could only imagine the effort it took. Finally, Josie dissolved back into the barn, and Emma did not notice her.

Josie turned and reluctantly walked back to the house. She stood in the large windows overlooking the back pasture and watched as Emma walked the horse and then encouraged him to go faster.

Josie sank into a cushioned chair and wept. Finally, she released her tension from the entire ordeal.

After a few minutes, Josie stood again to see if Emma still cantered in the field. But Emma was not alone. A ranch hand watched her as she made circles in the tall grass. Josie squinted her eyes to recognize the man, but they were too far away.

Josie was glad someone was there to help if Emma needed it.

CHAPTER 52

EMMA

Emma's knees and thighs burned. She had not ridden in so long, her body betrayed her years of expertise and fought against her. Still, she loped the horse and made lazy circles.

Out of the corner of her eye, she saw a man standing at the pasture's edge.

Did my mother send him to check on me?

Emma ignored him and continued her ride. Finally, she acknowledged she was too tired to stay on the horse and turned toward toward the barn. The ranch hand walked toward her and grasped the halter. He looked up at her and said, "It is nice to see you feeling better."

"Thank you. It's good to be back on a horse."

She shaded her eyes with a cupped hand and looked at the back of his head as he led her horse. He had shoulder-length dark hair that he had pulled into a ponytail. It protruded from under a wide-brimmed hat. He had the standard ranch uniform of a faded denim shirt and dark blue jeans with boots and a wide leather belt.

Should she know his name? She racked her brain. Tommy? No. Brad? Why couldn't she remember the tiniest details of her life?

Once, she could line up one-hundred ranch hands and tell them their names and their wives' and children's names. Now, she struggled with those who had been with them longer than she had been on this earth.

Something about his erect posture and the width of his shoulders indicated she knew him. He seemed familiar, but not really. She could cry with frustration, but that wouldn't do any good.

They reached the stable, and the man led the horse toward the stump where she could dismount. Emma hesitated when she tried to throw her leg across the horse, fearing she might fall. The man turned and lifted his arms to show he wanted to remove her from the horse. She leaned toward him, and he positioned his hands under her armpits and placed her feet firmly on the ground.

"Thanks."

"You are welcome. See you again." He walked into the barn leading the horse, and she followed the path to her house with one more look toward him.

"Mama, are there new ranch hands, or have I just forgotten their names?"

"A few new ones since you've been gone. Jay and Tim retired, and we replaced them with younger guys."

Emma huffed with frustration. She wanted to look at her laptop and see what other events had occurred during her disappearance. Maybe something she read would jog her memory.

Emma did not want to be like an amnesia patient from a TV drama who had been in an accident and couldn't remember her husband, so she fell in love with her brother-in-law. She remembered soap operas and daytime dramas from watching them during class breaks. So why couldn't she remember the year's gap?

She opened her computer and scrolled the news pages. Then,

she typed *Rosales girl disappeared*. The entire screen filled with news sites and reports about her time away. The stories began with crews and satellite trucks lining the road outside The Thorn gates. She saw photos of all the reporters sticking microphones into her parents' faces as they pulled out of the driveway in their trucks. *What a terrifying time it must have been for my family.*

A close-up photo of her mother as she stood before a crowd and spoke into a microphone showed a lined brow and crow's feet where she had never had them before.

The title of the article was "Mother Grieves for Lost Daughter." Emma's father stood behind her. Emma could see his hat over her shoulder, but Josie Rosales was in the forefront, asking for leads to find her daughter. She offered $100,000 to anyone whose tip located Emma. The more Emma read, the sadder she became.

How did this happen? Emma leaned back in the chair. She forced herself to remember any clue, any incident. But, after Honey Boy's death, she drew a total blank.

Her phone rang and startled her. She had not had a phone call since her return.

"Hello?" Her voice sounded frightened.

"Emma? This is Jeff. I'm happy to hear your voice."

Emma bit the inside of her cheek.

"I'm sorry for everything you went through from my parents— the district attorney and everything," Emma said.

"It was a hard time. But I knew your parents were worried about you. They wanted to blame me. My mother's still angry about it, but I'm not. I'm just glad you came home. We, well, we thought you were dead."

Dead. That word lay between Emma and Jeff like an explosive device.

"I still apologize."

"I called you to ask forgiveness for the way I treated you. That's all I could think about while you were missing—the last thing you heard out of my mouth hurt you." His voice was soft in her ear.

"Thank you for calling. I hope we can all get back to our normal lives now."

He agreed, and she hung up the phone.

At dinner, she told her parents Jeff had called to apologize. Her mother gritted her teeth, and her father just looked down at the table.

"That's the end of a terrible time. Now, we're back on track for your wonderful life. Did you know Emma rode a horse today?" Josie's voice brightened as she changed the subject.

Her father looked surprised, and they discussed horses born while she was gone and in what pastures the cattle grazed.

"Oh, I almost forgot. A horse was born on your birthday, and we named him Safe Return, nicknamed Ree. He's waiting to meet you." Josie smiled.

Her parents gifted her a horse to replace Honey-Boy. Emma mourned one and welcomed another. Then, they discussed her parents' anniversary, and Emma encouraged them to go into town, have a nice dinner, and maybe see a movie. But instead, they argued with her because they didn't want to leave her alone.

"Alone? Flora, Pedro, Abuelita, all the ranch hands? I'm never alone."

Finally, they relented and made a reservation at the King's Inn, known far and wide for its fresh seafood platters and onion rings.

"Just bring me a piece of their cheesecake," Emma teased.

"We definitely will."

The next afternoon, her mother and father stuck their heads in her bedroom door and told her they were leaving for their anniversary date night. Josie wore a pale blue dress, and John had shaved. Emma could smell how the citrus tones of her mother's perfume mingled with his musky scent.

She smiled to see how much her parents still loved each other, even after all these years. Then, Emma walked them to the porch and said, "Be back before your curfew."

They laughed, kissed her, and walked to the big white Ford F-250 truck parked in the circular drive. Emma sat on the wide swing and threw her legs up on the comfortable mattress, watching the truck until she could no longer see the tail lights blinking in the distance. This spot was where her mother had found her when she returned.

She moved back and forth, back and forth. Emma closed her eyes and blended into the mass of pillows leaning against the back.

"Hello," a deep voice greeted her.

"Yikes. You scared me." She opened her eyes to see the same ranch hand who'd walked her horse the day before standing in front of her.

"I am sorry. I just wanted to check on you."

"Do I know you? I mean, were you working here before I left?" She stared at the man holding his hat in his hand. His gaze was intense as he looked into her eyes. She noticed his deep brown eyes, so dark that there were no pupils.

"I wasn't working here before you left."

"That's weird because I feel like I should know you."

"I feel the same way about you. Maybe we had the same dream."

"Have a seat." Emma scooted to one side of the swing, and he joined her. Emma's pulse quickened.

He acted as if he did not understand small talk and knew little about football games or rodeos around the state. But there was something about him. She could not put her finger on it, but the curve of his jawline, those eyes, black hair, and deeply tanned skin seemed recognizable.

"You are very familiar to me." Emma cocked her head to the side and bit her lip.

"Maybe in another life, Emma?" His lilting pronunciation of her name triggered her heartbeat to pound faster. What was this? Why did she feel comfortable with him?

"What's your name?"

"Kai."

She squinted at him. Kai pushed with his feet, and the swing swayed. He looked at her expectantly, too. Emma knew her mother had instructed the hands not to ask her questions about her days away from the ranch. The doctors said it might put too much pressure on her mind until she fully recovered.

They rocked in serene silence. Then, long before Emma was ready for him to leave, Kai stood and said, "I'm looking for strays tomorrow. Would you like to ride along with me?"

"Yes," she said. "Yes, I would."

The next morning, Emma rose before the dawn. She dressed in jeans, a long-sleeve shirt, and a light jacket. When Emma reached the stable, Kai waited with two horses saddled. He laced his hands together, and she stepped into them. He lifted her onto the horse's back.

They walked the horses slowly in the darkness until they reached a far pasture near a line of brittle old oaks. Oak wilt had wreaked havoc on many beautiful trees and left them dying. Their large, crooked branches looked eerie in the hours before dawn. Emma and Kai rode side by side, and both stopped when the sun made its way into the sky. Emma had seen thousands of sunrises on the ranch, but today's was spectacular. The vivid fuchsia, crimson, and ginger colors made Emma squeal with delight.

Kai watched her and smiled. "Do you believe our ancestors are smiling down on us?"

"You mean they're sending us this beauty?"

"Yes. You are now well. I am fortunate to work at this elegant ranch, and we are getting to know each other. I think my grandfather would be proud."

Emma turned in her saddle to look at him. He did not speak like most cowboys or boys at college. Instead, he had a formal lilt to his voice and a hesitation, like he practiced speaking thoughts in his mind before opening his mouth.

"Is English your second language?" Emma asked.

"Is it that obvious?"

"You speak very well. Did you grow up near here?"

"Not too far away."

"Does your family still live there?"

"All my family died."

"I'm so sorry." She watched his expression.

"Your manager, Bob, found me camping near the river and asked if I needed a job. He said two of his helpers had left. He brought me to the bunkhouse, found me clothes, and showed me what I needed to do."

"Was that while I was in the hospital?"

"Yes. It took time for me to become accustomed to my chores, but I enjoy them, especially working with the horses."

Emma and Kai spent the day circling a vast area of the ranch. Finally, they found two calves and shooed them toward the cattle pens. Emma thought of returning home after being lost and was happy to see the recovered calves suckling at their mothers.

"Tomorrow, Kai?"

"It would be an honor, Emma."

The first stray search turned into many rides. Emma and Kai discovered being together was their favorite thing to do.

One morning, Kai asked Emma if she thought they were "compatible." She laughed and said, "Too early to tell, but we get along pretty well." He nodded and smiled.

The next day, Emma asked her mother if she could invite a friend to dinner.

"One of your college friends?" Josie asked.

"No, one of the ranch hands."

Josie drew a deep breath. "If that's what you'd like."

When the clock chimed six times, Emma answered a knock at the front door. Kai stood there, nervously twisting his hat between his hands. Emma smiled at him and took his hat. Then, tossing it onto a hook, she grasped his hand and guided him into the dining room. Kai looked from Josie to John and bent his head in greeting.

"Kai, these are my parents, Josie and John. Mama, Papa, this is Kai."

John scrunched his forehead and narrowed his eyes.

"Are you the man they call the 'horse whisperer'?"

Kai smiled and nodded. "That is what the hands call me."

John looked at Josie and explained. "Even the most difficult horses are tamed quickly by this young man. He's earning quite the reputation. Our neighbors are bringing their horses here to train, as well."

Emma reached for Kai's hand under the table and squeezed it as if to say, "See, meeting the parents is not bad after all."

She noticed Kai staring at the mixture on his plate. She pinched Kai's tortilla and showed him how to roll a taco. Josie and

John shook their heads. How could he have grown up in Texas and not known about tacos? Kai's eyes widened with his first bite of the concoction. Then, he rolled his own.

After Kai finished four tacos, he thanked his hosts and asked John if he might speak to him the next day. John gave him a time to join him in his office. Josie and Emma looked at each other quizzically but wished him good night.

EMMA TIPTOED TO HER father's office door when she heard Kai's voice.

"I see you there, Emma," John called. "Why don't you join us?"

Emma wore a self-conscious grin as she shuffled toward her two favorite men.

"Is it okay that I'm here, Kai?"

"Yes. Please stay."

Kai turned to Emma's father and said, "Mr. Rosales, I have items left me by my grandfather. I don't like to leave them in the bunkhouse unattended. I wonder if you might store them and offer any advice about their value?"

"Well, sure. I'd be happy to place them in my safe."

John entered a code and swung open the safe's heavy door. He accepted the box Kai handed him. Then, reaching inside, he palmed silver coins and one piece of jewelry after the other.

"These are resplendent—rubies, emeralds, and a diamond ring. They look like antiques, for sure. Do you have any idea how much they are worth?"

"No, I do not know."

"Well, you're a wealthy man with this stash."

Emma's eyebrows raised at the sight of all the fancy jewelry.

John picked up the parchment paper and unrolled it. His eyes widened, and he sat down hard in his chair. Then, spreading the document on his desktop, he exclaimed, "This is worth far more than the jewelry."

He whistled low. "This looks like a Spanish Land Grant for an immense piece of property adjoining The Thorn to the west. I've never known who owned those sections but assumed they lay unclaimed in Mexico. Now, it looks like they belong to you." John scratched his head in amazement. "This name looks like Elisabeth de la Ortega. Do you know her?"

"My great-grandmother's name was Elisabeth. She was called 'Bet.'"

"Let's lock this away, and I'll contact someone about your property claim."

Kai nodded. "It is the land where my ancestors lived. I would like to have it returned in its entirety to us. We have occupied only a small part of it."

From watching her father's expressions, Emma knew this young man could not possibly understand what they placed in the safe and how it would affect his life.

Her eyes watered. Kai had a birthright, just as she had, and both were bound to this land and heritage. Kai would have a future here or anywhere he wanted and not be dependent on his employers.

LATER THAT AFTERNOON, EMMA brushed her new colt, Ree. Kai joined her as she knelt beside the horse.

"He will be a fine horse for you, Emma."

"My mother said he was born on my birthday, and they named him 'Safe Return.'"

"Very appropriate because you are now here."

"Yes, safe and sound."

He smiled at her and took the reins from her hand.

Returning to the hacienda, Emma looked back at Kai, leading the horse away.

She shivered, and goosebumps prickled on her arms despite the harsh Texas heat. Suddenly Emma had a premonition. She could see herself with this man in her life. Was this the lightning bolt her mother described about knowing your husband when you met him? The same emotions Rosales women experienced when they met their life partners?

This relationship had progressed quickly, but Emma thought they could make it as a couple. Just as her father knew the minute he saw her mother, Emma recognized that this man was good and kind and would make someone, maybe even her, a committed husband. She had dreams about his lips on hers. But was that a memory or a present longing?

Did she want to remain on the ranch? Her mother asked her about that desire recently. Emma remembered she had once dreamed of attending vet school and owning a clinic in a small town.

"If you want to move off the ranch and begin a life somewhere else, I will understand," Josie said.

Emma had stared at her strong, proud mother. Her disappearance and illness had a profound effect on the entire family. Yet, Emma never imagined receiving her mother's blessing to leave The Thorn.

All the emotions Emma had felt since her childhood, her reluctance to manage the massive ranch, the fear of not being capable as the women before her, now slipped off her like a lizard shedding its skin.

Emma smiled at her mother. "No. I'm meant to live here as all the women before me. I don't have *all* my memories, but I remember my love for this place." A myriad of possibilities stretched out in front of her.

And, for some strange reason, Emma did not think the history of only one child, a sixth daughter on The Thorn, would continue. Instead, the more she and Kai discussed their hopes for a future together, the more she imagined a ranch full of rambunctious children.

THE END

I hope you enjoyed the book. If you did, please leave a review wherever you bought the book. An honest review means so much to authors and allows us to get back to the writing business, instead of marketing! Just a couple of sentences about your initial impression of the story will thrill me.

I would love you to join my team and leave your email at my website at www.juliadaily.com. I give away monthly prizes like Kindle Fires, gift cards, and free books, so please sign up. You'll be the first to know about my next book before it is published and receive discounts, as well.

To inquire about scheduling me for a book club discussion or event, please email me at julia@juliadaily.com.

Thank you so much for reading my novel.

Happy Reading,
Julia Daily
www.juliadaily.com

ACKNOWLEDGMENTS

To the family cheering me at every turn—Janie, Sam, Jack, Lily, Angela, Jefferson, Robinson, and Samantha Giffin; Elizabeth, Paul, and Emerson Tripp; Blaine Sullivan; Jim and Cathy Brewer; all Brewer relatives; Norma Jane and David Blanchard; Barbara and Jim Howard; Blain and Stevens cousins, especially Susan Stevens Shuler; newly-discovered sister Lily Cohn Elliott and first cousin Gordon Cohn; friends in Mississippi and Texas, including our canine life companions, Memphis Belle and Texas Star.

I thank Kathy Tolan, who walked with me through the original draft; Lorri Kendrick, Claudia Edgerton, and Cyndie Williams for loving support—in spite of having heard more than they ever wanted about my retirement careers; my editors Stacey Swann, Sara Kocek, David Arnette, Andrea Vanryken, and Ericka McIntyre; Johannah Hochhalter and Sarah Clark, sensitivity readers; my incomparable book designer Domini Dragoone; the Writer's League of Texas; the Women's Fiction Writers Association; Women Writing the West; Kathy L. Murphy, The Official Pulpwood Queens and Timber Guys Book Club; Keri Barnum, New Shelves Books; Dr. Rob Carpenter, Books to Big Screen; Suzie Abdou and Arlene Silguero, Good Life Management LLC agents who believe my books should be film adaptations in Hollywood; Jenn Vance, Books Forward; the incredible writers I've interviewed on my podcast *Authors Over 50*; and to my publisher Lara Bernhardt, Admission Press, Inc., who continues to believe in my stories.

Last but not least, to my supportive and loving husband, Emmerson, who eats peanut butter and jelly sandwiches too often, so I can pursue uninterrupted writing time.

1. *The Fifth Daughter of Thorn Ranch* is a family saga with a mother and daughter holding different expectations. Have you experienced a conflict with a parent about your own life's choices? How did it resolve, if it did?

2. The novel has several points of view. Does this allow the reader to get to know the characters more than one point of view?

3. Which character was your favorite and which was your least favorite?

4. If you had been captured and held captive, would you have made the same choices as Emma or done differently?

5. Were you surprised by the ending or confident that is how it would play out?

NO NAMES TO BE GIVEN

The award-winning debut novel by Julia Brewer Daily is a glimpse into the lives of women forced by society to gift their newborns to strangers. Although this novel is a fictional account, it mirrors many of the adoption stories of its era.

When three young unwed women meet at a maternity home hospital in New Orleans in 1966, they are expected to relinquish their babies and return home as if nothing transpired. Twenty-five years later, they are brought back together by blackmail and their secrets threatened with exposure—all the way to the White House.

How that inconceivable act changed them forever is the story of *No Names to Be Given*, a novel with southern voices, love exploited, heartbreak, and blackmail.

MAGNOLIA HOME HOSPITAL

Men loved Sandy's body. She didn't have the option of leading with her wit or intellect. Her looks arrived first. It was both a blessing and a curse.

Now, Sandy placed her hand on her formerly taut stomach. It felt bloated and mushy. How long would it be before she was back in her sparkly dance costumes and performing for audiences? The provocative bustiers and garter belts would not fit her now.

She slid up in her hospital bed and peered through a crack in the curtain. They were all in the same recovery room, separated by thin blue fabric. She heard the other two moaning as they awakened. A nurse worked among the three of them and whispered, as if the others were out of earshot, "What a coincidence y'all went into labor on the same day. We were inducing you next week."

An acidic smell of disinfectant and the rusty odor of blood invaded Sandy's nostrils. She swallowed and found her throat parched and lips chapped. Her head throbbed with a dull drumbeat, and she tasted a metallic tang.

What have I done? Why did I think this was the better choice? Sandy's thoughts jumbled, like a bad movie looping in her head. She squeezed her eyes shut as she remembered how her heart once pounded whenever she heard Glen's voice. The curtains separating the roommates' beds reminded Sandy of those in her home in Illinois, and her mind projected Glen's image into the hospital room.

"You see what happens to trashy girls?" She imagined him sitting at the end of the bed, sneering at her. Sandy's teeth chattered, and her body quaked in small jerks. Her chest rose and fell so rapidly, she became faint. Sandy imagined dying in the hospital. Women died from childbirth all the time. Would her mother ever find out? Probably not. Sandy covered her tracks pretty well. Glen would think she got what she deserved.

"Becca?" Sandy leaned forward and yanked back the cloth separating them. Becca twisted from side to side. Sandy hated seeing her roommate in such distress. Becca might have been a princess-like creature in her former life, but Sandy admired her rebellious streak. How many other white girls had the guts to fall in love with a Negro?

Becca broke the silence. "I cannot believe our babies are in the nursery down the hall, and they won't let us see them," she whispered. "Maybe we can sneak down there."

"Don't. It may make things worse." Sandy wanted to avoid all maternal feelings and didn't want to see a child who might look like her or Carlos.

"I can barely walk to the bathroom." Faith's voice trembled. Her pixie haircut, unwashed and dishwater blond, was in spikes and her eyes seemed too large for their sockets.

"Hey, Nurse Carter. If you let me go to the nursery, I won't bother you anymore."

"You know that's not allowed." The nurse frowned at Becca.

"I promise to stand behind the window. I just want to see my baby. One time. I promise."

The nurse's response was to leave the room.

Becca whispered to Sandy. "I just want to see the skin color. I want to see if the adoptive parents will know it's a mixed-race baby."

Most of all, Sandy knew she longed to hold her child. Becca still declared love for her baby's father. Sandy was still in love with her child's father, too, but he would be no help to her from behind prison bars.

"I'll go on a hunger strike. Do you want me to barricade myself in the nursery?" Becca made her announcements in a loud voice.

"Hush. You're disturbing the entire home." Nurse Carter poked her head back in the doorway and spoke harshly.

Perspiration beaded in the hollows of Becca's cheeks, and Sandy watched as she swiped it away with her palm. Her beauty dulled only slightly with her auburn hair in a messy knot on the top of her head and her freckles dominant on her ivory skin. Becca's startling blue eyes were now the color of a very stormy sea—gunmetal and glinting.

"Everything's gonna be all right," Sandy cooed. She feared Becca would spring from the bed and run toward the nursery.

Sandy watched Faith with her hands clasped as if in prayer.

"Faith, are you okay?" She always spoke to Faith as if she were a child. They were all about the same age, eighteen, but Faith's innocence made her seem so much younger.

"I'm miserable," Faith said.

"Me, too. I feel like a medieval torture device stretched my limbs," Sandy said.

Faith chanted prayers for her baby. "Please, Lord. Please let my baby have the very best parents. I know you'll take care of him—or her." She hummed the lyrics of "Jesus Loves the Little Children." "Red and yellow, black and white, they are precious in his sight."

"How are we expected to walk away and pretend nothing happened? They knocked us out before we had our babies and won't let us see them? We don't even know if we had a boy or a girl," Becca blurted out.

Sandy did not turn to Becca. Instead, she watched Faith twist her hands. Faith's frame disappeared from view under the sheet. Sandy was afraid her tiny limbs, awkward and knobby, would vanish altogether without the bed to contain her. Every time Sandy looked at Faith, she remembered Faith's description of her assault.

Now, a living reminder of it existed. Faith had said she didn't want this baby carrying the blame for its conception. Suddenly, Faith began gulping breaths like drinking water with a cupped hand from a bucket.

Sandy tried not to look at her own reflection in the mirror. Her hair, not dyed since entering the home, showed roots black and wide like the stripe of paint against a hot asphalt roadway, only in reverse—her platinum locks clung to the dark center.

Towering above Faith, she saw how sallow her skin was and how lackluster. She needed her eyebrows plucked and her nails painted—no time to worry about all that. Sandy required all her strength for her own recovery and assisting her friends. She tucked Faith and Becca's blankets around them, raised their hospital bed rails, and crawled back into her bed.

Tomorrow, they had plans to make.

Julia Brewer Daily is a Texan with a southern accent. She holds a B.S. in English and a M.S. degree in Education from the University of Southern Mississippi.

She has been a Communications Adjunct Professor at Belhaven University, Jackson, Mississippi, and Public Relations Director of the Mississippi Department of Education and Millsaps College, a liberal arts college in Jackson, MS.

She was the founding director of the Greater Belhaven Market, a producers' only market in a historic neighborhood in Jackson, and even shadowed Martha Stewart.

As the Executive Director of the Craftsmen's Guild of Mississippi (300 artisans from 19 states) which operates the Mississippi Craft Center, she wrote their stories to introduce them to the public.

She is a member of the Writers' League of Texas, the Women Fiction Writers' Association, The Official Pulpwood Queens Book Club, Women Writing the West, and the Women's National Book Association. Daily is the host of the popular podcast *Authors Over 50* which celebrates debut authors after the age of 50.

A lifelong southerner, she now resides on a ranch in Fredericksburg, Texas, with her husband Emmerson and Labrador retrievers, Memphis Belle and Texas Star.